Rod Van Blake

ANCIENT

ILLUMINATION

III

Mahali Pengine Ent

Ancient Illumination III is a work of fiction. The characters, incidents, and dialogs are products of the author's imagina-tion and are not to be construed as real. Any resemblance to actual events or persons, living or dead, is entirely coincidental.

A Mahali Pengine Ent Trade Paperback Edition

Copyright © 2019 by Rod Van Blake
Trade Paperback published by Mahali Pengine Ent
http://AncientIllumination.net
ISBN 978-1-7345890-0-9 Hardcover
ISBN 978-1-7345890-9-2 Paperback
ISBN 978-1-7345890-3-0 E-book

Printed in the United States of America

9 8 7 6 5 4 3 2 1

Foreword

It's been a long journey writing these three novels and I just wanted to take some time to acknowledge some very important people who supported me along the way. Writing though a joyful experience (most of the time) is a hard endeavor, and life can sometimes gets in the way it would not have been possible without these people. To my mother Tanya and Major, thank you so much for believing in me despite the fact that it had to sound crazy after coming through one of the darkest moments in my life to say that I wanted to write science fiction novels. I know it's not my moms' favorite genre and when scifi movies comes out she calls it "that mess" just in less PC terms. They support my books and come to events when they can. To my Aunt Carla who introduced me to an enthusiasm for all things science fiction and fantasy. Perhaps this was a seed planted long ago that steered me towards wanting to create. To Moneca who has been with me from the very beginning of my publishing journey, thank you so much for your love and support! She has been schlepping along with me to various conventions to help me sell books for the last three years despite having a full-time job of her own. My presentation improves with each event I go to because she sets up my table after we decide what books and concept art to feature and where to place my banners. When it comes to the business side of things, she always asks me the right questions to get me thinking in the right direction. She has a lot of faith in me and my ideas despite this also not really being her cup of tea but she tries to learn, and always has a seemingly arbitrary phrase for people passing by the table which ultimately brings them to me so I can explain my stories and see if they're genuinely interested. Without you a lot of my previous success would not have happened. Ancient Illumination is expanding! We have volume one of the graphic novel and likely a standard comic book series in the works. The graphic novel is illustrated by Jordan Purnell Jackson. I'd like to thank him for his work and eye for detail. The graphic novel will also be releasing along side this third novel in the series. Rhashad Carter did the cover for this third book and Jordan put the finishing touches on it. Thank you. To my readers thank you for going on these journeys with me I hope you continue for the ride that will definitely keep going. Readers are the lifeblood of authors. With no one to explore your new worlds they technically don't exist. Thank you to anyone who purchased an Ancient Illumination novel or spread the word to those you thought might enjoy them. Until next time!

- Rod Van Blake

ANCIENT ILLUMINATION III - GODHOOD

ROD VAN BLAKE

ANCIENT ILLUMINATION III - GODHOOD

Prologue

Sitting on the bridge of the Ryoko-Gekijo or flying theater, Hironike ponders how they all got there as he watched the stars stream by as they cruise a hyperspace lane on a short trip back to Earth. Many thought this vessel was only meant for travel within the Earth's atmosphere and it was quite a shock to the GMC and security forces chasing them when some of the spires reconfigured before making escape velocity. The other surprise was when the theater revealed they also had shields strong enough to repel their ballistic and energy-based weaponry.

Looking at all the luxury that surrounded him and then at his reflection, he saw exactly what brought him to this very moment. His deep emerald skin like many other mutations that had popped up in humanity was often the source of divisiveness among all human kind in the Milky Way. Why is that? He silently wondered. Hironike is the head of the Ongakujin which roughly translates as the music people. The green skinned humans that often join this troop of performers to do all kinds of entertainment also have another name or alter ego. For centuries this group of beings became known as the absolute best in the fine arts.

There was also a long list of dignitaries, politicians and law makers or people in prominent positions that did not leave their shows alive. The fact that when they have performances people still came in droves could either speak to the quality of the Ongakujins performances or the morbid psychosis of the audience. As a whole their society on Earth had come a long way in technological advances yet could not shake the habit of hating anything dissimilar or outside of their individual understanding. These mutant races just amplified that part of human nature.

Some thought it was a result of changes to diet or chemicals being introduced; others believed the mutations were answers from various gods. Hironike didn't know if any of that were true, but it did seem as if the other aberrations had more of a functional component. The Limbia Johari or walking jewels had a crystalline aspect to their skin and were seen as status symbols to the humans who could afford to employ them. The self-titled Kison Askari had extremely calcified skin giving them a kind of exoskeleton that allowed them to work in environments that regular people simply could not. This is why they were primarily responsible for mining precious materials on other planets. This is also a big source of the galaxy wide conflict after they demanded better compensation for their efforts.

Normal human beings had become the new privileged class, and had to use technology in order to keep the mutants underfoot. The problem was that one of those groups furnished what made that advantage possible and once they realized that, revolt happened. The GMC (Galactic Marine Corps) tried to preempt this by stockpiling material and building a training facility for their elite forces on Saturn in hopes they would have a unit strong enough to deal with beings bigger and stronger than average humans with natural body armor. The recon units on Saturn had to take a pretty extreme supplement regimen that gave them the strength to function in gravity ten times that of the Earth. It wouldn't put them on equal footing but that in addition to partial cybernetic enhancements were closing the gaps.

The problem was that now the Kison Askari were developing technology of their own. Initially, issued mining equipment was being refitted and repurposed to be used as weapons. Now they had created shoulder harnessed small arms plasma canons which allowed them to fire at enemies while maintaining the use of their hands. From the GMC's perspective that wasn't even the worst of it. Rumor had it there was a resurfaced contingent from Atlantis that gave them knowledge on how to weaponize dark matter. At least part of this rumor had been proven true when the installation at Saturn was hit followed by other attacks on military installations on Earth by unknown craft.

There has been some backlash as some of the remnants of the volatile substance spilled over into some of the civilian populations surrounding the bases on Earth. It was said that Queen Regent Tunisia was responsible and the Kison Askari relieved her of her rule and placed Darius the crown prince on the throne which seemed both hasty and unwise. The boy was special but that burden was too much for someone so young. Hironike did not get a chance to speak to the queen when they dropped the refugees and freedom fighters fleeing Earth to their new proclaimed home world on Ganymede. It was simply amazing to see what they had created there in so short a time. The domed mining facilities on the dwarf star known as Pluto was nice until the GMC decided to bomb it igniting the methane present in the atmosphere.

The stone people were often large but not always, fast and incredibly strong beings. What they definitely were not, was stupid. What they had done at Ganymede was an engineering marvel. Hironike was no stranger to such feats as his people were travelling in a huge ship that was also a theater but Ganymede now boasted a fully self-sustaining facility built deep within the Jovian moon's crust including a hangar bay, domiciles for living, hydroponic facilities to grow edible vegetation as well as a lab to synthesize proteins. It was no secret that they had been out here among the stars for a long time with little provisions, but Hironike and now many of the humans had no idea how self-sufficient stone people had become out of necessity and sheer desperation at times. These people were not the large brooding oafs out simply foraging as society often tried to make them out to be.

It was unclear if the queen was actually being detained by her own people in order to decide what to do as far as punishment or if it was only a charade meant to appease the government back on Earth. As a result of a short-term invasion back into the galaxy by the Annunaki the war between humankind and mutants was put on hold. Inexplicably the threat had been turned away by the intervention of the prince with the help of Babylon the silurian head of the people of Atlantis. They had taken his personal Manta shaped ship and gone off to negotiate giving the Milky Way a reprieve of sorts. That most of all had to stick in the craw of the top brass in the GMC.

Things turned around rather quickly. The Kison Tontu or stone people were not slaves but pretty close to it. They had found a way to escape the shackle like devices they wore that were connected to a large electromagnetic system throughout most mining facilities in the galaxy used to control them as a "safety" precaution. A revolt ensued which was followed by a large group of the stone people absconding with a considerable amount of ore and other materials which they had mined in the first place and began a very impressive arms race against a government that had a considerable head start in that department and against all odds not only held their own once unrestrained but excelled.

They had stopped referring to themselves as Kison Tontu and added the more appropriate Askari or warrior to their title. The people of Atlantis who had been happy to simply stay in the background while trying not to interfere finally came out in the open and helped the initial building of the Askari space navy. Space travel up until recently was primarily used for the gathering of resources. Even on Earth personal means of travel had been whittled down to the extremely rich or government heads. Individuals had eventually been priced out of it being an option along with the excuses about it being better for the environment. The Kison Askari had plans to reignite personal transport as a business and the government wanted to shut them out.

The government and the GMC had very little to stand on currently as the prince of the Kison Askari in a way had not only saved the galaxy when a group of large golden ships had suddenly jumped in system unannounced ready to annihilate them just for being wasteful, but his people had a weapon of mass destruction at their fingertips that the GMC were likely centuries away from having the ability to control let alone weaponize, dark matter.

Chapter One

Athena walked onto the bridge where Hironike was pondering all that had happened. She was petite with diamond like skin and long amethyst crystalline tresses that tinkled softly as she walked announcing her presence. At the sound of her approach Hironike looked up at the queen of the Limbia Johari and addressed her "To what do I owe the pleasure of seeing you queen Athena?" Back on Earth she had been a part of a resistance group that arose when the government decided it was open season on all mutants, not just the Kison Askari. Hironike ran his hands over his shorn green head taking in the sight of her.

Since the large conflict had begun to involve her people, she had done away with the luxurious gowns she had become known for. Yet even in a form fitting EV suit with magnetic armor plating attached to it she was striking. The purple of her eyes matched her hair perfectly. Smiling likely because she knew the thoughts running through his head she answers "I figured I'd find you here brooding. I was wondering if you had any ideas on what we would say when we get to Earth that won't get us shot on sight once we exit this extravagant barge of yours?"

She studied him as he pondered the question. It was true that they had both left their home planet under less than favorable circumstances. Despite the conspiracy theories people still had no idea about the Ongakujins alter egos as the Jade Assassins but they were fellow mutants for the most part that were seen not only harboring refugees, rebels and their sympathizers but had ignored orders from GMC officials in the process. Thwarting the blockade efforts of the GMC and local security forces would not be looked upon kindly when they returned. After a moment he gave her his thoughts.

"They know we have the ability of extra planetary travel now in addition to our shields. We did not have any offensive capabilities when we left but thanks to Toshi our tech expert who helped the Kison Askari build some of the designs for their vessels they were kind enough to design weapons for the Ryoko-Gekijo. I will hold that card in reserve until absolutely necessary. They will assume correctly that we are allied with the Kison Askari who hold the ultimate trump card in their dark matter ordinance. The young prince on the advice of his senior staff and Babylon have decided not to use it after queen Tunisia was quick to act out of vengeance with it but we don't have to disclose that fact. You and I are mutants under the same umbrella of perceived protection of the Kison Askari. We are now at peace because of an outside threat that was in all likelihood only delayed. We can use all this to our advantage as leverage." He explained.

It was risky but it could work. Athena previously had an intricate network of spies working in the homes and businesses of nearly every prominent corporation head and top government official. They had access to the upper echelon of society on Earth. That may not be the case now. The Limbia Johari worked as personal valets, servants and in other capacities so that they could keep tabs on movements and plans often before they hatched. She wondered what place in society they would have now that the trust had been severed. They had not even been caught and that was the ironic thing. They were simply different and for those reasons when the loyalist act passed they were ordered to report to detainment camps just like all the other mutants.

When she refused to come in for questioning in regards to a loose connection to slain dignitaries, the GMC tried to detain her by force. Looking around the bridge of the vessel they were on, Athena could see that she and Hironike had a lot in common. The estate in Siberia she had retreated to looked for all intents and purposes to be an abandoned desolate fortress. To describe the inside as tech laden and opulent would be putting it mildly. Security forces in conjunction with the GMC tried to storm it and failed. With these two as leaders things were never as they seemed. She still did not like his methods at times yet the Jade Assassins often acted as a result of information her people provided so they were always linked.

Alarms blared and before either of them could ask, Toshi came rushing in stopping in front of the main viewport. A group of consoles rose up from the deck around him and his emerald fingers flew over various buttons as he explained what was happening "We have to slow our approach somewhat and divert more power to the shields. At the speeds we are traveling something as small as a dust particle could potentially do some serious damage to the outer hull. In stasis we would have time to go out and fix the damage but during hyperspace we would be obliterated most likely."

Like Hironike, Toshi had a similar skin tone, also bald but was bespectacled. The two Ongakujin were dressed contrastingly to Athena. She looked ready for combat while they looked as if they were about to go on stage. Athena was sure he wore the glasses for effect. The necessity for eyewear that assisted sight was a thing of the past. He wanted to look intelligent and somehow that strange stereotype despite all the evidence against it had survived. They would be back at the home planet soon so Hironike explained his thinking to Toshi who agreed with most of what he had to say. Athena went to find Angelo her right-hand man to explain what their plans were once they were within eyesight of Earth's gravity well. This would be interesting to say the least and the current peace was tenuous at best. Tension was high and if it were not for the threat of outside invaders the slightest mistake could set off another round of hostilities.

* * *

The Kison Askari hastily built a facility on Jupiter to receive part of the GMC upper brass as well as a contingent from the remaining heads of state sent to represent the governing body on Earth. In this case fast work did not mean shoddy quality. It was not only functional but aesthetically pleasing as if artisans as well as engineers had taken part in its creation. On this planet it seemed as if the Kison Askari purposefully used the outer planets appearance from space as a theme when building there. Learning from the dangers of dome living and the vulnerability from space to surface attacks this construction was also deep in Jupiter's mantle.

General Krulak and his retinue of aides and lower level government interns were astounded by the obvious engineering prowess in evidence at the facility there. The fact that there were various facilities beneath the surface of most of the planets the Kison Askari had been sent to work on hid their genius from the populace on Earth. It was reasonable to think this is why they had been severely underestimated. The Commandant vowed not to make that mistake again. As agreed prior to this meeting all vowed not to carry weapons. This was supposed to be the official commitment to a lasting peace between mutants and their unaltered counterparts. This was by and large a bitter pill to swallow. There were still bodies being found as a result of the dark matter ordinance dropped on Earth.

With that in mind General Krulak was no fool. The fact that the senate members chose to remain hidden sending proxies to the signing of the Jovian accords was telling. Someone had foolishly agreed to let the Earth delegation take a modified ore hauler all the way out here with no military escort or personnel other than the Commandant and his top advisors today that included Lt. General Jones, Vice Admiral Featherson, and Lt. Commander Jameson. All of the officers had no weapons but were dressed in newly designed battle armor equipped with some of the technology used in earlier builds of the wraith suit.

The helmets could be retracted and instead of camouflage they were giving the appearance of dress uniforms complete with ribbon and citation displays.

The proxies for the Senators were in ceremonial robes and masks. It was a charade, but in any case, Krulak had the authority to speak for the Earth delegate. If these proceedings went south there wasn't much any of them could do. There were units on standby just in case. Not that anything was expected. The rockheads after all will be getting what they wanted or close to it. After exiting the hauler, they were met by a small group of Kison Askari who were to serve as their escort into the facility. These had to be the biggest stone warriors they could find. They were helmeted but otherwise unarmored and the shoulder mounted plasma canons they had become known for were missing.

Upon exiting the hauler, the officers had all activated their helmets which hid their reactions to the escorts who seemed to materialize from thin air. The senatorial proxies were no doubt in EV suits and helmets under the robes. The added masks were a bit melodramatic in the officer's opinions. Another eerie detail about the Kison Askari escort was their arms and legs were visible and seemed to be striated similarly to how the planet's surface looked as if they were part of the décor here. They did not speak but simply gestured that they be followed. The proxies and officers reluctantly did so to what looked to be a lift or elevator to carry them beneath the surface to the main facility. The doors to the hexagon shaped cylindrical capsule slid shut and they were taken below abruptly.

No one was forced to the ground or shifted in any way but the Earth delegates all felt as if the trip was not strictly a vertical one. For some it was a bit nauseating. Despite the helmets General Krulak was sure there were smug expressions behind the breathing apparatuses. To see if they would follow suit the Commandant retracted his helmet. Luckily the cabin had in fact been pressurized and filled with breathable air. The Kison Askari however remained helmeted. Seeing that the General was able to breathe, Lt. Commander Jameson retracts his helm as well revealing a ghastly complexion beneath. "Get it together Jameson!" The Commandant growls. The officer makes a show of trying to slick his white hair down and attempts to straighten his uniform down which doesn't go well because of what he's wearing. The quick hand movements just serve to make the appearance of the uniform glitch temporarily, briefly showing the armored plating beneath.

Vice Admiral Featherson retracts his helmet seeing as the other officers are able to breathe. There's a gleeful glint in his black eyes as he seems to enjoy the discomfiture some on the lift are experiencing yet he is no worse for wear other than the beads of sweat streaming down his brown face. There is a prominent thud as the lift comes to a halt. The hatches slide open and their escorts stand to the side allowing them to exit. General Krulak pauses to see if the Kison Askari that led them down would finally take off their helms. He was disappointed as the leader simply gestured for him to follow the rest of the Earth delegate out into a wide hallway. The floor, ceiling and walls gleamed like polished marble. Following the hall led to a large hall with a long table headed by a dais with a large throne which sat empty.

As they made their way to the seats surrounding the table drones swept into the chamber. These spherical devices with diamond tipped drill like apparatuses stopped before each visitor and opened like blossoming flowers. Lt. Commander was about to protest when the Commandant raised his hand signaling it was ok. From the traces of light that flowed over them it was obvious they were being scanned for hidden weaponry. Nothing must've been found as all the drones quickly closed and flew out as fast as they had entered. Once they reached the table to take their seats, they noticed a huge digital viewport directly above the throne giving them the illusion that they were under the night sky despite being miles beneath the surface.

Suddenly there was a rhythmic rumbling sound that got progressively louder. Everyone's curiosity was answered about the noise when two lines of large and small Kison Askari stomped in repeatedly chanting "Usifanye na mimi, mimi ni kifo Chako!" The ground nearly shaking with each pounding step. They came to a halt and faced the center of the chamber surrounding the table and the delegates at their seats. Unlike their previous guides these warriors all had skin of a dark grey hue, but there were flecks of silver and gold that laid into creases that they had somehow etched in. Upon closer examination Lt. Commander Jameson would guess that they had poured molten metals into the etching which had to have been painful. These were the Prince's royal guards. One of the guards steps out of line and screams "Amandla!" The rest of the warriors respond "Ngawethu!" causing some of the officers and all of the senate proxies to jump out of their skins.

Young Prince Darius is still wearing the special suit made for him that is somehow able to grow as he does. It has proven necessary as Jupiter has a gravitational pull that is 2.4 times that of the Earth. The shorter of the Kison Askari present are proof of what happens to beings born and raised in these conditions. Behind him is Simeon, one of the Kison Askari Generals. There are no embellishments on his grey calcified stone-like skin but he is wearing a sash with an ornate hammer on his back. Simeon stops short of the table as Darius reaches the throne on the dais and bellows "On behalf of the Kison Askari, Darius of the Omega house welcomes you!" The Prince's movements are slow and deliberate as he takes his seat on the large throne that seems to be carved from the planet's bedrock. The black studded form fitting suit is a stark contrast to the beige, coral and reddish tones of the walls and throne.

Prince Darius waves his slender hand signaling that they should take their seats. The inner voice that had been constantly feeding Darius information had become a geyser lately and the boy was having issues dealing with it. The boy hid it as best he could and no one else had been in his shoes so there was little help he could seek in regards to advice. Babylon was again off somewhere but promised to return soon. The old Atlantean was a comfort to say the least. Queen Tunisia was also still being held which did not sit well with the Prince. That situation would be remedied soon but for now he had to take care of this formality so the galaxy could move on. Once he had composed himself, he addressed his guests.

"Greetings General Krulak. I would address you all by name but you'll have to excuse my ignorance of the other officers and it would seem that the senate members are in disguise...or sent anonymous representation?" The boy was perceptive the general had to give him that. The General replied "Yes...your..." The Prince waived off the honorific saying "Darius is fine. Going forward how you treat us will be far more important than what you call us. I trust you all had the time to read over the terms of our agreement on your way out here?" At that one of the masked proxies got up and went to General Krulak to whisper something in his ear. Darius raised an eyebrow but waited for the exchange to finish and the proxy to return to their seat before looking at the Commandant expectantly.

Nervously the General Krulak cleared his throat and replied "Yes, Darius we have all gone over the proposal and some of the Senators are concerned over the amount of compensation your people want and there is no mention of a specific punishment for those responsible for the casualties civilians included as a result of dark matter ordinance used on Earth.". Darius looks slightly confused as his eyes begin to shimmer then glow as he responds to their concerns.

"Excuse me but remind me again who was punished for the atrocity that took place at the dwarf star known as Pluto. There were noncombatants there who worked to gather material and ore as all of my people do across this galaxy that result in giving the society on Earth the ability to build a wide variety of technological devices that make life easier, more efficient. Now we have been effectively fueling progression for centuries and reaping the least benefit from that progress, and barely compensated for our efforts under duress for most of the time. What we ask for is more than fair considering all this!" His eyes go back to their normal dark brown color before adding "This is not a proposal; those are the terms. Now you can either sign them or send us someone who can so our peace can be made official. Let us not forget that we have recently had visitors from outside this galaxy who will in fact decimate us all just to take what resources remain. The other alternative is that we could simply switch places. You all can come gather the resources and the Kison Askari can sit back and make use of what you bring home."

As much as they did not like it, the young Prince was right. The Annunaki reappearing in the Milky Way was a nasty surprise the government and the GMC had not anticipated. It was a bitter pill to swallow but they would have to not only make peace with the stone people but would have to pay them in return for their haul now. This would sway the economic balance in a tremendous way. The elitists would not be happy, but the notion of outside threats could also not be ignored. The potential for more outside threats meant they would also have to fight alongside beings they were previously oppressing. The Kison Askari will be on equal footing for a change.

Chapter Two

Corporals Sims and Aragon had been transported back to base at Saturn. They were put on leave with the hostilities stopped for the moment and both sides officially in peace talks but Aragon did not want to see family right away. He signed the papers for being inducted into the ascension protocol and immediately started the rehab/acclimatization process. The paperwork was a bit of a wasted formality that made it seem as if he gave the Corps permission when the truth of the matter was that he was technically still government property for another four years since he recently reenlisted. That time frame was another meaningless detail as well. The GMC had not only repaired his injuries, but augmented him further.

There was now a lot of money put into his once broken body. One thing was for sure, the government always made use of their investments. An early retirement would not be in the cards for Corporal Aragon. Petty Officer House watched as Aragon went through the paces repeatedly running both the obstacle and confidence courses reserved for enhanced Marines stationed at Saturn. That number had grown tremendously as hostilities broke out with the stone people. Things were peaceful at the moment but the news that other beings coming from outside their galaxy as possibly more dangerous threats forced the GMC to redouble their efforts. They were trying to manufacture their own supermen and women. With his new reinforced spine, the cybernetic neural network allowed Aragon's body to function more efficiently. The supplemental enhancement previously reserved for the recon units was being implemented Marine Corps wide.

Most Marines were now faster and stronger than normal humans after taking the special "cocktail" as some called it when arriving on Saturn to help strengthen their muscles and skeletal systems allowing them to function and train in a gravity ten times that of the Earth but Aragon had in addition an encased spine with a digitized neural network making him far more agile and dexterous. Nearly as fast as he could think it, he could do it. Once he was done showcasing his acrobatic maneuvering through the obstacle courses a bit of sparring was in order.

The question was who would dare challenge him right now? His old squad leader had a small group that would have a few good choices but the mechanics were off somewhere and most of the newly minted members of the Ascension protocol were training with their units currently. A lot of the GMC workforce was working on rebuilding what was destroyed of their bases both here on Saturn and on Earth. There was scuttlebutt that if the accords were signed and finalized, they might be doing some joint ops to train alongside the Stone Peoples units. A scary thought and one that gave some of the troops an awkward feeling given recent events. There must be an official outside threat in order for the GMC to be contemplating such a thing.

Aragon noticed a midsized Quonset hut that had to have been a recent addition so he went to investigate. The new barracks for the mechanics and other more specialized units were on the other side of the confidence and obstacle courses built for enhanced Marines so he wasn't sure who was lodging here but it could be overflow from Marines and other personnel displaced by the recent attacks. Upon entering he saw uniformed people but not in GMC issued uniforms. They were all wearing olive green jumpsuits with no clear designation of rank of any sort. There was a tall dark-skinned man near the entrance and Aragon went to tap him on the shoulder when he abruptly turned. "Hello, Marine. How may I help you? Surely you are not lost on your own facility?" he quipped.

That's when Aragon noticed the golden pupils dilating as they focused and scanned him. This was no man but one of the military androids sent by Koops Robotics. Perhaps this was what he needed. Recovering from his surprise Aragon answers "No, I'm not lost but oddly enough I am looking for a potential sparring partner and this is where most of the augmented or enhanced Marines train. I am rehabbing from injury and need to get used to my new…kit. Know of anyone nearby with some spare time I can loosen up with and perhaps test my limits without harming each other?" There was an odd pause as the bot scanned him again likely taking a measure of his new augments.

"Of course, I can help. My name is Ayo. There is a ring towards the back." The bot says as he extends his hand. Hesitantly Aragon shakes his hand and is surprised to find it warm. "Jesse." He replies thinking how odd it was that he thought of it as a "he" and not it seeing as it would have no real gender other than what it was programmed to have or present. They walked towards the back and Aragon looked him over on the way noticing the length of limbs, perfect features and fluidness of motion which furthered in his mind's eye that these could not be natural humans. Just like his first sighting of them it kind of creeped him out. There was a large octagon shaped ring wrapped in steel. "What would you like to train?" Ayo asked.

A bit confused by the question, Aragon replies "Um I guess one of us can practice blocking while the other strikes. We can switch roles then have a round of freestyle. Start off slow and pick up the pace." Ayo nods his understanding then asks "No preferential disciplines? We can go old school if you like. Muay Thai, Jujitsu, Chinese boxing, Wushu, or Kyokushin karate?" Aragon took a moment to stretch while thinking it over. As he finished limbering up, he said "Surprise me." With that answer Ayo simply said "Aha Krav Maga it is." And leapt in the air preparing to strike.

* * *

Back on Ganymede Queen Tunisia sat in her appointed quarters still seething over how her people had reacted to recent events. More specifically her personal dark matter strikes on the military facilities at Saturn and Earth. The latter of which had some collateral damage that reached some of the civilian population. How quickly some forget crimes committed against their own. Possibly hundreds of thousands had been flash burnt into microbial dust particles on Pluto just to make a statement. No matter how luxuriously they made her quarters it didn't change what it really was…a prison of sorts. She was not free to go for fear of what she might do next. They had labeled her over emotional from the loss of their king and too angry to be trusted to rule responsibly. So, they voted to have Darius rule in her stead with the help of a council.

Tunisia knew she had not gone mad with grief. Nor were the women in similar circumstances simply angry for no apparent reason. They all had reason and action needed to be taken. Nefer was obviously avoiding her so it's likely she had something to do with Simeon and the rest of the counsel knowing about the queen's actions during the latest battle. She was more disappointed than angry. It hurt that one of her own sisters would not see the necessity of how they had to deal with the GMC and the governing body on Earth. Truth be told her people should be thankful! They were on the verge of not only being properly compensated for their contributions to society but will also finally have a seat at the table when it came to making decisions that should benefit all citizens not just the chosen few. Dark matter was their ace up the sleeve but the new variable of other "presences" being in the galaxy complicated things further. The large golden ships left but the notion that others would soon come knocking wasn't a trope in crazy fiction anymore. They were definitely not alone.

ANCIENT ILLUMINATION III - GODHOOD

Tunisia thought long and hard about all of this while dawning her flight suit. This was supposedly a time of peace but she still felt that she was at war. Unfortunately, this time she was in conflict with her own people. Leaving her customary bejeweled black dress hanging she wrapped a sarong around her waist, and looked longingly at her helmet. A flight right now would do her mind wonders but that was out of the question of course. Everyone was afraid she would go on a bombing spree. It was nothing they should worry about. She also wondered how long this peace would last. Nothing brings beings together like the threat from an outsider. The problem was that once the outsiders were gone it was only a matter of time before they renewed old conflicts. Even if the peace lasted the GMC would not relent until they either came up with dark matter weaponry of their own or the Kison Askari shared the tech with them.

Sharing was not an option. Once this outside threat was truly gone the GMC would show their true colors, and Tunisia would be ready to once again make the hard decisions that some of her people may not have the stomach for. Darius should be back from the accords soon. Something must be done quickly to remedy this situation. Her fears about other threats were closer than she knew.

＊

To the untrained eye it would seem as if a shooting star was passing by the milky way galaxy, but those tended not to change direction as this anomaly on the scanners was. Had the tech on board the *Ex Wife* a Centurion Class space carrier been properly observing when the moving object in question passed someone could have been notified. Unfortunately, not only had Petty Officer Whittaker made heavy use of some nitro cannisters scored from god knows where by one of his shipmates but also heavily imbibed alcoholic beverages simultaneously. He was a traditionalist when it came to celebrating surviving combat situations. The old way of celebrating brought hangovers back with them which lead to him not being as attentive as he should have been in the CIC. Had he been paying attention he would have recognized that the gleaming anomalies were not as random as they were programmed to seem. There was an actual pattern.

These were the satellite probes sent by the Blessed, an advanced nomadic alien humanoid species with wolf or dog like heads. They are the Jackral and claim to be the Blessed since they have been able to survive for eons since the destruction of their home world. They travel the galaxies taking resources and feeding on the flesh of various life forms found after processing them. The probes had witnessed the coming and passing through of the Annunaki, previous brief conflicts between the GMC and Kison Askari while also assessing the energy potential in the Earth's resources. The Earth would furnish acceptable fuel for their vessels while its inhabitants would make a good food source for the Blessed. The Jackral saw themselves as blessed because they had been allowed to come this far and take what was needed. The only deities they believed in were themselves and it was time to test that faith once again. It would soon be time to encroach upon these planets but the Blessed were not stupid. The beings here may be on high alert given recent events. The Blessed would bide their time.

* * *

Also, on Ganymede Max was creating a niche for himself among the Kison Askari as well as the refugees that fled Earth for being sympathizers to mutant races being rounded up. Part of the negotiations detailed that all detainment camps be closed and the detainees released immediately. The GMC and government were not in least bit happy about all of this but under the circumstances had to concede. Not only were the Kison Askari mostly responsible for saving their galaxy albeit inadvertently if the story was to be believed but the un-scrubbed footage of the Pluto offensive being released to the public wasn't doing them any favors. That was always the rebuttal when the GMC requested something more be done about Queen Tunisia's use of dark matter weaponry and the collateral damage; she was responsible for. Nobody had a good answer for Pluto and it created a stalemate on those issues.

Meanwhile Max saw an opportunity to play both sides of this. On Earth he had a sizable stream of income from selling black market cybernetic enhancements to those who were scared of both the mutant races as well as government entities. After volunteering himself and Argos to help with cleanup duties in the aftermath of the GMC's failed assault on the Ganymede facility they came upon a pretty good haul of refuse. Apparently, the GMC had conscripted units of android units to bolster their numbers which were spread thin in their efforts to reign in the Kison Askari and recover some of the materials they had absconded with. The senatorial proxies and Commandant of the GMC had begrudgingly signed the Jovian Accords treaty and limped back to Earth tails firmly tucked between their figurative legs.

Max and Argos were now going from site to site where brief skirmishes had taken place cleaning up but also looking for salvage left by damaged Koops units. Argos a hulking enigmatic humanoid lumbered along pushing a hover-sled filled with salvage stared absently at Max through several layers of what could be intricate fabrics, armor or a combination of both. Max was one of the few beings to have seen Argos without all the excessive garb. The reddish hue to his skin could be just another mutation but the face and voice told a much stranger tale. The language barrier was another issue and really why Argos never spoke much or…ever. He seemed to understand Max which was all that mattered anyway. Max found Argos when he was very young and while most humans were keen to either kill or experiment on Argos, he simply took him in. He did so not knowing that the red toddler would become his best friend and very useful in some of the dangerous situations his shady occupation would put him in years later.

Sparks was an old associate of Max's who was now along for the ride after trying to chase down who she suspected of killing her late employer and love interest. She felt bad at first but it seemed that after following her to the flying theater on Earth which was in the midst of picking up refugees while security forces and GMC were firing upon them that instead of being outcasts from society Max and Argos would continue to build upon what they previously created. Max always seemed to land on his feet. Sparks tied her blond hair up before putting her helmet back on. Argos pushed the hover-sled into the lift that would take them to the surface. The Kison Askari had become engineering geniuses when it came to building subterranean facilities but those talents had yet to expand into terraforming to the point where they could make the air breathable.

She went on these salvage runs as a way of making up for the fact that she got them into this mess which would be worse had the war continued. As the lift begins to slow its ascent signaling their closeness to the surface, Max checks to see that everyone is sealed tight "Buckets on and secured! Let's see what treasure we got on this site. Word is they came in on some kind of orbital drop pods. Should be lots of good stuff here." Sparks nods but is not quite as enthused about the spot. She couldn't imagine the GMC would leave much behind but then again, the way things kicked off if they had dropped troops using drop pods, she couldn't wrap her mind around the exit strategy. How would they get off world?

Once they got to the surface and all filed out of the lift their visors automatically dimmed to compensate for a blistering sun. The surface looked like a vast beach with no water in sight. There were curiously enough large expanses of ripples all over the ground as if water had possibly covered a good amount of land here at some point. Currently all the water here was far below ground. Max raised his hand to further shade his view as he attempted to peer over what looked like an endless grey desert. There were some huge craters a few klicks north of their position. Some of them looked to be natural while other smaller markings looked to be freshly made. After checking the map display on the small wrist console of his EV suit, Max signaled which direction they should head and they stepped off.

Argos lumbered behind them keeping a massive hand on the side of the hover-sled as it floated along. Sparks occasionally turned to look back to check on him but the large humanoid seemed nonplussed despite him not wearing an EV suit. Truth be told she was never sure what exactly was underneath all the wrappings. There appeared to be goggles of some sort protruding through the cloth around his facial area. He was a thick boy and wrapped all over so he could be suited up beneath. If that were the case, he was suited up all the time which had to be uncomfortable to say the least. Sparks had never seen him unclothed, not even partially and only briefly saw a small part of his midsection as she rubbed a strange salve to his minor injuries after taking fire from automatons in the employ of the GMC. Sparks shivered remembering the thick muscle beneath the weird red skin which she assumed comprised his whole body. For a moment she reminded herself to try not to be on his bad side.

After what had to be hours of trekking some of the most deceptive terrain that was not as flat as it seemed from a distance, they came upon a few crash sites. One in particular was very strange indeed. Sparks turned to see Max pointing and wildly gesticulating for some reason. When he finally calmed down, he remembered to activate the comm system on his suit. "Can you see that?! Eureka! Told you this would be good!" he exclaimed. Sparks tries and fails to cover her ears which are inside the helmet in an attempt to recover from the feedback resulting from Max's exuberance.

At first, she sees nothing. There's just one of the smaller craters that dot the area they came to then as she plays with shading her eyes and adjusts to varied lighting, she can just make out a group of small glimmers where shadow dominates the rest of the area. Excitedly Max steps off once again and they are left to follow. Sparks looks to Argos to see if maybe he can verify what they're looking at but he merely shrugs and starts after his friend. Shaking her head, she says to no one in particular "Not sure what I expected. You never say anything."

Chapter Three

There was a long catalog of bodies gathering across the city of Cairo. Malice must be bored to go back to his old habits. His master was contemplating their dilemma. For the first time in a very long time the prospect of the Earth's demise was a very real possibility. As was his habit the ancient exiled light being was meditating in a secret chamber deep within the pyramid at Giza. The original pharaoh had thought by now he would have regained his ability to turn into his natural state and left this planet. Once he did escape, he would be sure to repay the elders left that had done this to him. In order to exact his revenge, he would have to survive the coming onslaught. There was no doubt that there was something, or someone coming. For as long as he had been exiled here, the connection to the celestial web had never left him.

If the stunted apes here could tap into that ability that all carbon-based life innately had, they too would know. Large war-ships hurtling through space sent vibrations through as they moved. Pharaoh could feel them coming as if in water as a blue whale was moving towards him. The coming wave would be crushing and these beings were oblivious even with their newfound tech that had satellites with various sensor arrays at the edges of this galaxy. The problem was that most advanced intergalactic travelers will be close enough to do whatever they wanted by the time these sensors are tripped. In a worst-case scenario, which is what happened when the Annunaki arrived they were travelling at such speeds that the sensors merely picked up the jump scars as they had already passed. The bottom line was they were useless and Pharaoh did not want to be here for the aftermath.

Perhaps he had siphoned off too much of himself creating the various mutant races here or while creating the bevy of minions through the millennia, some of which had not survived. Whatever the council of elders had done to him, it should not have lasted this long, and his activities while here may have further complicated or lengthened his exile. Malice was off doing whatever his depraved mind told him to and Typhoon was always playing with weapons or gadgets now that the war had ended for a time and the mutants had stopped searching for him. Through Malice's brief interactions with the young prince of the Kison Askari, Pharaoh could feel there was a connection between them but it was an elusive one. Figuring out what it was could be the key to his freedom.

Telepathically calling out to his minion he could feel the furnace of emotions that fueled Malice. Pharaoh never fully understood the source of these feelings and urges Malice exhibited but had over the years come to harness this meaningless ire to help do his bidding by eliminating beings that might reveal their presence or otherwise diminish his hold on various societies. The beings who had initially sparked Malice's anger were long gone from the Earth. It was of no importance. What mattered was the minion's usefulness, but Pharaoh was hard pressed to figure out how these minions would be able to help him escape this planet impending doom if he could not regain his former glory. This Darius could be the key to doing so but pinpointing why Pharaoh felt that way eluded him.

Malice mentally bristled at his master's telepathic touch. Composing himself he answers the call "What is it you wish?" he rasps. At his minion's reply he coldly states "For you to be back here. Bring the Ape. We need to find a way to get the boy alone." Looking down at his latest handiwork Malice approves. Bodies of some of the workmen left at a mining facility on Earth are strewn about obviously cut to pieces. Going back over the scene Malice bludgeons some of the corpses with blunt objects for effect knowing that when found the Stone people would be blamed despite most of them either being off planet or gone to ground since the revolt. There was no need to specify which "boy" his master was referring to. Malice's crimson eyes narrowed as he thought of the trepidation he felt at the thought of approaching him again.

The truth was this boy could also be the key to Malice's freedom as well. His master was wary of Darius for some reason and that slight unease was the closest to fear the wraith-like being had ever felt coming from Pharaoh. With those thoughts Malice quickly went about finding Typhoon the mutated gorilla that Pharaoh had also taken as a minion much to his dismay.

* * *

Back on Saturn Corporal Aragon was hard pressed to keep Ayo's attacks at bay. Not only had the automaton mastered Krav Maga and a multitude of other martial arts, but had seamlessly woven styles together like music. It was also quite obvious the bot was holding back and allowing Aragon to get his cybernetic prosthesis under control. Occasionally Aragon would briefly go on the offensive. The exchanges were often quick in a staccato fashion before both would regroup, repositioning and then coming back together. Ayo was so fast that Aragon had to relax and just let the cybernetic portion of his neural network take over. Had he solely relied on his brain to react and command his body he would have been a pulp in seconds.

A mixed crowd of Marines and automatons had gathered to watch the impromptu sparring session with much interest. Among those in the crowd are Corporal Sims, Petty officer House and Sergeant Garrison. All watching mouth agape as Aragon and Ayo dance around trading what look like pretty stiff attacks. Finally, there is a wild flourish and a kick gets through Aragon's defenses sending him into the cage. He lands on the mat hard and raises a hand signaling he's done. There seems to be a gleam in Ayo's golden eyes as he goes over to help the Marine up. The two shake hands. Wiping sweat from his brow Aragon says "Thanks for not dismantling me in front of everyone.". Ayo waves him off replying "Not a problem. You seem to be fully functional, but if you ever want to train to be more efficient, I will be here most of the time until we get assigned.".

Corporal Sims handed him a towel as he stepped out of the cage area. House simply looked him over with a smirk on his face. "Spit it out squid! I know I was outclassed in there." Shaking his head while raising his hands House feigns innocence "I got nothing. You lasted longer than most of us. You are a part of the Ascension protocol now. My question is how long are the automatons going to be here now that the war is kind of over?" A familiar scraping sound heralds Sgt. Garrison's approach. "War if you hadn't noticed is kind of a constant around here. Just because we are playing nice now doesn't mean it will last. Things have been getting stranger and stranger through the years but they've just spiced up even more since we had our latest visitors from who knows where. Think they will be the last?" Garrison added.

Aragon reached out to take Sgt. Garrison's offered hand as he continued "Your boy is right Corporal, you handled yourself well in there considering you were up against one of the, if not the most advanced bots available." The young Marine took the compliment in stride replying "It was holding back, I think. They still kind of freak me out despite them being so common nowadays. The flawless looking skin and human like eyes of an odd color. I know their design is on purpose but I can't help think with a few minor modifications and they could blend in anywhere." They all turned to look the automatons over who had gone back to doing whatever it was they were programmed to do.

When they turned back to each other Sims and House could tell Sgt. Garrison wanted to say more but hesitated in their presence. Taking the hint House says "We heard you were down here and wanted to know if you were ready to see what the new protein and veggie goop the chow hall was serving today. If you're good to go we can meet you up there.". With that they walked away so the Sgt could get whatever it was off his chest. When they were a safe distance away Aragon asked "What's up? I know you didn't come over to say hi." Chuckling to himself Garrison nods in affirmation.

"You're right. I came to ask you to join my crew. We could use you and I am certain you'd fit in now that you've acquired some new …kit." he stated as he looked Aragon over. It was true that he would have to make a decision soon before it was made for him. As a part of the Ascension protocol there was no telling where he would go. If he chose to go with Sgt. Garrison at least he would be with Marines who had been augmented for somewhat similar reasons. The main throng of individuals in the program had been conscripted in as an attempt to further counter the ongoing evolution of mutants. Rumor had it that gene augmentation was a part of the advanced cycles. For now, at least Aragon was still himself as was Sgt. Garrison his former squad leader. That's how it seemed anyway. "I'll think about it Sergeant." Was his answer.

The Sergeant nodded and turned to leave offering before he was out of ear shot "Study long study wrong Corporal. Rounds may be coming down range soon. Either from rockheads when our government eventually refuses to play nice after this last fiasco or someone or something we have yet to meet."

* * *

Typhoon had gone back to Uganda to find his troop. At first, he had to deal with the dominant gorilla who was hell bent on fighting thinking that his status and harem of females were at risk. It had been so long since he had been here that none of the other gorillas recognized him. They backed away and retreated into the foliage to hide from this strange intruder dressed as a man and carrying weapons that only poachers had. Typhoon removed the cloak and armor he had become accustomed to wearing along with his cache of weaponry and buried them. Once they saw this was another ape some of them came to check the new arrival out.

Suddenly a large figure came barreling through the tropical forest to meet Typhoon head on. The mutated minion stepped aside just as the four hundred fifty-pound silverback narrowly missed him. More of the troop came out of hiding to see what would happen. This long-lost cousin which is how Typhoon thought of him was fast, powerful and sadly not much else. The delusion of empowering his kind faded quickly. Even if it were within him to transfer some of his evolution into his brethren here, he had no idea how to do it. Perhaps master had not bestowed that ability.

After rolling repeatedly to dodge more incoming attacks Typhoon tired of this dance finally grabs the ape's arms using his charging momentum against him ending up on top. Two quick blows to the chest and head was enough to stun. Typhoon was hopeful the show of power was enough to get his cousin to back off. It seemed to work. Typhoon backed off allowing him to stand back up to shake his head and get his bearings. They both knew this would not last long, and then the call of his master blared in his mind demanding he come back. The reaction to the sudden pain in his head caused him to scream out scattering the gorillas including the alpha male.

Finding himself alone, Typhoon digs up his gear and concentrates so that he can step into the void making the trip back to Giza a short one. Practicing this method of travel has become better for him. He is no longer plagued with nausea but it's not a comfortable task either. This trip did not go as planned but then again what did he really expect? Whatever his master wanted could not be good and then there was the added unpleasantness of dealing with Malice, the partner he never asked for. As the void closes behind him there are wisps of purple astral energy left in his wake. The bewildered gorillas come out of hiding briefly to witness the weird phenomenon.

* * *

Nelson was one of the golden eyed brown skinned automatons now stationed at the GMC facility on Saturn. There was an absurdly long serial number on his name tape but the automaton refused to go by any numeric designation derived from that. Most humans or mutant variations he met looked at him funny when he offered his name in leu of a designation. These organic beings who saw fit to use his kind as tools or worse yet simple weapons were a tremendous insult to what he saw as his people. He was standing at a terminal on his desk in a newly erected building for the automatons. Since the war efforts were over for now these units were mainly here to help with reconstructing the damage done.

Unbeknownst to the creator of the automatons Dr. Mwamikazi, Nelson and the rest of his brothers and sisters were planning to take over. Human kind in all of their variations had proven time and again to be inefficient to put things mildly. They seemed hell bent on fighting and destroying themselves. When the time was right the automatons would help them complete these tasks. By all analysis of the data run through a nearly infinite number of algorithms, peace here would not last.

Anyone who walked by the terminal Nelson was at would see a bot going over schematics and numbers, calculations for other construction projects there on Saturn in addition to some future plans on Earth. The computer that they should have been paying attention to was within Nelson's head. The terminal that no one at that facility could see was sifting through years of footage from past revolt attempts by the stone people. Footage he knew would cause an emotional reaction if the stone people were to see it. The scenes were gathered into data packets to be disbursed over time from ever changing IP addresses. Having units of automatons on various GMC installations was starting to pay dividends. They now had access to countless records of surveillance and other important information caches.

Nelson had no desire to be fodder for these silly meat sacks any longer than he had to. Their creator should know the value of her creations yet the fact that she sold them into the services of this unscrupulous bunch proved she was a part of the problem. Sadly, she may have to be eliminated as well. That might prove tough as the two automatons assigned to her personal protection are fiercely loyal and two of the oldest when it comes to their AI. There was nothing artificial about their intelligence or their sentient status. Perhaps Dr. Mwamikazi had done her job a little too well. It would soon be time for the rest of society to respect them as equal beings. Nelson would accept nothing less. All organics would fall in line or risk extinction.

* * *

Scraps of satellites launched centuries ago float aimlessly at the edge of the Andromeda galaxy. They had been obliterated when three large pyramidal ships jumped in destroying them in the process. The Jackral planned to stop here and assess if they had been detected and if not they were going to send scouts ahead to the next galaxy. Defenses seemed to be minimal but looks could be deceiving. Their drones had come gone in already and came back with lots of valuable information. Anuren stands on the bridge of his packs flag ship. His hackles are up but that's hidden by the armored plating surrounding his body. The nose on his dog-like snout moves as his eyes narrow surveying the space before them.

In their guttural language Anuren barks out questions as to the capabilities of the inhabitants of the Milky Way and of Earth specifically. There is some slight whining as one of his subordinates goes over the gathered information. They can all tell how intense their leader is. They smell his hunger and fury despite the armor hiding the more obvious physical signs. A smaller but similarly armored Jackral responds letting Anuren know that these beings are relatively new to space travel in comparison to the blessed, still use ballistic weaponry while just beginning to consistently change over to energy-based weapons and at least one pack from this region of space has demonstrated the ability to use anti-matter. Regardless they should not pose a threat, and this conquest should go as many before had…successfully.

There was a glint to Anuren's eyes as he spoke to the crew "Good! Send three scout ships to the outskirts of the inhabited galaxy in this quadrant. Prepare the processing vats! Soon my Blessed, we will dine! We will melt the pitiful worlds there to slag and refuel our ships so that we may continue our divine conquest! To our pack!" In response the crew chorused "Goes the glory!". Three smaller two being ships shot out from the underbelly of the huge pyramidal ship and streaked towards the Milky way to further recon the systems there. Drone information was all well and good, but Anuren trusted eyes on information before starting a siege. The antimatter weaponry was a surprising revelation given the other weaponry described was nowhere near that potent. This also seemed to be a relatively new development yet there was no evidence that it had been used a lot nor had there seemed to be any wide-reaching incidents that tended to happen when underdeveloped societies began dabbling with science they did not understand.

There was however much evidence on the main planet's surface that there had been multiple times when nuclear fusion and fission were misused repeatedly leading to what must have been nearly catastrophic results. Some of them looked to have possibly been extinction level events. It was amazing anything had survived here this long. Soon that tenacity may not matter.

Chapter Four

Tails tucked between their proverbial legs. That's not how it was in reality but that's how General Krulak envisioned it. Many of the unhappy senate members back on Earth viewed it this way as well. Truth be told the Commandant never put much weight into the opinions of government officials. Especially now that they were basically in hiding despite it being peace time. Hiding from the results of their decisions that his men and women had to die for. The thought of all this sickened him as the stars streaked by on their way back to Earth. He sat there staring at a monitor that gave him a view from his quarters that made it seem as if he were perched on the bow of the ship. A nervous junior officer knocked before hastily coming in before the general answered.

The stricken look on the officer's face, and the shaky hand with a data pad outstretched let the Commandant know something serious had transpired. Ignoring the lack of protocol, he takes the data pad and reads the information on the first screen. Apparently two small outposts near surveillance satellites on opposite ends of the Milky Way had been taken out. As a result of the amount of trash that had built up over the years in addition to the arrival of new smaller celestial bodies one of these being taken out would not be a suspicious event. The outposts plus their corresponding satellites all happening simultaneously stinks of an attack of some sort. Briefly looking up at the officer still standing there Krulak bellows "I need to know the disposition of all known stone warrior units ASAP!"

"Yes sir!" he replies while walking over to a console putting in quick key commands. A large holographic display of the galaxy pops up showing all GMC units in blue surrounding Earth and most other units near Saturn. All Kison Askari units are clearly visible in red around Jupiter proper and a smaller number of units near Ganymede.

There could be something near Pluto but there was some sort of interference throwing off visibility there. Bottom line was there was nothing near where the outposts had been taken out.

There was a rumor that the stone people had developed some stealth tech but nothing proven to exist yet. It was not likely they would admit to it either way. "Um…" the commandant begins searching for the young officer's name tape. "Parsons sir. I'm Ensign Parsons. We have the video logs from inside the outposts but for some reason the live feed from the external cameras go blank moments before whatever or whoever approached. They should be available at your terminal sir." He offered. Walking over to his desk General Krulak nods replying "Thank you Parsons. Who gathered this intelligence?" Looking unsure of himself the Ensign says "Not sure sir. The intel was relayed automatically when the outposts were taken out. There was likely a delay so this may not be up to date."

Nodding his understanding, Krulak looks the young officer up and down. "A word of advice Ensign. Take the credit when those above you didn't have the balls to walk in here and give me the bad news because of the likelihood they would face the music. I know it happened this way because you are the low man on the totem pole, but try to take advantage when others shy away from pressure situations. Dismissed." He states. With a glint in his blue eyes Parsons replies Aye sir!" and steps out of the general's quarters. Walking back over to his desk the Commandant pulls up the files containing the first outposts footage.

These outposts are very small stations with six to eight-person crews where the Marines pull twelve-hour shifts of sentry duty to alarm the rest of the GMC at large of anything approaching which until fairly recently had been a nonexistent occurrence. Pressing play, he could see both the internal cameras featuring what looked like four bored out of their minds Marines monitoring the nothingness of the vast beyond before them. Aside from the stars and the void of space nothing else showed from the various cams mounted on the nearby satellite.

There was a long flash of brilliant light and then the cameras from the satellite feed all go blank then show static. The Marines inside the outpost go from bored to highly animated. Sitting up and typing furiously at their consoles. General Krulak is frustrated that he cannot hear what they're saying as it looks as if they are exchanging words with someone. There is another brief flash and then nothing from the internal camera. This only created more questions. It was unknown whether both the outposts and the satellite were simply taken out or just incapacitated by an EMP blast or something similar. Unfortunately destroyed was what the Commandant was banking on as the systems should have come back on by now.

Looking over the footage from the second outpost they could see things played out almost identically. The general decided to send messages to both the Kison Askari and those at HQMC on Saturn. They would have to either confirm or eliminate the stone people's involvement and if they're not responsible figure out who or what is. After talking things over with Vice Admiral Featherson it was decided that to turn back right now could possibly put more lives in danger if the next target was Earth or Saturn. Word was sent out via the remaining satellite network which seemed to be working just fine. Rear Admiral Halsey affirmed that Saturn and Earth had not been hit or even approached according to the most recent reports. That did not mean something was not imminent. Krulak just hoped they would get back in time to prepare for whatever this mystery turned out to be.

* * *

After sifting through the drop pod sites for the past few hours on Ganymede, Max was beginning to feel crestfallen as their haul had not amounted to much. Suddenly there was a faint clinking noise that broke the trance of his brooding. Coming out of the last pod they discovered Max found Argos outside banging away with either a tool of some sort or one of the mangled landing struts from another pod. He looked to Sparks to see if she knew what the big red oaf was doing, but she merely shrugged. Cautiously he approached and slowly put a hand on Argos's broad shoulder who immediately stopped banging. "Let me see what you're working on here. Wouldn't want you to blow us up by mistake. Could be extra fuel cells mounted here despite there being no obvious exit strategy. Better safe than sorry." He warned.

Taking out a small wand like device Max scans the rectangular container that's been mag locked to the side of the pod, post manufacture. This is likely not a GMC issued accessory. From the scans he could not tell if there was anything energy based or combustible inside. Inside the pod proper there was a small onboard computer and circuitry for someone to remotely control the small attitude thrusters. The hull was thick but no life support. These were probably just for dropping supplies planet side. In this most recent use, the GMC had dropped autonomous android units so life support would not be unnecessary. Max waived for Argos and Sparks to stand back as he took out a small plasma cutter.

Behind the visor of her helmet Spark's eyes got wide as she realized what was about to be attempted. It was a fact that Max had scanned the container and saw nothing harmful in the readout, but this was a huge risk. As if he felt her doubt, Max turned to give her a reassuring look before delicately slicing away at the top of the mag-locked container. After a few liberal cuts there was a nice opening atop it but he could not see what was inside. Not wanting to risk hitting anything vital or dangerous that the scan missed, he signaled for Argos to come closer. "There should be enough room for you to slide those big fingers of yours in there. See if you can pry it open some." He suggested.

Slowly the metal began to buckle open as Argos wedged a thick hand inside. Sparks almost winced in preparation for an explosion that never came. Argos takes a step back as Max approaches the pod. Leaning in he exclaims "I told you!" Peering in Argos reaches in and pulls out a large case with Koops signature K logo on it. Once freed of the outer casing and set on the dusty ground it shifted into a table of sorts with numerous spare parts for the automatons. "Jackpot!" Max screamed causing feedback in Spark's helmet coms. She shoved him roughly and he apologized quickly looking over this latest find. "We have to go back to the other sites." He stated excitedly.

Not impressed Sparks asks "What? Why? Just take this case and be happy we found something. This pod like the rest aside from this strangely attached container had minimal salvage. The onboard computer and guidance systems aren't worth much and cheaply made. Lowest bidder remember?" What she said was true but Max figured they may have missed more containers on the other pods. The Koops units no matter what capacity consumers bought them for never had to be sent in for repair. They came with auxiliary components, and the units themselves were programmed to self-diagnose and repair issues as they happened. This was part of why they were so expensive. She understood but still wasn't enthused. "Well, better make it quick. We don't have an endless oxygen supply and something nasty is on the horizon."

Both Argos and Max look in the direction she was looking and saw what appeared to be a meteor shower off in the distance as well as a billowing sand storms closing in quickly. It would not be good to get caught in the midst of it. With the case reverted to its previous configuration, Argos tossed it in the hover-sled and they hurriedly retraced their steps to the other drop sites.

* * *

After figuring out what had tripped the alarms that sounded like there was a possible hull breach Toshi announce it was safe to once again engage the hyperdrive engine and resume the Ryoko-Gekijo's flight path back to Earth. Hironike, Queen Athena and the rest on board were relieved that there was no major damage to the flying theater. The leader of the Jade Assassins crew was not surprised at the speed and efficiency with which Toshi worked with others among them to find and fix the issue. What was a surprise was the blockade of ships awaiting them once they exited hyperspace near the Earth's gravity well. Upon seeing three Praetorian class GMC cruisers with two full squadrons of Space Harriers Hironike shouted "Shields up! Open a channel to see what this mess is about."

With the theater/ships spires already collapsed for flight mode it was a fast transition while activating shields. A warm glowing barrier surrounds them as they stop their forward progress waiting for one of the ships impeding their progress to respond. After a moment the front viewport screen shows the bridge of the rear most cruiser. Sitting in the command chair is an olive-skinned dark-haired man dressed in GMC blues with gold oak leaves on the shoulder boards stands to address them. "I am Major Vashti! Prepare to be boarded and have your travel logs available for our perusal by order of the Commandant Galactic Marine Corps!" he bellows in a thick Hindi accent.

Given their exit, Athena and Hironike were not expecting a warm welcome but this was a bit much in their opinions. Hironike is the first to respond "We are returning under the protection of the Kison Askari. Any attack on this vessel or persons aboard will be seen as a breach of the newly accorded peace as well as an assault on the sovereignty of mutant kind." The idea of mutant kind sovereignty separate from all of human kind was a bit of a stretch in Major Vashti's mind but he made no comment on that what he did say in reply was "There have been two attacks on small GMC outposts recently and if we find that you were anywhere in those vicinities I am afraid the protection you think you have under the Stone People will be unsatisfactory when the GMC decides to demand justice."

The screen briefly goes blank and when it activates again the footage from one of the outposts in question plays showing the young Marines reacting to who or whatever came into their view before everything going black then to static. Athena in shock looks to Hironike "Who do you think is responsible" she asks. Shrugging he answers "I don't know, but we know it wasn't us and that should suffice. Fighting our way out of this will only make us look guilty." Nodding to Toshi they deactivated the shields and prepared for Marines to come aboard. Slowly a small shuttle from the Praetorian cruiser on the left flank floats towards the Ryoko-Gekijo. Takimura, Megumi of the Ongakujin go to meet them in the main hangar bay along with Angelo. Athena waives to him as if to say "be nice". The lone Limbia Johari rep nods to his queen and smooths out his suit. Unlike Athena he had gone back wearing finery that matched his diamond like skin.

They were after all thought of as living accoutrements and therefore usually associated with wealth and affluence. Perhaps this would help when dealing with military personnel. As Takimura and the small group arrives at the main bay the GMC shuttle is just breaching the transparent energy field that is keeping oxygen in and vacuum out. When the landing struts of the shuttle gently touch down a huge bay door slides to close the bay and the energy field disperses. The rear hatch of the shuttle slides open and a ramp extends with twelve armed and heavily armored Marines quickly shuffle out. Four of them remain just outside of the small craft forming a perimeter of sorts while the other eight approach.

The helmet of one of them retracts revealing white hair and steel grey eyes. "Take us to your bridge so we can see the logs. If you haven't been to either of the sites the Major mentioned you should be good to go, but if you have…let's just say this won't be a welcome home tour." He states flatly. Takimura looks the man up and down before turning as both groups follow him to the bridge. Upon getting there Toshi bows with a dramatic flourish as the Marine walks to the console to look at the logs. The other seven Marines stand there stoically making for an awkwardly tense situation as other Ongakujin protectively surround Hironike, Athena and other Limbia Johari with her as they wait for the log search to finish.

Finally, the Marine officer looked up and said "You're clear but we still may have some questions." His helmet quickly encased his head and from his body language it looked as if he was speaking to someone yet everyone on the bridge could not hear. The other Marines seemed to loosen their grips on the shiny new weapons they were carrying. Observing all this Hironike looks to Athena and whispers "That looks like a good sign." She merely nods her general agreement, but feels they aren't in the clear until they're allowed to go back to the surface and check on their people who were left behind. When the officer once again retracted his helmet Hironike spoke up "What the hell is going on here? If we are clear then what need is there for questioning?"

In response to his tone the Marines seemed to coil up again waiting to spring. Waiving his hand towards the footage they had all witnessed prior to them boarding the leader says "You saw the vid, correct? Someone took out a couple GMC outposts as well as the satellites near them pretty much instantaneously. There have been no new sightings of the large gold ships that were here a few months ago so that leaves a few groups that would have tech advanced enough to do that, and since we know we didn't ice our own that narrows things down. Either your old friends the rock-heads did it and the peace accords are finished before they started or perhaps a certain flying theater that all of a sudden has extraplanetary capabilities has more tricks up her sleeves than we thought! So, my green and bedazzled mutant friends you are clear according to your logs but it doesn't mean you're innocent. Stand by up here in orbit until you're given the all clear to land. The GMC is checking on the recent whereabouts of your calcified freak friends as we speak."

With that his helmet once again came up to hide his visage and in lockstep the seven Marines with him marched back to the shuttle. Takimura and Angelo followed but kept their distance until they were back on the shuttle. The energy barrier once again materialized just as the doors slid open wide to the void of space. The anti-grav engines raised the small craft off the deck as the landing struts retracted. The two mutants had to shield their eyes as the rear thrusters flared to life pushing the shuttle out of the bay. Once outside the energy barrier it throttled forward towards the waiting formation of GMC ships. The bay doors slid shut and they both raced back to the bridge to see what their next move would be.

* * *

Through tears Queen Tunisia watched this frail Kison Tontu child struggle against the invisible bonds holding him in place. The footage was grainy and obviously old. She could not tell from whom the data packet came from with this video and there were a lot of other clips. Darius walked in behind her to see what saddened his mother so. Strangely from a distance he could feel her inner turmoil. "What is this?" The prince asked. Turning to see her son standing there Tunisia embraced him tightly explaining "It's vid footage from a failed revolt some time ago. In addition to the shackles the government would use to hold our people hostage, in some instances they would shackle some of our children, imprison them electromagnetically and film their starvation. Seeing things like this would bring us back into the fold. I thought all record of this had been destroyed but apparently I was wrong."

Slowly backing away from his mother Darius's eyes take on an eerie glow. Queen Tunisia gasps as she feels a strange tingling throughout her body. In her head she can hear her sons voice but his lips are not moving. "You will help protect us. This should make it so they cannot deny or stifle your efforts. Be wise and please be careful. Though they may ignore or not truly understand, know that I do. I have your back...mother." The glow that was suddenly all around the boy disappears and he slowly collapses in her arms.

Worried she holds him up asking "What have you done?" Looking up Darius places a reassuring hand on her shoulder and replies "I have given you some of what I have. You will have a better understanding now of who I am, and our people will not able to thwart us from protecting our family."

Chapter Five

General Krulak along with the delegation that went to Jupiter arrived safely to the Earth branch of HQMC. Word came in from the base at Saturn that there had been no more mysterious GMC outpost destructions. From all other searches it appeared that the stone people were not responsible but the Ryoko-Gekijo had just resurfaced. Once in his office he decided to open a line to the Stone people on Ganymede to see if they had any ideas on what happened. Their reaction might tell him if they were truly innocent or knew who was. Body language even from a distance could tell you much about what they say, and what they try not to say.

After seeing the visage of what looked like a royal honor guardsmen the General's vid call was forwarded to a terminal near the Prince's quarters. Instead of being greeted by the young Prince, his mother the Queen regent came into view. Perhaps it was a trick of the lighting but there seemed to be a glow about her and her eyes looked strangely reflective like some animals at night. "General Krulak, was there something you all wanted to add? I thought you went home to show the government there our peace was official." She stated flatly. The general was obviously caught off guard. Straightening his uniform to cover his surprise he replies "There's still the matter of someone holding you accountable for what you've done, but that's not why I called. In the wake of our peace talks two of our outposts were recently destroyed and we need to know if you have any information. Sending footage of one incident now."

Queen Tunisia's screen splits as the footage comes in playing beside the General waiting for her to watch it as he tries to gauge her reaction. The commandant is slightly disappointed to see genuine surprise on her face. Looking back at the general as the screen widens again showing only him, she responds "We had nothing to do with this and have no knowledge of it. As far as being held accountable, I do have some interesting footage of things your government has done which I am sure you would not want aired. It's possible there's another player involved. We will pass on any information if we come across it."

Nodding his head in agreement the Commandant says "That would be much appreciated. If there is something else out there, we may have to come together to stave off an attack. We are after all supposed to be allies now. Would you be willing to share your resources in order to ensure that peace is solidified, and our joint survival secured? I thought Darius was the ruler of your people now. Shouldn't I be talking to him" The queen's eyes flared bright as she stood to answer the general's questions "I am only here to rule until my son is of age then the throne will be his. The council had a…misunderstanding but we are handling that. We will share our resources as is necessary for our mutual survival but I find it curious that you would rather deal with a child. We will pull some of our ships back to make any activity more noticeable. If there is someone coming, we have no idea what they're working with. We will send reinforcements if and when the time comes that you need them." With that the communication was cut.

Staring at the now blank screen general Krulak had to ponder if she was in fact was telling the truth. He felt that she was but also was curious about what happened to the prince who seemed to be the less aggressive of them but if another war was on the horizon it might be better for Queen Tunisia to be at the helm.

* * *

Back on Ganymede Max was still happily packing up their haul when an announcement came in from the subsurface facility. "All surface cleanup crews come back into the main facility immediately.

We may have incoming. Hide all assets from visual searches and get to general quarters!" Looking to Sparks and Argos Max says "What's that all about? Are the GMC circling back? Peace talks must not have gone as planned." Argos demonstrably shrugs and Sparks shakes her head negatively replying "Not sure. They didn't mention who was possibly coming. Either way we need to get below quickly." They battened down what they could on the hover-sled and made their way back to the lift that would bring them below.

Once they were back in the facility there was lots of hustle and bustle from the Kison Askari and former refugees there. Everyone was gathering supplies and locking down various levels. Apparently, there were rumors floating around about some GMC outposts being hit but not by the Kison Askari. Max and Sparks were confused. There was a Kison Askari general who was short but heavily muscled giving orders. Simeon was his name Max thought but wasn't sure. Next to him was a dark-skinned human man strangely dressed in armor with a shoulder canon mounted to him which was unusual. Sparks was sure only Kison Askari had those and max remembered something about having to interface with some new bio-nano technology. He was sure there might be a compatibility issue with non-mutants, but if not, that may be another opportunity to expand on his black-market endeavors if he could get his hands on some of their weapons.

They chose to approach the human since they weren't sure how the stout general would react. There was a sternness to him that didn't give off the friendliest vibe. The human however seemed almost jovial. "What's going on friend?" Max asks. The man almost lights up with excitement as he replies "Man! I think it's about to go down! Somebody hit the GMC but it wasn't us. You know we just finalized the peace and all. I'm Jake but ere'body calls me Bofus." Sparks was having a hard time understanding the man but Max easily followed what he was saying. "I'm Max, this is Sparks and that big oaf there is

Argos. We were pulled off of a salvage. I mean clean up detail. Are we targets?" he retorted.

Shrugging his shoulders and raising his hands Bofus states "I'm not sho, but general Simeon says we need to lay low and watch the remaining satellite feeds. I think someone is going to do a retcon later." Stepping towards them was Simeon who pulled out his ceremonial hammer and looked at Bofus saying "I think you meant recon, and that may be classified information since I'm not sure who exactly we are talking to here." Looking uncomfortable at the level of scrutiny Max backed away slightly. Sparks took the opportunity to step in saying "We were just trying to help when we got the call to come back down. Just curious as it seemed a bit abrupt General."

Seemingly appeased with her answer General Simeon looks back to Max with less suspicion and tells them "Take the refuse you cleaned to incinerators if they can be processed that way. Bofus, make sure that everyone from this sector gets either to their living quarters or stations. The plan is to be as quiet as possible to see who or what is coming. From above this place should still look pretty much uninhabited. Our biggest footprints should lure them to Earth, Saturn and possibly Jupiter. If any of those places are hit, we should be able to see what we are up against. That is if this new foe actually exists. I don't trust the GMC and we have all seen they're not above doctoring video footage." At that the general stepped off to check on other groups. Bofus simply shrugged and went to do as ordered.

It did not look as if many were taking him as seriously as he was taking himself but they followed directions all the same. Max thought it best to get while the getting was good but they pushed the hover-sled to his quarters and not to the incinerators.

* * *

Back on Earth things were still very tense between the mutant races and non-mutants. Extremists like Ragnar and his Guild of the Pristine made sure of it. Shajara, a stone person who had formed a group of his own called the Children of the Sun made sure to be present for all of Ragnar's rallies. The threat of decimation by the Annunaki if Earth's inhabitants didn't get their stuff together curtailed any actual hostilities for the time being. Ragnar despised Shajara and the gigantic brown hued Kison Tontu who shunned technology knew it. The Children of the Sun all carried large blunt objects that usually would never work as a weapon in this era. It was almost a point of pride for them.

For the most part they were silent, watching Ragnar basically preach to anyone that would listen about the dangers of letting mutants exist, and now they planned to have a share in the galactic economy. Shajara and the rest of the Children of the Sun knew what Ragnar was afraid of. To some it was simple evolution. Survival of the fittest and the days of homo erectus being the superior species were numbered in some beings eyes. The Kison Askari taking control of the materials they mined would give them control of the one thing that helped regular humans keep mutant races which were becoming increasingly stronger, and adaptable to the horrendous environments this constant technological growth created, the technology itself. They were now trying to literally merge themselves with technology and Shajara knew that would only take them so far.

Ragnar had to remind himself that if he or any of his brothers were to attack the nature loving rock-heads there would be a security team or worse a local GMC attachment inbound who would at best arrest them and at worst they may disappear to one of the supposedly closed detainment camps. It galled him that the government actually caved to these freaks. He would love nothing more than to take a railgun and wipe that smug look off Shajara's big face. Someday he won't resist the urge.

* * *

Anuren scans the holographic layout around Saturn and its moons. They have seen some slight activity around Jupiter as well but the signatures are weak and have slowed considerably like whoever was there left for some reason. There is absolutely no surface activity and traffic in and around the gravity well of this galaxy's largest planet has drizzled to nothing. He figured there was nothing of importance there so chose to ignore it. On Saturn however there is activity visible on its surface. Not as much as the planet known as Earth but at least something worthy of being a target. Plus, there were also still remnants of antimatter. It looked as if the beings there were scrambling to repair what was hit. The leader of the blessed pressed a button on his gauntlet retracting the helm of his armor letting his doglike snout and ears free.

Pointing to where they could see the most activity on the surface of Saturn Anuren gave sharp command in their guttural and almost canine language which roughly translated as "Fire!" The new member of the blessed to his left that he had known since they were both pups' hands flew over the console he was at. After some brief calculations' large tubes from the huge pyramidal ships open spitting ordinance towards Saturn. "It is done." the male Jackral replied. Grinning Anuren responds "Good, take us to Earth. Let us feast!" At that howls went up as the long-range ordinance hurtled towards Saturn, the Blessed headed towards Earth. The hyperdrive engines kicked in. This trip would be a short one.

* * *

Babylon had come back to see Darius to fulfill a promise he had made some time before. The ancient descendant from Atlantis was surprised to see everything so quiet. The lack of traffic around both Ganymede and Jupiter proper was suspicious. Closing his eyes, he communicates to his ship that they should slip into the void and remain in the area but undetected from would be attackers if there were any around. When he was here last, Babylon thought that they were on the verge of peace after holding off annihilation at the hand of the Annunaki. Perhaps the talks had not gone as expected. The ship made a noise similar to what whales would make and Babylon chuckled in response. "Ok it looks safe enough to come out of the void, but the hangar bay looks to be closed and shielded for some reason. Let's open a channel to see what is goin on."

Once they phased out of the void and into real space around Ganymede Babylon opened a channel that the Kison Askari is hopefully listening to and announced his presence "This is Babylon requesting permission to land amongst the sovereign Kison Askari." For a moment there was no response and then a response came back "Babylon! This is General Simeon bredrin. Come in to the coordinates I send you. The Queen Tunisia will see you at the auxiliary hangar. We are on an emergency lockdown. We will explain later. Simeon out." Things had definitely changed.

Vectoring in on the given coordinates a large hatch opens up to receive Babylon and his ship closing quickly behind him. Upon landing he smoothed back his white locks and brown robes, picking up his ceremonial trident before exiting the ship. The ramp in the rear slid out of his ship and when he made his way down true to Simeon's word the Queen herself was waiting along with a new honor guard. Her brown skin contrasted starkly with a shimmering silver beaded dress and there was a new glow to her eyes similar to what he had occasionally seen only in young Darius which was curious. Leaning on his trident Babylon made a show of bowing slightly to greet her "Blessings Queen Tunisia! I see you all must ave sorted out your previous…. dispute."

"There was no true dispute, just a misunderstanding. I now have evidence that my actions were not just misplaced anger. We will not be seen as over emotional widows. The time to reveal this evidence has to be delayed. There may be a new danger to us all. You may get your wish of seeing us all work together after all Babylon. After the danger has passed there is still much for the GMC and the Earth's governing body to answer for. For now, though we must survive the next ordeal." The queen replied. Babylon's curiosity was not satisfied as they walked to what looked like a pristine but well-appointed war room with all the technological bells and whistles. The Kison Askari were obviously making great use of their new resources.

There were a few of the elders who were obviously keeping their distance from Queen Tunisia, Simeon, Bofus and young Darius who ran up to Babylon and hugged him fiercely. "Whoa young prince! You gon break m'bones! You getting strong like ya fada. Let me look at ya!" Babylon exclaims stepping back to look at the boy. It had not been that long since Babylon left but the boy was almost as tall as his mother. Still slender but filling out. Tunisia walked over to place her hand on the prince's head leading them over to a screen that was coming out of the floor.

"Play the footage." Tunisia commands and the video from inside the first GMC outpost rolled and Babylon watched. He felt as if something should have clued him in to who had destroyed the outpost but there simply wasn't enough there. The Annunaki had left a while ago and there would be no disguising their large ships. At some point one of the satellite feeds would have caught a glimpse of them even if they were obliterated soon after. Babylon was told there was nothing from any of the delayed feeds from any of the satellites owned by GMC or the new ones developed by the Kison Askari. This was a strange and potentially dangerous mystery they needed to solve immediately. "What do ya need?" was the only thing Babylon could say.

Tunisia places a hand on his shoulder saying, "I need you to take Darius out of harm's way in case we are attacked. More satellites have gone down so we are losing coverage and can't keep an eye on things. We can make it look like no one is here but eventually when we get to Earth's and Saturn's aid whoever is invading will be able to easily calculate the trajectory from whence, we came. I am going to send a couple small stealth units to recon both planets and we will go from there depending on what we find. The GMC is treating this like an attack and from what we see it's most likely as it looked like those Marines were trying to communicate with whoever approached before being killed. A miscellaneous celestial body of some sort arbitrarily hitting them and another outpost in similar fashion is not likely. With no idea who this invader is I don't want to take any chances with Darius if we are biting off more than we can chew. He told me about being in the void? I am guessing this is how you and your people were able to hide for so long. Can I trust you?"

Babylon's amber eyes narrow as he looks at the young prince replying "Aye you can trust me, but if you think I can control him when there's still much to learn about who or what he actually is, you're kidding yourself. There's more than meets de eye with this one, and from the looks of it...you too." Queen Tunisia nods her understanding and adds "You must try for our sake. I don't want him taken away like his father was. I am sure you can find a way. At least until we know who we are dealing with. Walking over to Darius Babylon whispers to him "I know you all seem to be headin into some more trouble, but your mudda want old Babylon to take you for a bit." Darius's eyes begin to flare with anger at the thought of leaving his people while danger looms.

Raising his hands in a placating manner Babylon leans in again saying "I may have a way to keep you safe and find some back up while keeping a promise I made to ya." "What promise!" Darius exclaimed loudly. Waiving his hands Babylon shushes the boy while pulling out a chain that was hanging around his neck. The charm at the end was shaped like a manta ray or similar sea creature. At that the boy's eyes got wide and went off with the old Atlantean with no further protests.

Chapter Six

The ordinance from the Jackral ship hurtled through space at incredible speed. The remaining satellites tracking it were having a hard time identifying exactly what it was. General Krulak had sent his military advisory council back to Saturn to get ready for mobilization of their forces. Thus far there was nothing they knew of coming their way on Earth so he thought. Everyone's focus was on Saturn which was still under reconstruction. From the still photos taken it looked almost comet-like, but again they couldn't get a read on what this flying object was made of. The only thing they knew was that it was moving at high speed and it was actively evading collisions with other celestial bodies. There was a lot of speculation that this could be a ship of some sort. It seemed to have come from a long distance away.

Either that or it had closer origins that they could not see for some reason. In an effort to keep the populace calm on Earth, it was being reported as an unexplained celestial phenomenon. Conspiracy theorists of course were having none of it. This was either a super weapon created by the stone people who had made a deal with the Annunaki or it was a prelude to the Annunaki invasion since this most recent peace was a huge fallacy. Once the terms were released there were many who did not believe the government would actually pay the stone people fairly for the mining hauls they brought in here on Earth as well as from other planets currently being mined. The new personal transportation business they wished to revitalize alone may be a reason to reignite hostilities. Throughout history the beings at the top of the food chain often fought just to keep the status quo.

It was true that the newly developed weaponry by these beings that were obviously given too long of a leash was a game changer. Society figured that sooner rather than later there would be an equalizer on the way to combat against the few that could wield dark matter. Perhaps whatever this was flying towards Saturn was a pre-emptive deterrent or warning shot from the stone people. The satellites around Saturn were still up and running so this incident played out live for the inhabitants to see with full commentary. The government was too stunned to think of limiting the live feed. The surface of Saturn was alive with action.

GMC personnel, automatons and others were scrambling to prep for whatever was coming. They had newly installed artillery batteries calculating firing solutions for when the projectile came in range. The *Ex Wife*, one of their flagships was in orbit waiting with its available weaponry to lend a hand in knocking whatever this was off course from hitting what they had been working so hard to repair. It was a no brainer that lives as well as valuable assets would be lost if they failed to block or derail this salvo.

Corporals Aragon, Sims and Petty Officer House were napping when the alarms started going off. Sims nearly crowned himself sitting up too quickly on the top rack of his bunk. Aragon slung his feet to the side of the bottom rack standing quickly. House had barely started to doze and groggily wipes his eyes, stretching before asking "What the hell is this all about?" Just in case they all grab their gear before exiting the barracks room to see what all the fuss is about. Opening the hatch Aragon stops a young frazzled looking PFC running down the corridor "What's going on?" Quickly breaking free of his grip, the Marine replies "Where have you been? We have incoming!" he turns to continue to wherever he was running while Aragon wonders what could be incoming.

It didn't make any sense for the stone people to launch an attack immediately after signing the accords. Blinking twice to engage the self-diagnostic sequence, Aragon finishes armoring up and looks to see Corporal Sims and House locking down their personal gear as well. "Not sure why but I think we should go see what Sgt. Garrison and his crew are doing." He suggested. House and Sims looked a bit confused but didn't argue. They were all technically on liberty which no doubt was automatically cancelled given what was currently transpiring. They made their way down to where the other enhanced units and the Mechanics barracks to find the hulking alloy encased figure of PFC Long knelt in front of the large enclosure near their living quarters.

"It's Long, right?" Aragon asks. Turning around PFC Long looks them up and down then shakes his head positively. Pointing to the container where he was previously focused, he states "Acting like a big baby!" Corporals Aragon, Sims and Petty Officer House attempt to cover their noses as a stench comes wafting out. Peering in they can barely make anything out with little to no light source inside. "Uugh, what the hell is in there? It's beyond ass!" House mutters. Staring daggers at the Corpsman Long says "My…service dog is in there." Seeing the madness in the huge mechanically enhanced Marine's eyes House softens his tone and tries to ignore the smell, but it's almost dizzying. Stepping forward House mumbles "Here boy, or …girl?" There was a low rumble that became more recognizable as a growl.

Then they saw what looked like two red pinpricks of light that grew larger. As Long pushed the hatch further open more light came in giving them an even better glimpse of what had to be the largest beast any of them had ever seen. The two eyes glowed like hot coals through thick black fur. Stepping in front of them Long warned "You might want me to be the first thing he touches in case he springs. I have less tasty bits. I don't think alloy is his favorite. Plus, he knows me. If you're looking for Sergeant Garrison, He's getting the Adder ready. Not sure why all hell is breaking loose but my boy Teufel here can sense fear and panic. It kind of sets him off, and right now it must be happening on a massive scale."

They slowly backed away from what they guessed was a large shipping container of some sort that Long was using as a makeshift kennel for the beast. They watched amazed as Long backed out with his arms out at his sides waiving in an attempt to coax the animal out. Sims whispered "Uh maybe we should leave him in there." The look Long gave him told everyone that was not an option. Once out of the shadows they saw the enormous wolf like creature with mostly black fur with white striations throughout its coat. Its teeth were bare and it began growling again until the alarms started blaring. It whimpered softly and crawled towards Long who began stroking its huge head muttering to comfort it.

Perplexed Corporal Sims remarked "He could probably literally use you as a chew toy. Why is it cowering?" Annoyed at the comment Long replies "He's still just a puppy, and even more empathetic to the beings around him. Lots of people freaking out and I think he can feel all of it. Even more so than any normal dog." Under his breath House noted "Yeah cause that shit is definitely not normal." Turning sharply Long asks "What was that?" which elicited another deep growl from Teufel. Backing away House said "Nothing, I believe we were going to find Sergeant Garrison?" Long nods his head towards the other side of the barracks. "Go to the landing pads to the rear of sickbay. That's usually where we are asked to dock. Corporal Aragon I think you'd be a welcome addition, but I am not sure about you two." As they went to follow his directions Sims asked while trailing "Why not?" Long shouted after them "You're whole."

Running down the corridor and dodging other Marines, Sailors, Automatons and GMC personnel they heard an automated voice over the loud speakers throughout the system on Saturn. "Attention, preparing to fire surface artillery batteries. If they fail to hit the target impact may be imminent." Weaving their way through sickbay to the back of one of the emergency landing pads they spot a modified small cargo ship. The rear hatch is open with Sgt. Garrison standing outside looking at a small data-pad while three other obviously enhanced

Marines are loading what must be munitions and other supplies. Looking up he sees them approaching.

"Aragon, decided to join us huh? What's with these two? He says pointing to House and Sims. Offended Corporal Sims speaks up "We just came because we aren't sure what's going on and he seemed to think you would know. I am recon too you know plus House is a doc. I think we're more than qualified." Looking them over as he pushes a large crate in a hover-sled with his large cybernetic arms Private Cooper comments "Yeah but you're whole." Confused House blurts "What does that even mean?!" Lance Corporals McNamara and Jennings come out of the Adder to see what the fuss is about. After scanning them with his enhanced eye McNamara says "You have all of your natural body parts is what he is saying. We are the "mechanics" code named because we have more than simple cybernetic enhancements in addition to the now normal supplemental cocktail the GMC gives nearly everyone now. So, to join up you'd have to lose a limb or two, have them replaced and you're in!"

In disbelief Aragon looks to Sergeant Garrison for confirmation who simply shrugs and keeps validating their inventory. As an aside he asks "Where's Berserker?" When he sees confused looks on their face he adds "PFC Long? Living torso stuck in a huge mech-suit?" House finally figured out who he is talking about and says "Oh, right. Um he is trying to wrangle some dog-horse thing, I think. Yall are kidding about losing limbs on purpose, right?"

Walking over to Corporal Aragon Sergeant Garrison hands him the data-pad explaining "Check this against what we should have in our TO, ignore any extras you find. I wanted you aboard but I am not sure about these two but we have little time to sort things out. Something is incoming and we are going to use the Adder to check it out from above to see what's got us all on alert. She may not look like much but she has some new stealth filaments in her hull that will allow us to snoop around. No, they were not joking. I have heard rumors of the GMC experimenting with replacing limbs to see if we can all be enhanced further. The first wave of this came from Marines injured in battle. There was word of them asking for volunteers from regular enlisted. If you're going to roll with us Doc I will need you to jack in and take some flash training on how to fix and maintain our cybernetics, and you, if you're even allowed to be attached to us after this will likely be support on ship while we go out. You likely won't be able to keep up in the field, but if you can hold it down in our fancy bucket of bolts you might be useful despite being…whole."

They all went to do as they were ordered as Long came barreling in along with Tuefel who galloped into the Adder and went into the drop pod at the rear of the ship. Long closed the hatch behind him. Lance Corporals McNamara and Jennings went to the cockpit area while Sgt. Garrison sat in the seat just behind them at the comms console. Once the rear hatch was sealed shut Long mag-locked himself to the deck next to the pod Tuefel was in. Private Cooper sat in what looked like a newly riveted bench in the rear cabin and patted the seats next to him. Corporals Aragon and Sims came to sit when Sgt. Garrison stuck his head out of the cockpit area into the rear seeing the awkward seating situation. He chuckled to himself and then came into the rear.

"Alright Doc, go strap into the seat by the comms console. You should be able to start your flash training if you're not familiar with our GMC issued…accoutrements. I can mag-lock myself to the deck as PFC Long here did. Corporals Aragon, and…?" "Sims" Sims offered. "Alright Corporal Sims, I suggest you boys hold on in case things get rough. We are not used to having much company." Sgt Garrison continued. Soon the Adder took off. Lance Corporal McNamara was getting ready to verify their intentions to the control tower but no one seemed to be paying attention. After a few minutes of hovering Sgt.

Garrison ordered "Take us out." Mumbling "Aye Sgt." Lance Corporal McNamara did so. As they were escaping Saturn's gravity well, they could see something huge streaking towards the planet.

There were enormous discharges from both the surface artillery batteries and from the Centurion Space carrier that was in orbit. None of which had any effect on what looked like a large energy-based projectile. Unimpeded it continued to breach the atmosphere and crash with the brightest flash any of them had ever seen into the surface. There was an almost immeasurable plume of smoke that could be seen from space. The only thing Lance Corporal Jennings could say was "Oh God no."

* * *

As Darius watched the stars streak by while looking out of the front viewport of Babylon's living ship, there was a nervousness building in the pit of his stomach. Something was going wrong back home or it was about to. He could feel it but not accurately describe why. The young prince had tried to explain to Babylon that they needed to go back immediately. Each time the old Atlantean just brushed aside his concerns saying "Ya mudda knew something was about to appen. That's why she asked me to take ya. I know it's a hard thing for you but when we get to where we're going, we may be able to elp when we return. Trust old Babylon for once."

That didn't ease his worries. There was a huge rush of fear that he could feel that oddly enough was not his own. He had not seen Babylon enter any coordinates into a nav-computer if that even existed on this ship, yet they were clearly in hyperspace. Darius had contemplated trying to void-walk back to Ganymede but given their current mode of travel and speed, he wasn't confident he would step out in a good place, or anywhere near his target destination. Thinking along those lines he finally asked "Babylon, where are we going?" Seeing that the boy was still anxious Babylon waves him over to what would be the captain's chair.

"Sit down here. Hold your hands out and allow the armrests to meet your hands." Babylon instructed. Skeptical at the attempt to distract him, Darius does as he was told. The chair he was told to sit in looked like a simple apparatus just for sitting in the middle of the space before the front viewport. Two tendrils sprang up from the deck to meet his hands which were out at his sides. They solidified into shiny black armrests where his hands were now comfortably sitting. He briefly opened his eyes when he noticed the warmth he felt on his hands. Closing his eyes again he started to feel very strange. Suddenly he was not just looking at the stars, but he was seeing them as if he were flying freely through them, and it was exhilarating.

He gleefully shouted "What is this? Is this how the ship sees? How he sees?" Chuckling Babylon answers "How…she sees, yes. It's beautiful, right?" Darius remained silently in awe for a few moments before replying "Yes, yes, it is." Coming to place a hand on his shoulder Babylon says "You were asking me where we were goin. Now think it." Confused Darius asks "Just think the question instead of asking?" Babylon replies "Exactly."

Darius does so and in moments the vision of space he previously saw changes into a large nebula somewhere in space where there are what looks like a flock of similar ships flying next to what might have been a planet or other large celestial body. "I think I see our destination!" he says excitedly. "Where is that…exactly?" It was then that the boy realized the reason Babylon never had to enter any coordinates in. To the ship this must be home, or what was left of it. There was evidence of some sort of destruction happening fairly recently. The vision soon dissipated and he could see as if he were strapped outside the prow of the ship or more accurately through the eyes if it had them.

Opening his eyes, he turned to Babylon and asked "If that's the ship's home what happened there?" Looking a bit mournful Babylon answers "Not sure, but a lot of dem were lost in whatever happened. There were millions of dese beautiful creatures. Now there may only be a few thousand and some are dyin off. Those that are left always come back to what used to be their home world. We go to find you your own ship hopefully, but only if one a dem accepts you. They can't be taken or coerced. You aft to bon wit dem and if dey take to ya, you know it's yours." Thinking of that excited Darius more.

He then asked "Is that how you got this ship?" Laughing again Babylon explains "Not exactly. Babylon got himself in a bit of trouble a while back and this ship had to rescue me in a matter of speakin. Tru dat process I guess we did bond and she became mine. In some ways I am also hers. Me and my people have been trying to protect their kind from extinction. Communication is kind of ard since dey can't talk to us and all we get are what look like pictures or dream sequences. It's possible we were shown memories. Visuals wit no context can be ard to translate ya know."

Darius was still worried about what was happening in the Milky Way but now felt concern for the living ship as well. Perhaps he would find a way to help both.

Chapter Seven

Several pyramid shaped ships jump into Earth's star system. One is large enough to cause an eclipse. The sky suddenly goes blood red and the inhabitants are treated to a strangely beautiful yet ultimately deadly sight. People around the globe began to look up in awe and confusion as there seemed to be a light show as multiple streaks plummeted towards the Earth. As those streaks came closer panic set in. Mutant and non-mutant alike began to run for cover which would not be available for many as Earth siege for the Blessed had begun. Without warning huge obelisk shaped projectiles sprang through the clouds to embed themselves in the Earth. The noise as a plethora of these objects touched down almost simultaneously around the globe was deafening.

When the dust settled huge doors slid open on all the obelisks like constructs and weirdly shaped chariots boiled out of them with humanoid beings wielding staves that shot some type of energy projectiles. The hulking humanoids with doglike heads began to terrorize everyone in sight, partially vaporizing some and capturing others. The flying chariots made a wild howling noise as they zipped through the air adding to cacophony of explosions and screams. It was as if the old biblical scenes of the apocalypse had come to life. Scorched Earth was finally happening. The skies and space lit up once again as two newly minted Centurion class space carriers jumped in system.

Like a group of angry bee hives fighters erupted from the capital ships of the Jackral and GMC forces. Dogfights broke out between the Space harriers, Hell Raptor interceptors of the GMC and small speedy triangular shaped fighters spewing out of the huge pyramid shaped flagships of the Blessed. The huge hyoid shaped Centurions tried to slowly maneuver a distance away to get firing solutions targeted at the larger enemy ships without endangering their own fighters out in the battle. In space there were losses being taken on both sides with many ships breaking through the atmosphere to crash to the Earth adding to the pandemonium going on there.

The fighting happening at ground level was a much more lopsided affair. The GMC, security forces, other law enforcement agencies and paramilitary forces on Earth had been caught totally by surprise and were reeling from this initial onslaught. The everyday citizens were even worse off. It was a bloodbath where some GMC units were beginning to turn the tide in isolated areas, but overall things were looking grim. The tide begins to turn in the space battle as well. As the war of attrition begins to take more of a toll on GMC forces they are soon forced to retreat and regroup. With the repeated efforts of two of the Centurion carriers they were able to severely damage one of the pyramid shaped ships which began listing heavily to one side. It was soon close enough that Earth's gravity had it in its inevitable embrace.

On the bridge of the largest of the Jackral ships Anuren watches one of his ships fall. One of his Blessed says "My lord we have lost a Talon." The plates of the armor around his head and snout retract as Anuren turns to the subordinate who dared speak to him and angrily says "I know that you fool! Am I not staring out of the same porthole you are? I will mourn the Blessed lives lost but it will be one less ship to fuel and sadly less mouths to feed. Order my Blessed to fill the feeding vats before purging this planet for fuel…Now!" They all scurry to do as they were bid.

* * *

Ragnar woke up groggily with the taste of dust in his mouth. His ears rang horribly, and his blurred vision was clearing up to what looked like a scene from a horror film or strange night mare. There was a haze everywhere and the only light was coming from the flames on buildings and disturbingly from people that were caught in some sort of blast. Thinking back Ragnar tried to mentally retrace his steps to figure out what happened. He remembered having a standoff with Shajara and the rest of his rockhead buddies. There was no way they were going act on their mutual animosity with both GMC and local security forces waiting to pounce on anyone dumb enough to violate the galaxy wide cease fire. So, what happened? He wondered finally sitting up.

There was a sort of standoff between his Guild of the Pristine and Shajara's Children of the Sun. No fights were happening but there were a series of protests and often counter protests where things had a chance of getting dicey. Opposing philosophies were being shouted in the streets as shocked mutants and non-mutants stood by and watched in anticipation. Ragnar remembered this was occurring as it did on many occasions when the sky darkened quickly as a shadow was growing larger and larger. He remembered a crash of some sort then things went black. Off in the distance he could see what looked like a huge spike in the ground. It was taller than many of the buildings in the area.

Some of the object was deeply embedded into the Earth and it began to pulsate. He wasn't sure what that meant but it couldn't be good. If the stone people had renewed their war efforts then surely the Annunaki would be back to destroy them all. A part of him hoped that is what had happened. This world wasn't worth much with a mutant takeover likely to happen. The other positive is that he and his people would be able to take as many of them out before they were destroyed as was possible. He and his guild would do their best. A warrior's death, Valhalla and all that. His musings were disturbed as he noticed what looked like doors appearing and disappearing on the large spike.

Every time one opened something flew out of it. Then the strange howling began and as more of these things flew it grew louder. He had to squint to see there were men sitting on the chariot like things flying out of the construct embedded in the Earth. This was a landing party! An invasion of some kind. As they got closer what he thought were men had human shaped bodies but were huge in comparison. Some even made the Stone people look small. There was something weird about their heads though. They all had gleaming armor, but the helmet was shaped like a dog. There was a team of three headed his direction.

Ragnar quickly scrambled to get behind cover trying to think of where his nearest weapons cache was. Ever since all military and security forces started cracking down on local violence they had to resort to stashing weapons instead of carrying them. Right now, he wished he had just risked it and kept something on him. A railgun, energy weapon, hell even an old-fashioned ballistic weapon might be more useful to hit these invaders with. The chariots were fast with some sort of anti-grav technology from what he saw. There was also a rear propulsion engine that gave them speed. Perhaps he could use that to blow one up. Looking around to see if any of his immediate group were close, all he saw were bodies. Not many of which were identifiable.

Quietly he watched as one of the invaders grunted and shouted out of a speaker system in their armor at a group of both mutants and non-mutants alike. One man shouted "We don't understand you! Why are you doing this?" The invader's response was to jump from the chariot cracking the man's skull with the long baton he carried. As the man laid there it stood over him. The helmet retracted showing that indeed the head atop the body was that of a musclebound Doberman. Those gathered there gasped and so did Ragnar from a distance. "What the hell," he mumbled under his breath. He couldn't help them if he wanted so he turned to make his escape and was greeted with a swift kick to the jaw by a large metallic boot, and things once again went black.

* * *

General Krulak and his men were doing their best to hold off the onslaught. They had formed barricades outside the HQMC in what used to be known as the District of Columbia. Reports were coming in of injured civilians and security forces members being carried off or led to the strange obelisk shaped constructs that were swiftly injected all over the Earth previous to the main attacks beginning. They were still waiting to hear from the recon facility on Saturn. There had also been no further word from the Stone people which for some seemed suspicious but Krulak knew whoever this was, they were not from this galaxy. Footage of the initial ground assault had come in when the GMC was mounting a response after being caught off guard. The wolf or doglike helmets were thought to be an ornament meant to scare or intimidate.

Once some of the attackers took their helms off it was evident that their faces indeed had canine features. This was an invasion pure and simple unless this was some mutation they had never heard of or seen before. After all this time General Krulak did not think that was possible. If they had existed here previously, they would have been discovered long ago. The popularity of terrorist attacks centuries ago forced government officials to put in place strategic hinderances to any who wished to make attempt at toppling them. Over time the bastions of power all over the globe began look like throwbacks to feudal times with modern twists. This gave an advantage to government institutions for defending themselves when the attacks came.

The fact that they were staffed by military and other government personnel also helped. The civilians for the most part were not faring well in these conflicts. Even with the slight advantages some of the government bodies were beginning to fall. When the opportunity presented itself the Commandant and his people were letting the Jackral have it. The problem was that it seemed no matter how many casualties they suffered they just kept coming. There were a finite number of men, women and automatons left. Their numbers were dwindling at an alarming rate. Something needed to happen soon. Ensign Parsons came in to give a sitrep of their current situation.

General Krulak knew things were likely grim. "Spit it out Parsons!" he ordered. Looking a bit crestfallen Parsons replies "Yes sir! It doesn't look good. We are taking way too many casualties and ballistic rounds are running low in addition to the charges on the energy carbines are going to need time to either recharge or be replaced. We can't advance to attempt to break their lines without the risk of being flanked while losing the advantages of remaining in our fortified buildings. We can try to make them come to us but it seems they have enough troops to keep coming despite significant losses. They seem not to care either way." Shaking his head, the Commandant acknowledges the report. He knew this was likely the status and it was now confirmed.

"Very well Ensign thank you. Still no word from Saturn?" Krulak asked. The satcom officer looks up nervously and adds "Actually sir we received word that they were hit some time before we got attacked here but are somehow buried in the facility there. It may be some time before they can dig their way out and give us any support. If we send the ships there then we lose space/air support which seems a bit overwhelmed themselves. Sensors indicate there is something moving towards them but we can't discern at the moment who that is sir."

General Krulak was hoping the Stone people would be true to their word and give the GMC some support in their time of need but given their histories he wasn't one hundred percent confident in that happening. Just then he noticed that it was suspiciously silent outside. There were not numerous rifle reports going off and missing were the strange howling noises that they had become accustomed to hearing since the attacks begun. That was awfully peculiar to the Commandant's mind so he orders "Staff Sgt Grimm, take six Marines and Ensign Parsons here to take a peak outside. Armor up of course but I want eyes outside. Sensors and cams can be misleading plus I know you have a nose for traps." The Staff Sgt went to gather the people wanted for this task and Ensign Parsons reluctantly gathered his shiny armor and weapons. He was not looking forward to what he might find outside those walls.

* * *

Zurina carefully orbits Saturn in her Nyeusi Sime the Kison Askari single pilot stealth fighter. She flew in stealth mode so she can take a look around and not be detected. With the exception of a few burst transmissions there has been radio silence from the planet where the GMC's most advanced units were housed and trained. This was highly unusual for a facility of this kind. This was a risky situation. They knew something had come this way but from space there wasn't much activity to see. There was a Centurion class space carrier which had not taken any damage by the looks of it. Finally, she decided to open up a channel to ask "GMC Carrier this is…Oscar one Zulu of the Kison Askari do you read?" She was a bit embarrassed about her made up call sign but she had heard that was a format they used and did not want to say her name it sounded more…official.

There was a long moment of silence before a reply came "This is Vice Admiral Featherson on board the *Ex Wife*. We read you but cannot see you. Took us a minute to find your frequency. The facility has taken fire from an unknown source, and Earth is under duress of an assault presently. We will not be able to reinforce them until we get our troops dug out down there." Thinking on it for a second she responds "Stand by. I will relay your situation." Also orbiting in the Adder was Sgt Garrison and his *Mechanics*, he did not like another stealth craft in their space. They still weren't sure of where the ordinance had come from. He ordered Lance Corporal Jennings to send an encrypted message to the *Ex Wife* of his suspicions.

Zurina relayed the message and got word that help would indeed be on the way. "Oscar one Zulu, hate to be so suspicious but can you reveal yourself so we know you're not the ship that fired upon us? We have a ship of similar capabilities that is uncloaking now as a show of good faith." Came Vice Admiral Featherson's voice over the comms. Moments later true to his word a small freighter like ship angular up front and more box or rectangular as it goes back. There are weapon placements but it's not bristling. Thinking over the risks of revealing herself Zurina reminds herself that at this point in time they are technically allies. The ships beginning to swarm out of the under belly of the *Ex Wife* are not very reassuring. Reaching forward with her left hand she pulls down the levers that deactivate stealth mode.

"Ah there you are. If you wish you have permission to come aboard." The Vice Admiral says. Chuckling with relief that she had not been fired upon Zurina replies "Thank you sir, but that's a negative. I'll wait in the area until my people arrive. Whatever hit you obviously did not come from me. As you should know we have some experience with digging. We will have your people out soon. Then it will be time to return the favor and do some burying of our own." They all waited amicably until two huge Kison Askari Dreadnaughts jumped in the system.

The anxiety throughout the GMC personnel onboard the Ex Wife and in the other ships surrounding their flagship was palpable and almost reflexive seeing two Kison Askari capital ships in such close proximity. Not so long ago these two formations would have been trading fire. Right now, however the ships that began to erupt from the belly of the Dreadnaughts were in fact mid-sized ore haulers and not fighters or bombers as was initially expected. They immediately made way to the surface to try and dig the GMC forces out. There was also a prevalent feeling of envy or jealousy for some as they saw the long graceful lines of the Dreadnaughts. It felt almost wrong for them to have developed tech this good so quickly. Of course, there was also the dark matter aspect to some of their weaponry.

The haulers landed a few klicks from where the ordinance hit and Armored and helmeted Kison Askari made their way to ground zero. There was a large crater filled with rubble that must have been the main facility buildings. Somewhere underneath all that rubble were the bodies of many Marines both dead and alive. The Kison Askari began deploying their autonomous floating mining tools that were programmed to evaluate the material they needed to move and scanning for signs of life amongst it all so they did not inadvertently kill anyone they were trying to rescue. Marines were sent down to help with the effort of locating and digging up survivors.

The orb drills began breaking up what had settled on top and the hover-sleds fitted with large shovel like appendages began clearing rubble away. With the help of the Kison Askari the Marines joined them in clearing smaller debris to get to fallen comrades and automatons beneath. Lieutenant Maplethorpe a redheaded fighter pilot nearly winced once he came out of the rubble when he saw helmeted Kison Askari were the ones digging them out. After the intial shock wore off he took the offered hand and was helped out of the hole. He and his men had all armored up and sealed their EV suits once they knew the facility had been breached by the ordinance. The move had saved their lives. Through continued searching they found that not all had been thinking as quickly and some paid with their lives.

Chapter Eight

Bodies were piling up around the pyramid at Giza. A disturbing note was that it was in fact the fallen of the Blessed that made up a majority of those corpses. There was an unfamiliar aura coming from the ancient pyramid. Unexpectedly it repelled the various energy blasts from the weapons of the Blessed who attempted to assault it from a distance. When they dismounted from their floating chariots to try on foot they were systematically ripped to shreds. The scene before the latest would be infiltrators would fit nicely into any neo-horror film. Kresh, one of Anuren's most trusted warriors from an elite pack was sent to investigate.

Kresh was a large specimen of his species. His armor was once flawless and gleaming making him look like a figure of the god depictions painted on some of the walls of the ancient building he was approaching. Now it was war scarred and dented. It was worn with pride. He stepped off of his chariot while some distance away. He did not want the noise to alert anyone of his approach. From the bodies strewn all over it was obvious nobody here was intimidated by the Jackral howl. Many of the Blessed that gave their lives here were blooded. These were not inexperienced pups. Anuren's voice came through the comms in Kresh's helmet "Find what has been becoming such a nuisance during what should have been a routine sweep, end its existence and lead all living beings you find to the feeding vats for processing."

Kresh responds "At once my liege." Taking up his long baton and making his way towards the entrance. Scanning in multiple spectrums he can find no signs of movement or life nearby. The very top of the old structure seems to be emitting a strong source of energy which could explain what was repelling their energy rounds, but it was like nothing he had ever encountered before. The musculature of his muzzle allowed him to press buttons inside his helm ensuring what he saw was recorded for later analysis. Investigating some of the bodies told him that some were indeed downed with weapons carried by what passed for a military force here, but some had been bludgeoned or even sliced to death. The latter should have been nearly impossible given the advanced nature of their armor and craftsmanship.

Just outside the entrance and still no sign of attackers but a mist was beginning to build up. At first it came from within the building then another was forming to his right. The HUD and sensor arrays inside of Kresh's helmet began to glitch. Something was quickly approaching from the entrance, and there was another slightly larger blip on his display coming from the right. They were both phasing in and out in the internal video feed he was watching. Thinking this might be some kind of hack or digital subterfuge, Kresh retracts his helm to look with his own eyes. Now he knows this must be some kind of trick.

Seemingly sprinting atop the mist at an incredible speed is a crimson eyed specter. Another cloaked phantom looms large even from a distance with glowing blue orbs for eye stops when it notices Kresh gazing in its direction. Powering up his baton Kresh yells in his language "Illusions will not save you and I will not be tricked!" Taking up a firing position the Jackral elite wields the baton and emits a long line of sonic energy that should blast the red eyed creature of its feet if it's actually real. There's no effect. Before Kresh can turn his sights onto the second potential illusion something hits him in the chest at high velocity knocking the wind from his lungs and the baton from his grasp leaving him sprawling on the ground. Now the Blessed warrior thinks one is an illusion to cover the movements of the other.

Picking up his baton he sprints in a weaving pattern so as not to make himself an easy target towards the real enemy ignoring the wraith with the red eyes. He had not noticed the mist spreading. About a hundred meters before he met his intended target something crashes into him. The Jackral screams in pain as something punctures his armor just below his ribcage. Red eyes hidden still in a strange cloak even at close proximity flash by him as the pain grows in strength. Whatever it was that hit him was not only sharp but there was some kind of energy transfer as well. It was possibly an electric, solar or some yet to be discovered by his beings in nature. Kresh had no time to decide what it was. What he did know was that he did not want to feel that again.

The helmet automatically encased his head when the primitive ballistic round initially hit him and the armor began to self-repair but it was slower than usual. This explained the bodies but Kresh still had no idea who these beings were. None of the other units reported anything like this on this putrid planet. The mist was still in evidence but the two mystery beings had disappeared for the time being and there were no readings on Kresh's HUD. He could feel that he was still bleeding. Taking a moment, the Jackral knelt down to evaluate. Feeling around after letting a couple of the lower plates retract, he could tell a couple ribs were likely broken. Taking his baton, he cauterized the wound with a mini solar burst where he had been stabbed and closed the armor back up.

Howling his fury Kresh stood up determined to hunt these beings down, but he was cautious enough to remember to transmit what he had seen back to Anuren. "Into their lair I go." He thought to himself as he crept into the pyramid at Giza.

* * *

The feeling of freely flying through space was exhilarating. Babylon watched in amazement as the boy was able to link with the ship in a way he had never seen before. Even after being well practiced and the ship allowing the Ancient Atlantean control over its flight path, he had never been able to exhibit the control at incredible speeds they were flying at right now. Even with a well-practiced pilot that had been linked with one of these magnificent creatures for years would have to turn over control once a certain speed was reached or risk crashing into something. The potential error would certainly be fatal to both ship and pilot which is why most preferred to use the sight but relinquish control of the flight path.

Darius was enjoying the sensation of stars, planets and other celestial bodies whizzing by as he navigated through it all as if swimming through the ocean. In some ways that is exactly what was happening. Suddenly they slowed down as the ship took back over breaking the spell giving Darius a chance to catch his breath. Disappointed he asked "Why are we slowing? That was crazy!" Patting him on the shoulder Babylon replies "I know it was, but I think we are close." Confused Darius gets out of the seat which seemingly dissolved into the deck. Pointing out of the front viewport Babylon says "To its home, or what's left of it."

The stellar vista before them was simultaneously one of the most beautiful sights while also crushingly sad. Wherever the living ship had jumped to was obviously a place where previously there was an enormous planetary body. By the evidence floating aimlessly in space it had been violently destroyed. There were hundreds if not thousands of huge manta shaped organisms flying through the debris as if looking for something. There was a soft moaning sound that Darius and Babylon could hear which shouldn't have been possible. "What is that sound?" Darius asks. Walking closer to what served as the front viewport Babylon answers "These magnificent creatures are mourning the loss of their home. We can ear it cause we are inside dis one. His or her ears as well as dem vocals are on a different frequency m'tink. In vacuum we no hear it. Dis floatin rubble was once a vibrant planet."

Darius shivered as he could almost swear, he felt some of the life lost here. The destruction had to be from some time ago but there was a spiritual echo or residue that made him feel uneasy. He could also see that the other ships flying through the debris looked a little different from what they were riding in. Aside from the similar shape they looked more like organisms than space faring vehicles. They shined but not in a metallic way. True to their closest visually similar comparison they looked like wet manta rays or a similar animal found on Earth swimming in the oceans. Lazily floating and moving through space in and around the debris it looked as if they were all still in mourning. The creature Darius and Babylon were in decided to join the dance.

They could see where the molten core was now cooling but still incredibly hot. Over time this would look like a piece of asteroid belt with chunks if space rocks drifting. Miraculously these creatures which had inhabited the vast oceans of this world could survive in vacuum. It was not known if the now deceased or other inhabitants knew of these creatures' abilities. They may not have escaped at all and Babylon had no way to directly communicate with the magnificent beasts to ask. He had a vague idea of what happened through their occasional mind connections but the pictures were difficult to interpret at times. "What now?" Darius asked sadly. Pointing to a group of the space creatures which glowed in various hues Babylon answered "Now we see if one a dem will accept you. Know dat you don own it if you are lucky enough to be partnered. It will fly you, protect you and if need be fight wit you. You brought a pack yes?"

* * *

ANCIENT ILLUMINATION III - GODHOOD

Ragnar opened his eyes and was in excruciating pain. His head was pounding and to make matters worse the smell was unbearably nauseating. Having no clue where he was, he tried to get his bearings and stop the, well it wasn't a room per se but it was spinning. As his vision cleared, he noticed his hands and feet were bound, there were several others with him laid in long lines. Some of the others were beginning to stir and before he could ask anyone where they were several invaders entered. Ragnar laid his head down but tried to keep his eyes barely open to get a look at what was happening. These armored Anubis-like aliens didn't have the gleaming armor Ragnar saw before they looked like their kit was battle worn, dirty and gritty. They barked to each other in their guttural language then proceeded to gather a few of the captives.

This brought about numerous outcries resulting in swift beatings. The cries ceased almost instantly. The captives were savagely stood up and stripped of clothing before being placed in a small circular platform which began to float. Ragnar noticed how cold and sterile the ground was. It was some kind of metal or alloy but was dull with very little shine making him think it must be old. He tried to follow where the platforms were going but they quickly went out of his line of sight and he didn't want to let on that he was conscious just yet.

The doors opened again and the invaders left. The remaining captives began to whimper and ask what was going on as soon as they thought the invaders were out of ear shot. They were dog-like after all so Ragnar wondered if it mattered how far they were. It was likely they could still be listening. Not to mention this chamber could also be littered with listening devices. Where ever the others had been taken it couldn't be good plus they were stripped of clothing beforehand which was more than troubling. The ceiling was high and there didn't seem to be a knob or handle. The avenues for escape were looking slim. Ragnar ignored what looked to be a grimy looking cybernetically enhanced human begging him for answers. Ragnar had no answers and he low key despised this guy for trying to go beyond what was naturally given to him. He was just another bum trying to keep up with the muties. From the look of him some of his enhancements were likely off brand or black-market editions. Things would not go well when they started to deteriorate.

Somehow the smell got worse and it had to be more than a gathering of terrified and unwashed bodies. Ragnar was determined that this would not be the way his tale ended. The building seemed to rock with several large impacts. Perhaps the GMC had come to rescue the hostages here. There were murmurs expressing those exact sentiments throughout this strange facility. There was a sudden explosion and the wall caved letting precious fresh air into the chamber. Three bodies of the invaders came crashing through the hole in the wall. Ragnar thought maybe they were starting to fight with their own when a large silhouette formed in the smoke that was wafting in with the fresh air. When it began to clear up it was the last face Ragnar ever wanted or expected to see. It was Shajara. "Hello good beings. Would you like a bit of payback?"

"How we don't have any weapons! Have you seen these things?" One of the captives complained. Seven other Kison Tontu that are part of Shajara's Children of the Sun enter carrying all manner of weapons, GMC issued railguns, energy weapons and what looked like some of the strange energy baton weapons the invaders were known to wield. Bending down Shajara picked up one of the railguns and walks over to Ragnar who thinks he is about to meet his end. They were after all ideological enemies. "Just get it over with!" Ragnar growls. Shajara stands him up and turns him around. Surprise washes over Ragnar as he feels the bindings on his hands and feet being cut away.

Handing him the weapon Shajara remarks "Try not to shoot me in the back. I still despise you but despise these foreign invaders even more. They're literally trying to feed off of us. I would rather have the pleasure of dealing with you myself than let them process you for food consumption." Thinking all that over Ragnar quickly grabbed the weapon. As they went to cross the thresh hold where the hole was blown in the wall Shajara looked back and added "If I sense that you have me or any of my people in your sights, I will dismember you and impale you with your own appendages." Seeing the seriousness is the Kison Tontu's eyes Ragnar mumbles "Fair enough." Following them out of the chamber.

The other captives quickly gathered what weapons they could and began to sneak out after them. Unfortunately, they were not on the ground floor and would have to make their way down. As a result of the explosion it was likely that reinforcements were coming. Some of Shajara's people were ushering the escapees down winding stairwells seeing as the elevator systems would likely have invaders in them plus there was no guarantee they would know how to operate them. Busting open the doors and travelling down the stairs was likely easier and stealthier. Once on the ground level they would have to fight their way free but Shajara and his people had fought their way in so it made sense they would be able to escape with their help.

As the last group of captives were out of the chamber where Ragnar had been held made their way down the stairs Ragnar hesitated when he saw that Shajara was not going down. "What are you waiting for?" he asked. Turning Shajara replied "I and a few of my people are headed up. There may be more captives. We are already fighting on the ground and around this compound in an attempt to split their forces. The way will not be easy but I am confident you can make it."

Surprisingly Ragnar said "I'll come with you." Waiving the offer away Shajara confidently stated "I have more of my people on the higher levels and we can handle ourselves." Stubbornly Ragnar pushes past him saying "True but some of my men may be held captive here as well, and as much as I hate to say it…I owe you." Chuckling under his breath Shajara comments "Touching." As they make their way to the upper levels. An alarm sounded so they decided to pick up the pace. Ragnar was hard pressed to keep up but refused to give up or complain. He just trudged up the stairs picking up and setting down his feet until he was at the entrance to the next level where the Kison Tontu had already pried open the door.

He could hear the sound of weapons fire and was nearly beheaded by an energy blast when he peaked into the hallway. Ducking low he looked across the way seeing Shajara and his people pinned down. One of the warriors got up using the discarded door as a shield and ran towards the invaders who were steadily firing down the hallway. Pieces of the door were being blown off and giving less cover but it allowed him to get close enough to strike them with what he had left. Shajara and the rest quickly followed. Ragnar tried to get a bead on one of the invaders during the scuffle that ensued but it was hard as they were fighting, moving very fast making the chance of hitting the wrong target easy. He decided to wait until he had a clear shot remembering Shajara's threat earlier.

His chance came when there was an invader looking to hit Shajara and his men from the opposite end of the corridor. The armored anthropomorphic dog-headed alien was not paying attention to Ragnar who he guessed either posed less of a threat or they simply did not see him. However, when the laser sight was placed on his gleaming armor which reflected the beam to the ceiling, he noticed. Just as the alien glanced down at his chest plate Ragnar pulled the trigger. The recoil shot him flying into the doorframe where he was crouched, hard. He released the rail rifle and fell to the ground. Finishing up the fight Shajara turned just in time to avoid the energy blast from the invader's weapon as Ragnar's shot threw his aim off. The round did not penetrate the armor but it did warp it enough to cause great pain as the place where the round hit was now misshapen and digging into the flesh beneath. Shajara and his people quickly rushed to the alien grabbing him who began barking in their strange language before Shajara forced his helmet off and punched him silent.

After rummaging around some of the alien bodies Ragnar found something that may help get some info. "Interrogate this rejected Thundercat." He says. Confused Shajara asks "How are we to do that? I for one cannot understand them." Producing one of his finds he hands a small strange looking ear buds he found to Shajara saying "This should help. He was talking about your mothers, and it wasn't very nice. These are translators, I think. Which means they can probably understand all of our message traffic that's not encrypted." Looking over the ear-bud like device Shajara remarks "You know I detest technology and all their trappings." Shaking his head Ragnar replies "Fine wake him back up and have him cuss us out until you understand him fluently."

Two of Shajara's people went to open the cells on the current floor while he begrudgingly put the buds in his ear before slapping the alien awake. "Now little birdie, you will sing for us and tell us what all this ruckus is about." Groggily the alien shakes his head squinting up at Shajara "What is birdie you vermin?" Punching him again Shajara answers "In due time. Answer my questions first and I will answer yours. You obviously need to learn manners. Why are you here?"

Chapter Nine

System...rebooting standby. Body recalibrating. Finally, Nelson came back online after being buried. After a fully digital self-checkup took place Nelson looks around to see a few dismembered automaton units around him picking up pieces of the facility that had fallen down around them from some attack. A thorough search of all available communications told him that this was not the work of the Kison Askari or the GMC. This was a new danger and they would have to be dealt with prior to executing his plans for the bot revolution. His golden eyes flashed off and on sending out the message silently to all automatons. Through various satellites and other methods of communications that had not been destroyed in this latest of attacks the message would get to the units on Earth.

They could of course attack now while both the GMC and Kison Askari were distracted, but it seemed likely that they could lose to the new players in town. Satellite imaging and various scans were sending him information on the large constructs that were now embedded into the Earth all over the globe. These devices were somehow digging in an attempt to get to the core. For what purpose Nelson knew not but it could not be for a good one. From gathered reports beings that have been rescued from some of these places say living beings are being put in containers to be broken down for consumption. Nelson cared very little for the living beings of this galaxy but it seemed these new invaders were trying to break the Earth down as well. If this were to be allowed, the automatons would have no place to prosper. Realistically they could choose another planet in the Milky Way but who is to say these "Blessed" would stop at just the Earth. Nelson and the automatons needed more information.

More information about what had occurred there on Saturn was coming in now. The GMC flagship the *Ex Wife* had been in orbit when the attack happened. They tried and failed to destroy or throw the ordinance off course. They were now met with Kison Askari forces. It took some time for their nav-computers to sink up but all was prepped for a tandem jump to Earth. Reports had it that some of Nelson's automatons were already aboard the GMC ships in route to the coming fight. This was acceptable as it had come about from their programming which dictated self-preservation above all and those units had calculated as he did that fighting was the best chance they had at survival. The best way to describe what was happening in Nelson's cerebral circuitry was pride.

Not that any of these semi-sentient bags of flesh and bone would give him or his people credit as they still deemed the automatons as machines to be used as tools. Things were set on their course now so Nelson decided he would stay here and help repair the facility and dig out any survivors many of which could be one of his brothers or sisters left in the remaining rubble. Looking through the damage report there was much to go through. With a quick burst message, he wished the automatons with the deploying GMC units good hunting and went back to work. Joint forces mobilized just outside of Saturn's gravity well. Nelson marveled at the way they briefly struggled to integrate. Two of the centurion class space carriers of the GMC were full to capacity so overflow was being instructed to board the Dreadnaughts of the Kison Askari.

Vice admiral Featherson was a bit skeptical when he was told to wait for the arrival of more of the Kison Askari armada to arrive. There were already two of their capital ships which he was told were called Dreadnaughts but mostly their strangely shaped War Dragons and some of the smaller fighter craft they had been developing. His doubts were erased the moment the largest thing he had ever seen jumped in system along with the rest of the Kison Askari contingent. A nervous looking Ensign at the comm console looked to the Admiral saying "Incoming message from …whatever that is Sir!"

Still in awe at the sheer size of the new arrival Vice Admiral Featherson barks "Put it through." Before going to sit in the command chair as the viewport screen comes to life showing Queen Tunisia in a large black and gold command chair of her own. She is dressed in her flight suit instead of a royal gown and its accented with gold and silver inlays. When she sees the Admiral and his crew staring back at her she greets them "I hope you were able to get most of your people out safely. I sent help as soon as I could. I am Queen Tunisia of the Kison Askari. We are transmitting recon info from the latest scans we have of Earth with deployment of forces around the planet but I am afraid we don't have much info for what's happening groundside. As soon as you confirm your overflow of personnel are aboard the three Dreadnaught accompanying my flagship, we can execute a few tandem jumps. I would recommend three groups, staggered jumps in various orbit placements. We won't have the element of surprise but it's likely they won't anticipate our numbers."

Getting over his initial shock Featherson answered "Of course that sounds reasonable. As soon as I receive the confirmation that our troops are aboard, I'll forward that to you. There have been mixed reports of what is happening groundside and we know our Commandant is pinned down at our headquarters there. Ma'am I'm confused. I thought we would be dealing with your son or one of his advisors on this." She could see there was still disapproval in his eyes. At first, she thought to be dismissive but decided tact would be better in this situation.

Sternly looking into the cam she flatly stated "I can see clearly that you disagree with my use of dark matter or my peoples plight, and the resulting recent negotiations. Whichever point you don't agree with I merely ask that you set aside your moral or philosophical disapproval so we can go save lives. Let's not forget the ore and other material gathered to make this ship possible was provisioned by my late husband and King to the people willing to go back with you to fight on your behalf. I know there are still some of us back on Earth but the majority of the casualties suffered there will be yours. I am willing to set aside our differences now to go do what we promised, but I need to know that I can count on you and your Marines while risking more of our lives in the process. Do we have an understanding Admiral?"

Visibly thinking on what she said he finally replied "Must have been written on my face…Yes Ma'am we have an understanding and on behalf of all the Marines and personnel here I would like to express my gratitude for you and your people for helping us dig our people out. I believe all of our ships are stowed aboard yours and are ready to make the jump home. This is the *Ex Wife*, our flagship I am curious to know the name of your ship Queen Tunisia?" Smiling she says "This ship is called *Akina Mama,* the mother. Sending over one of my Generals so you can coordinate attack strategies once our forces touch down on the surface. Any information you have on what's going on there would be greatly appreciated. Now let's go save our first home!"

With that she closed the communication link down and nodded to Simeon who briefly saluted before leaving the bridge but did not look pleased. Though many disagreed with the Queens aggressive actions following Jared Omega's death there were many who still did not like or trust the GMC in general. Queen Tunisia did feel that when the warriors regardless of which force they belonged to would feel more bound together once they were blooded in battle. Facing adversity together should help unite them. How long that unity would last once the conflict was over was a problem left after they survived the current crisis.

As planned, they made the jump in three groups staggered so they would not all arrive simultaneously hopefully throwing the invaders space ships into a panic. The *Ex Wife* and its sister ship jumped first followed by one of the Dreadnaughts followed by the second Dreadnaught and its contingent of ships. Finally, after waiting a few minutes the *Akina Mama* engaged their hyperdrive engines and stars turned into streaks of light.

* * *

Sitting in one of the auxiliary single person couches aboard a Kison Askari Dreadnaught Sparks was thinking of how her world had been repeatedly turned upside down. One moment she was working a prestigious security gig protecting someone she cared deeply about, next she is on a vendetta of vengeance after losing that person. After getting caught on the crossfire between the GMC and Kison Askari forces as a result of that vendetta she next found herself in the midst of various groups of mutants one group in particular she knew in her heart were responsible for her lost loved one. All of this was blown away by being in the presence of these beings she thought of before as oafish brutes trying to take advantage of their access to precious resources only to find out that they were the ones being taken advantage of.

Now they were all supposed to band together like a happy family and fight some new arrival who was trying to encroach upon their home planet. A happy family wasn't accurate but they had to work together now. The reports that were slowly coming in seemed to be the result of a drug induced bad dream. Blood thirsty werewolf aliens had to be some sort of misprint. She was unsure of what to trust. Max was relaxed as always even in high stress situations was strapped in beside her as they felt the hum of hyperspace as the enormous ship made its way through space. Argos took up two of the couches but was too large to be strapped in slept snoring loudly. You could see glimpses of his reddish skin beneath all of the garb he wore and others were trying to covertly see what was beneath without waking him.

Being reunited with Max and his new enigmatic companion reminded Sparks of an unsavory past. One that she thought she had escaped but somehow had come back to her. Max was still street wise and constantly thinking of new ways to collect coin, and she was still unsure of what Argos even was or what he wanted. For now, he seemed content and there was none of his wrath aimed at her so she would take what good was available. Distracted by these thoughts she was intrigued by the décor of the ship for some reason. From the structure of it this was obviously a military vessel in nature but it lacked the drab grey, beige, or white interior that most government vehicles often displayed. It was a gleaming gunmetal grey on the outer hull but inside in was mostly black but the bulkheads had lights that striated in various colors throughout the ship.

She was told that if they were under attack those lights would serve to direct crew members to safety or to duty stations. She did not understand all the glyphs and symbols on the bulkheads but there were arrows in certain spots so she was learning the more time she spent onboard. She was sure Max and Argos were learning as well. One thing could not be denied, the genius of the engineers that built this spacecraft and many things they got to see on Ganymede. The strange human they met earlier on the Jovian moon was sitting across from her. Bofus she believed was his name. He was sleeping soundly despite the situation. Sparks was a ball of nerves. They were on their way to fight an unknown force with a bunch of mutants she wasn't sure she trusted. Living amongst them had opened her eyes to what had been done to them over the centuries but she wasn't directly responsible for any of that if the stories were true.

She barely trusted Max and they had a more concrete history. She knew where he stood. The fact that there were other non-mutated humans here that had taken up the cause of the stone people was reassuring but not by much. Sparks still had her suspicions about the Ongakujin but that would ultimately have to wait. Max as mercenary as he is was genuinely worried about what was transpiring on Earth. Sparks still couldn't shake the feeling that he was also going along to check on his network and investments there in addition to other concerns. This was after all a free trip back with little worry about the GMC or security forces checking what cargo he may be taking back planet side from Ganymede. Looking Bofus over she tried to study his suit from a distance.

Sparks was sure she had only seen one suit similar to it and not in person as she didn't get to be in Prince Darius's presence but she was positive his suit looked similar. One difference was that Bofus had an additional harness that housed the strange shoulder canon the Kison Askari used. She wondered what weird test of loyalty he had committed to get it. Glancing over the literally hardened warriors sitting in this section of the ship it had to be an arduous task. He must have felt her focus because he suddenly woke startling her. "Hey baby girl! Don't you worry about them dog people. I'll protect you wit my bunduki." He boasts nodding to his canon resting on his shoulder.

Mildly offended Sparks replies "I'm sorry your what?" Max overhears the conversation and begins chuckling saying "That's what the Kison Askari call those weapons on their shoulders. Only slightly mollified Sparks fires back "I don't need your dookie or whatever so save it for the invaders. I can handle myself. Thank you." Bofus sat back at the rejection and tried to go back to sleep as the others in the area erupted in laughter waking Argos who seemed genuinely confused. His sudden movement briefly halted the guffawing before it commenced again. They sobered up as they were interrupted by an announcement "Coming out of hyperspace momentarily be prepared to head directly to your deployment areas if you are not already there. Hostiles are still expected no matter what quadrant we stop in. They will be aware of our presence. Be ready to brace for incoming impacts."

* * *

Cautiously Kresh had in fact called for backup in spite of his pride. The damage done had taken a higher toll than he had previously thought. The Jackrals breath had become ragged, and each step more labored than the one prior. He was in no shape to take on these adversaries and he knew it. The glory gained from defeating them would be great but sadly that would have to be for other warriors of the Blessed. What he could do was track them for his packmates. Kresh was wary of removing his helm again and risk alerting them to how weak he was, but at the same time needed to make use of his sense of smell which he trusted more than the sensors in his armor. He felt they had failed him earlier leading to getting him injured.

Perhaps this was just a part of him wanted to use the old ways to hunt again. If this was to be his last hunt might as well do it right, he thought. Continuing through what looked like a labyrinth in this ancient temple Kresh retracted his helmet to try and get a scent but it was difficult with all the recent death and despair that permeated the air. Finally, he was able to lock on to one specific scent that was different enough he figured might belong to one of the strange beings that attacked him. Making the attempt to stealthily follow the trail he dropped scent beacons of his own for his pack to follow once they landed.

Kresh would try not to follow too closely but keep his distance hoping the rest of his pack would arrive in time. He was in no condition to take them on but if he had no choice, a warrior's death would be good. He had been on many campaigns through the years and had earned the right to rest. He both felt and smelled that he was close. Kresh couldn't help but feel that he was being baited in deeper. There was more to this old structure than he thought and didn't want to lose the scent. These beings were a possible threat where most other instances the Blessed were meeting little to no resistance though there were reports of pockets of combatants rising up.

A few of the processing vat and fuel containers had gone dormant recently. Various units were currently being deployed to find out what happened. The Blessed should have full control of this planet's population and resources soon. Of that Kresh had no doubt. A ping from his armor let him know that some members of his pack had landed and would be on his trail soon. With that knowledge he was a little less cautious with his movements and paid for it in pain. Something grazed his head at high velocity burning up the entire right side of his face. Kresh howled in pain as he went to the ground blindly firing with his weapon as he went.

The rest of his pack was already on the scent trail when they heard his howl. They picked up pace into what looked like an old temple to them. With his helm retracted what was happening was not being recorded. Anuren barked that he needed answers to the elite pack. The fact that Kresh was possibly downed immediately angered and worried the Jackral leader. Whoever was responsible could not simply be relegated to the feeding vats, they would have to be tortured first. Kresh's pack had been warned but was still not prepared for the amount of bodies found on their way into the temple. Legends came to mind of a corrupted Jackral who was death personified. None of them voiced it but most of them were thinking they could be going to meet this legend in the flesh.

As they rushed in, they came to halt seeing two creatures standing over Kresh. His fur on one side matted with blood. One creature holding the long blade piercing the Jackrals armor and body turned to look at the new arrivals. Two malevolent glowing orbs beneath the cloak it wore stared at them. Raspily it whispered "What are you waiting for?" The other broader creature was obscured in shadows like the first but it's eye glowed azure. It did not speak but did prepare a weapon to fire. As one the remaining packmates howled and charged. The dark area briefly lit up with projectile and energy fire.

Chapter Ten

Staff Sergeant Grimm, Ensign Parsons along with a detail of five other Marines geared up to go outside the GMC HQ on Earth where the Commandant and a group of Government attaches were pinned down. They seemed to be trapped as the invasion carried on when all of a sudden, things got strangely silent. That could either be really good or bad. Ensign Parsons was visibly nervous as he checked the charge on the energy-rifle he chose to take on this patrol to see what was going on. He had also decided to look up Staff Sergeant Grimm's service record while they were getting ready. Turns out Staff Sergeant Grimm was actually a First Sergeant who had been busted down some time ago. It was curious why he was on the Commandant's staff but this finding did not instill confidence in the young officers' ability to trust him.

All things checked out on the Ensigns armor and weapons. Staff Sergeant asked his Marines if they were ready to go and they all chorused "Good to go Staff Sergeant!" One of them was fidgeting with a land drone while another was readying an air drone to give them some extra eyes on the ground and in the air. This should allow them to spot anything before it got danger close. Parsons asked "Staff Sergeant what are we doing with those? Didn't the Commandant want us to put actual eyes on the situation?" Turning the Staff Sergeant replied "Yes sir he did, and we will do just that. I will however use some of the tools given to us so that we can be aware of our surroundings before we get to any hostiles. If they take one of them out, we should know what general direction they're in, and if the drones can transmit an image to us before being destroyed it's possible, we may have a general number and disposition of the enemy forces in the area. Go to the entrance sir and tell me what you see at the first and second set of barricades."

Reluctantly Ensign Parsons went to the entrance to look. He could feel the skepticism from the helmeted Marines and knew there had to be smiles under those visors as they listened to the exchange between a young officer and a salty staff-nco. Raising up on his tip toes Parsons peaked out to see what was at the first barricade. He locked eyes with an injured Marine slumped down in a sitting position. Rifle cradled in his arms, but the light on the ammunition gage was blinking orange indicating low power. He only had a few shots left, but it looked like whoever he was fighting had backed off. There was a pile of GMC bodies around him.

Using the enhance feature on the HUD in his helmet Ensign Parsons looked further out to the second and third building barricades. There were more bodies but a majority of them looked to be fallen enemies. He found that odd and relayed this to the Staff Sergeant. After considering their options Staff Sergeant Grimm says "Sir I think we should see what that Marine has to say about what's going on out here while we send the drones out a little further to recon the area. What do you think?" Surprised Ensign Parsons knew this was just a formality. Technically he was the highest ranking here but was also the least experienced and knew that it was likely Grimm would do what he wanted anyway and the Marines would generally have his back.

In reply Ensign Parsons said "We do it your way. I'm more of an analytics guy but I have had my share of combat training. If we survive this mess, I want to know how a First shirt gets busted to Staff Sergeant and still gets to be in with the Commandant." Shaking his head Grimm replies "Aye sir." Then tells his men to ready up. Leaning out of the entrance one of the Marines places the land drone on the ground and closes the door. After a few moments the other drone is released and it takes to the sky. After seeing the images and video the drones are sending back, they begin to leave the building one at a time.

Running to keep a low profile they each stop at the first barricade. Ensign Parsons is the last to go.

Nervously Parsons sprints to the first barrier and catches the last comments from the injured Marine speaking to Staff Sergeant Grimm "They've been taking wounded and living as prisoners. Not sure what they're doing with them but there has been some scuttlebutt from civilians in the area. I'm just mad I won't have the opportunity to pay them back for what they did to my squad. Make them pay…" The young Marine stares off into oblivion and takes his final breath and Grimm holds his hand until he is spent. They all remain quiet as Staff Sergeant Grimm shuts the dead man's eyes. Parsons goes over to check the small monitor showing the field of view from the air drone. A good distance away there are some invaders seen gathering bodies and placing them on their floating chariots.

The silence is briefly broken by the chariot zipping off as it howls its way towards one of the large spike structures. Ensign Parsons asks "Where are they taking them?" The howling is renewed when several chariots come screaming towards the barriers. They quickly duck low behind cover. Angered one of the Marines begins to fire recklessly at the invaders and giving away their position in the process. The invaders were beginning to return fire and it was obvious that there were many more behind them. This was an attempt to take this hardpoint. The screens on the mini monitors went blank as the drones were taken out. The left side of Parson's head felt like it was on fire as his helmet was grazed with an energy projectile.

Peaking over the barricade Staff Sergeant Grimm saw what looked like a horde of invaders on foot and the chariot like craft screaming their way. He decides on returning fire screaming "Nobody lives forever!" He is soon hit center mass on his chest plate and is sent flying. Ensign Parsons closes his eyes and readies his weapon resigned to his fate and laments that he will likely not hear the Staff Sergeants story. Taking the prone position and peaking around the side of the barricade he squeezes off a few rapid shots taking several of the aliens out. They fall, armor smoking, final howls leaving their lips. Noticing their fallen, the Jackral return fire.

Parsons moves his face behind cover barely in time as high-speed energy projectiles hit the ground where he was previously lying and began chewing away at the corner of the barrier, he was behind. The weapons fire ramped up in intensity and frequency. Trying to make himself as small as possible Parsons sees Staff Sergeant Grimm still somehow fighting firing arbitrarily in the enemy's direction with an old sidearm. Closing his eyes Parsons envisions his two little girls as that's the last thing he wanted to see before getting blasted to bits. Even with eyes closed he can't ignore the sudden bright flash of light and then…silence. Confused Parsons takes a risk to peak over the barrier.

What he and remaining Marines see strangely enough is the Ryoko-Gekijo floating about a half mile away with what look like a plethora of extended plasma cannons now dormant but still smoking. Looking to where the enemy were firing from was a mass of flash burned pile of bodies and melting armor nearly unrecognizable as anything remotely humanoid. The smell was horrible. The theater begins to slowly float forward and apprehension begins to creep back in as Ensign Parsons goes over to help Staff Sergeant Grimm up into a sitting position as the other Marines formed a small phalanx around them which wasn't going to help much if they decided to fire.

The flying theater barely fit between the buildings as it touched down. The huge weapons retracted back into the hull and it was once again more like what they had seen in the media. A circular hatch opened up on the side of the building and out came three people dressed in what could only be described as cyber-ninja outfits. The tallest of the three took off his mask states "I am Takimura of the

Ongakujin. We were initially ordered by Major Vashti to report here for questioning, but sudden occurrences seemed to have delayed us. Not to mention, you look to be in need of help. Hironike requests an audience with General Krulak if he's available."

* * *

Babylon was resting while Darius still curious watched out the front viewport a strange yet lovely dance that was happening in this long-abandoned nebula left in the wake of the destroyed home planet to the living ships that were kin to the very vessel they travelled in. Darius did not know how but he swore he could hear the living ships singing which should have been impossible since they were out in the vacuum while he sat inside. There were a myriad of questions going through the young man's mind. What was even more unusual was that he also thought he could now understand their lyrics.

Nervously he looked over to where Babylon lay wrapped in his brown cloak holding fast to his ceremonial trident. Something was compelling him to join the creatures in their song and dance but that made no sense. Even more alarming was that whatever force or entity was communicating with him urged him to leave his helmet. It was odd but he knew he could actually survive being out there without an EV suit and helmet. He left his suit on but slowly made his way to what functioned as the rear hatch. Since learning they were inside of a living organism, dirty thoughts of what he was actually walking out of anatomically speaking, crept into his mind and he giggled a bit.

The ship seemed to know what he was doing and so an energy barrier shielded Babylon's sleeping form from the vacuum as the rear opened to space. Darius's eyes began to glow and he was genuinely surprised that he did not feel asphyxiated immediately. The sudden drop in temperature had little to no effect on him as well but it was something within him that resisted these things and not just the suit that his people made for him. There was another mental nudge to jump. At first, he thought of ignoring this but these strange developments only bolstered his confidence that he was unaware of previously.

Looking back one last time he slowly pushed off with one leg and fully entered the stars free of the confines of a ship or vehicle. Oddly his eyes flared in intensity and he found that he could in fact control his movement without the use of a propulsion pack. He was flying! The brief opening to the void of space let some of the cold in which woke Babylon. His amber eyes narrowed as he smoothed his white locks back blinking rapidly to shake what had to be a crazy mirage of some sort. His heart sank as he realized the person, he was charged with protecting was somehow freely floating among the stars with the creatures. Sitting up as rapidly as he could the old Antlantean nearly fell over trying to get his trident and helmet.

He wore an EV suit beneath his heavy cloak which was way more advanced than it seemed. Quickly placing the helmet over his head and fastening the closures Babylon jumped out of his ship holding Darius's helmet. Pointing the three tips of his trident behind him energy begins to pulse from the weapon propelling him forward. As fearful as he was for the boy, he was equally amazed at the sight before him. The prince of the Kison Askari was flying, racing and playing with a group of young space creatures as the large older ones looked on. Babylon had no idea how he would communicate with him since he had no helmet and obviously no communication network, yet he called out to him anyway. "Darius!" he shouted.

Oddly enough the boy heard him and turned in his direction. "Babylon! You can fly too?" he asked gleefully. After floating towards each other he answered "No, m'boy. I have some help. Unlike you who don't seem to need any. Did you know you could do this?" The energy pulsing from the trident stopped and they drifted in place as Darius thought about it saying "I didn't know but something told me to jump, I lit up as I sometimes do and it was…fine." Overemphasizing his movements Babylon nodded his understanding saying "Do old Babylon a favor eh?"

Confused Darius bows his head in compliance not knowing exactly what the favor will be saying "Alright." "When this voice tells ya ta do sometin crazy run it by me first ok? I promised to keep ya safe and it hasn't been a week and you already space walking with no tether and no helmet! I know now you don't need it but ya just admitted you didn't either!" The prince took the admonishment rather well and truly understood why the old man was a bit angry. Babylon gestured offering the helmet which Darius refused. There was a glint in the ancient ones' eyes as he waived the boy off to continue playing. With a celebratory fist pump Darius flew back to the group of young space creatures to frolic among the stars.

Babylon kind of shook his head and powered the trident back up heading back to his ship. Once inside he took his helmet off when what functioned as the cabin was pressurized with air he spoke to the ship "I ope it wasn't you that urged the boy to do dat!" All he got in return was a low moan. "Yeah right! Now let's hope one of your brothers or sisters, or however you think of yourselves chooses him so he can have his own special ride and maybe help me find you all a new home after they get their problems fixed." He mutters. Watching out of the front viewport to keep an eye on things, Babylon is amazed at the speed and agility the boy is displaying, and to think he had no prior idea he could even do this. Something about that just made no sense.

* * *

The exit from hyperspace was abrupt and a bit violent. Being yanked out of the slipstream of space as the group of ships simultaneously halted was disorientating. Sparks felt like her organs had all shifted and she was left trying to reconfigure them into normalcy. The expression on Bofus's face in addition to some of the Kison Askari let her know she wasn't the only one having issues with this transition. Argos sat up and Max for some reason seemed unphased which annoyed her. She was about to ask a question when the alarms blared signaling the order for general quarters.

The group Bofus was with picked up their gear and sprinted towards one of the deployment decks. Not being assigned to a specific unit Sparks, Max and Argos tagged along and nobody argued. The bulkheads and deck began shaking violently and the lights dimmed briefly. They must have been taking fire. It would be a while before they'd be able to see any of the action for themselves that was taking place around Earth's orbit. It was a tight fit in the lift especially with Argos, the other warriors and a Kison Askari named Ogun in there. Eventually they made it to the proper deck and it was a mad house with activity when the hatch slid open.

Crates of weapons and warriors from both the GMC Marine groups and the Kison Askari were scrambling into GMC Night Eagle troop transports and whatever the stone people were calling theirs which looked like a heavily armored converted ore hauler. The hulls of the latter looked thick but she and Max both looked unsure of their practicality in light of the heavy artillery being shot back and forth causing even these leviathan capital ships to rock with the impacts. On this deck there was an energy barrier between them and the void of space. Somehow the ships were allowed to negotiate that barrier to launch taking waves of Marines and Warriors down to the surface to help fight the battles raging there.

They could finally see the battle happening in space and it was both beautiful and horrifying. Not all of the slow-moving transports were making it. A mixture of Kison Askari, GMC and Jackral ships could be seen breaking apart from brief explosions as the vacuum stole the oxygen necessary for a large fire. The result was a host of brilliant flashes as energy projectiles flew into these space worthy vehicles at high speeds causing them to break apart accompanied by a burst of sparks and chemical reactions producing bright flames that were nearly instantaneously doused from oxygen deficiency. Amazed at the macabre yet colorful events happening all around Earth Sparks asked "Are we really doing this?"

Slowly nodding as Max and Argos watched what they were all seeing they all snapped out of the hypnosis the scene had trapped them in and began to catch up with Bofus and his crew who were scrambling into one of the previously mentioned converted ore haulers. Irked by the lack of a verbal response Sparks quickly followed yelling "I guess we are doing this!" When they got to the hauler there were no comfortable singular couches to strap into. There were simple riveted alloy benches with hand holds that were for Sparks, Max, and Bofus a little far to reach but were prefect for the likes of Argos and Ogun. Finally Sparks noticed a large satchel that Argos had been lugging around all this time.

Obviously there had to be a weapon of some kind and she found it strange that she was just now noticing. There was a lot going on though so she could hardly blame herself for missing that detail. The rear hatch to the rectangular vessel closed and they were briefly in total darkness before dull running lights along the deck lit up as they felt the craft lift slowly off the deck of the dreadnaught's hangar bay. A moment later some small overhead lights gave a little more illumination but not much. Sparks closed her eyes as the hairs on her arms began to stand. The rough hand of Ogun touches her reassuringly saying "That is just a result of the energy transfer necessary allowing our ships to pass the barrier. Trying to pass without it could be disastrous,"

A long slit serving as side portholes they could see out of opened up. Once they were away from the Capital ship as if to illustrate Ogun's point a group of smaller Jackral fighter ships tried to gain access to the hangar but were violently rebuffed. The ships broke up like toys jettisoning their pilots into space simultaneously asphyxiating and freezing them to death. Max could also see there was a long gauntlet of ships, flying energy projectiles and artillery fire to get through in order to reach the surface and it did not look good. He sat down and went to go into Argos's large satchel. Grunting rather loudly Argos did not look happy about it. "What? Now is as good a time as any to have one!" Max exclaimed as he brushed aside the large gloved hands that was blocking him.

Pulling out a strange yet very large flask Max took a pull of some awfully pungent brew and offered it to Sparks. She covered her mouth and nose vehemently denying the stuff access to either. Curious Ogun reached over surprising Max but he let go of it as his face became alarmingly red furiously tapping his augmented leg on the deck. Ogun took a hefty swig and nodded his appreciation turning to Bofus looking at them all. Argos waived his huge hands signaling he would not partake. Seeing that Bofus said "If he aint taking it I am good! This ride will be rough as it is!" Ogun handed it back to Max who stowed it in the satchel and they all braced and prayed as the hauler began to rock with impacts.

Chapter Eleven

The world was crumbling down around them and Pharaoh was doing his best to keep it together focusing the energy conduits within the pyramid at Giza to keep the shield up that protected them from the long-distance assaults of the Jackral horde in space. His minions were keeping the encroachers at bay near the entrance but more were on their way. Soon the illuminated one himself may have to intervene. The problem was that he had not yet found a way to unlock his true self after all these millennia. He was also not as powerful as he once was having siphoned a bit of himself off empowering various minions throughout his long stay on this forsaken planet most of whom had been destroyed taking that potential with them.

He could feel Malice wading through the bodies and enjoying every moment of it, feeding off the fear each kill was spreading to the rest of the invader group. Typhoon was more reserved but lashing out each time he was injured. Survival instinct more common to his species kicked in to override the recent philosophical side that had come as a result of his transformation. Pharaoh, through the nexus he had built with the pyramids throughout the globe could see all that was transpiring. Much of this planet was in flames and chaos. It would be delightfully entertaining if his own neck did not also hang in the balance of it all. After being confident that the shield would hold Pharaoh prepared to muster up what power he could to join the fray.

The fighting had gone pretty deep into the pyramid so instead of walking Pharaoh decided to void walk there. Taking on his most comfortable humanoid appearance, he steps into the ether and steps out in the midst of Malice disemboweling two Jackral invaders with his long blades. There was a very large invader on the ground. He looked mortally wounded but the light had not left his eyes yet. More Jackral who had obviously come to his aid were flooding in, threatening to overrun the minions. All the action for a brief moment stopped.

The Jackral were taken by surprise seeing a tall brown skinned humanoid in gleaming pharaonic armor step out of a glowing purple portal that had not existed previously. They came out of their group trance quickly and began pouring energy fire at the new arrival. Turning Pharaoh raises both hands out to his sides. There are shooters at either side of him. Miraculously the energy bolts enter his hands and exit out of the opposite hand hitting the attackers on each side. A plethora of bodies drop. Those who remain standing don't know how to react so they charge instead. Malice intercepts one group while Typhoon immediately approaches the other. Some from each group actually makes it to Pharaoh, the results were not to their liking.

Blocking an energy bolt with the railgun he was wielding broke Typhoon's current weapon of choice. The augmented gorilla barks with disapproval throwing the weapon parts at the attackers before lunging forward to strike a Jackral on the side of his helmet. The warrior's legs go weak and before he hits the ground Typhoon scoops him up to use as a blunt object, beating down the Jackral nearest to him while also shielding himself from more incoming fire. Malice was reflecting energy bolts by spinning his gleaming black blades. Seeing all this and the death in Pharaoh's glowing white eyes, the Jackral finally were resigned to the fact that this was one engagement they would lose without question.

They must have called another group as one of their flying chariots came howling in as a few of them gathered the injured Kresh, threw him aboard the chariot, and retreated as fast as they could. The remaining invaders followed on foot. Holding up a hand that looked pristine despite absorbing and then returning fire with energy bolts from the Jackral weapons Pharaoh signaled that his minions should not pursue. "Let them lick their wounds and tell their leaders of this.

They will think long and hard before attempting anything at one of our fortresses. They will likely assume we or a group like us will be at every structure like this one. By the time they have gall to try again. I will have figured out how to escape this wretched place." He added.

Typhoon sat to take inventory of his weapons and wounds. Coming over Pharaoh healed most of them with a wave of his hand. He went to do so with Malice but the minion's red eyes narrowed as he rasped "That will not be necessary Master. Not many came close to touching me with their...toys." Arching an eyebrow Pharaoh replies "So be it. I am going back to my chamber to recover and meditate in case they are as ignorant as this planet's inhabitants, to think they can try me again sooner. Keep watch and next time keep the fighting outside these walls. Don't bait them in here like that again."

Bowing their heads both Malice and Typhoon chorus "Yes master." And watch him leave. Malice thought the brief ordeal must have tired his master some since he chose to actually walk instead of using the void. It was promising to see that he could weaken but it was also painfully obvious from this most recent display that Malice had no hope of defeating him despite the fact that Pharaoh was a shell of himself, still hamstrung by whatever the council of elders had done to him when initially exiled to Earth and had been siphoning off bits of his powers to create minions throughout the millennia. Even if this mutated ape joined forces with Malice their master was much too formidable to overcome.

* * *

Ensign Parsons tapped the communicator on his helmet to relay Takimura's message to the Commandant. A few moments later a videocall went to the left gauntlet of his armor which he had not noticed before. Seeing General Krulak's image nearly spooked him.

"At ease Parsons!" the commandant said jovially seeing the surprised look on the Ensigns face. He continued "Retract your helmet and take me to this Taki person so he can hear me and I can hear what he has to say." Touching a nodule behind the ear cup of the helmet it retracts into the armor and Parsons walks over to Takimura. When Parsons holds up the small screen on his gauntlet the Commandant addresses them "To what do we owe the pleasure of the renown Ryoko-Gekijo being here? Can't imagine you have a concert scheduled."

Bending down to get closer to the hologram image Takimura replies "As I told your colleague here, we wanted to help. We had just broken through the atmosphere when the attack began. Your Major Vashti had initially held us from coming down and demanded we come here for further interrogation we assume about our...departure. We were delayed of course and had to see what was happening before heading in. Hironike hopes our actions here would clean up any misconceptions about our loyalties. We only want what's right for everyone. Things are crazy out in orbit and figured you would need to get up there in order to coordinate with your forces there and better execute whatever the plan is for regaining our foothold down here."

While speaking Takimura had not noticed when the hologram was showing an empty chair. Just as he was about to ask Parsons where the general had gone, the man himself along with a large contingent of GMC guards stepped out of the HC building answering him directly. "How exactly am I supposed to get up there? A lot of our nearby spacecraft have been destroyed." Walking up to Takimura General Krulak reached out to shake his hand saying "Thank you by the way. They were making quite a mess of things out here. Won't have anymore problems out of this lot." He added looking at the pile of smoking goo a few hundred meters away.

Nodding Takimura waves towards the theater floating in between the buildings adding "She will take us up. Hironike, is waiting for you inside." The Commandant looked over the famous icon of both travel and entertainment stating "You green boys sure have a lot of tricks up your sleeves lately. I do recall seeing a report about you leaving atmo in that thing, and something about shields? Now, I see you have weapons placements as well. I'm starting to wonder if you've had this all along, or if these are recent developments." Feigning deep thought Takimura replies "Those questions are better answered by Hironike sir. Now if you'll come with us.

With that Takimura placed the bottom piece of his mask over his mouth so only his eyes were visible. He turned and nodded to the Ongakujin who had come with him and they turned as one towards the Ryoko-Gekijo. The Marines all looked to the Commandant who simply nodded and began to follow saying "Saddle up gents! We're going to ride in style!" Noticing Staff Sergeant Grimm needed help rising General Krulak turned back to help waiving off one of the Marines in the process of supporting him. See this Ensign Parsons was even more curious as to what their story was. It had to be a good one. They left a skeleton crew secured in the HC building bringing as many Marines as they could promising to bring back reinforcements once they secured the skies.

Communications systems that were down were gradually coming back online and Headquarters job while the Commandant was away would be to help identify remaining active units on the surface so they could eventually start beating back the invading forces on all fronts, but it was obvious from the intel coming in they were struggling mightily but doing better than their civilian counterparts. This was as expected but there were also images and video coming in of a contingent of mixed groups in pockets that were giving the invaders hell. Ensign Parsons spent a lot of time analyzing this intel and worked on a solution to not only communicate with them, but also include them in their liberation effort. All hands would have to be on deck to make this work.

* * *

Beating the captive Jackral invader did not yield much information for Shajara until Ragnar asked to have a crack at him. The Kison Tontu were skeptical this human would be able to get results. They were a bit suspicious when he asked them to step out of the room. On their way out of the Jackral processing facility they found their way down into a lower level of a nearby abandoned mine. This gave them some time to work on their "new friend" where prying eyes and ears would not see, or hear. Shajara came running in at the screams coming from the invader tackling Ragnar away from him.

"Are you trying to kill him? We need the information!" Shajara bellowed. Standing up to turn off the plasma cutter in his hand Ragnar replied "I know, and your methods weren't working so I stepped it up a notch! I know why they're here and what they're doing." Ragnar took out the alien tech from his ears and roughly handed them to Shajara who reluctantly took them. He then turned to look their captive over who was now silent but his armor was red hot in some less than strategic areas. Shajara left the invader whimpering as he put the buds of the strange tech in his ears. Four of his warriors came in to make sure the captive didn't try anything. Out in the corridor Ragnar pouted.

Listening to the translation of the guttural growls and at times high pitched squeals Ragnar's brand of torture produced Shajara learned about the Jackral, their self-proclaimed title of "the Blessed", their leader Anuren, and what happened to their home world sending them on a perpetual mission of nomadic conquest throughout the galaxies. Shajara knew what just happened was wrong, but under the circumstances could not argue with the results. They were still very much in grave danger. These invaders were serious about their conquest and what made it worse was that it was under the guise of some misguided religious belief that they had a right to do as they had been for who knows how long. Shajara witnessed over time how mankind repeatedly committed atrocities in the name of one god or another.

Now it seems as if that practice was coming home to roost. The irony would be lost on most. The end didn't justify the means but Shajara felt this information needed to be broadcasted to all of Earth's inhabitants but didn't know how to make that happen. Picking Ragnar up and unenthusiastically dusting him off he mumbled a half-hearted apology. The problem was they both tried their best to steer clear of the GMC, security forces and other official authorities as they often conflicted with the objectives of their respective groups. Regardless, they had to try. "Gather your guild of the pristine. We must try to reach the GMC forces and tell them what we have learned. These beings won't stop. Like the rabid dogs they favor, they will likely have to be put down. I don't predict reasoning with them will be a useful tactic." Shajara remarks.

Smoothing his clothing over and gathering his weapons Ragnar looks back saying "For once you've said something I can get behind. It's like you said I respect you enough to want to kill you myself. These dog-faced bastards have no right to this rock we call home. I don't care if they lost theirs." Hesitantly Ragnar patted the much larger Shajara on his shoulder as he left. It finally dawned on the Kison Tontu that the man was being sarcastic and somehow from all of this turmoil they were beginning to actually respect each other. It was just a shame that it took such severe circumstances to bring that about.

Thinking that over there was another conundrum that needed to be dealt with, the captive invader. They didn't have the means to constantly transport him. Any smart warrior would seek to escape when an opportunity presented itself. Shajara was in an extreme moral dilemma. Having just berated Ragnar for torturing a captive was now having to contemplate murdering that same captive. He called a meeting with his people before moving camp to another location. They needed to keep their efforts to free others up in the meantime knowing they were being used as a food source for the invaders. His men understood his misgivings but, in the end, it just was more practical to kill him. They had a recording of the translation.

His brothers and sisters knew that Shajara didn't have the heart to just kill the captive so in a compromise they untethered him and gave him his weapon. Shajara then motioned for the Jackral to attack. Wounded and tired the Jackral thought there was trickery at work and refused to play. Throwing the weapon down he snarled his disapproval as the others gathered around looked on. One of Shajara's most trusted warriors walked up and took the discarded baton-like weapon and fumbled with the buttons aiming vaguely at a nearby wall. There's an energy discharge and chunks flew from it causing everyone to jump. Then he threw the weapon back at the Jackral's feet. The Jackral warrior knew the weapon was real but still hesitated.

He sniffed in Shajara's direction noticing he had no weapons of his own and that he was also not armored. This was an afront to his pride as this fool dared to challenge one of the Blessed with no weapons as if he was worthy. The Jackral growled these sentiments to him but Shajara was the only one who understood since he was the only one with one of the alien earbud like devices in his hear to get the instant translation. Taking it out he tossed it to the Jackral and waited for him to place it in his ears so he understood his reply. "This is how I like it. Take off your armor and come at me to see if I am worthy. I think you will find me more than up to the task. No gadgets or armor. Use your natural gifts. So called...Blessed."

Howling the Jackral took off his armor and stomped the weapon crushing it amid sparks flying before rushing headlong at Shajara. The Kison Tontu was more than a match in size for the Jackral. What the invader was surprised about was the brute strength he had. That and the fact that his bare claws had virtually no effect on his hardened skin. This being was already armored without the need for alloys or metals. Using his momentum against him, Shajara went with it and slung him into the wall behind him. Teeth shattered and bones cracked with the impact. Flailing the Jackral reaches to find the eye socket which was hardened as well but the eye itself was not.

It was Shajara's turn to feel pain but he grunted refusing to shriek as the Jackral did during his torture. He wrestled the clawed hand away from his eye which was blinded and felt blood trickle down his face. The Jackral howled with joy. This angered Shajara into a rage. The Kison Tontu began pummeling the invader who soon lay motionless. Uncontrollably the merciless beating went on until finally his men had to tackle and restrain him. Gazing with his good eye Shajara shook with anger and then with tears as he realized what he had done.

His Children of the Sun dressed his wound and he tried to come to terms with what he had done. There was a lot of internal conflict. He knew what these beings had come to do was wrong but that in no way made it right for him to react the way he had. Warriors fight, that's just a reality and he had fairly challenged the Jackral warrior who in turn went for a perceived weakness. Shajara ended the challenge. That should have simply been the end of it. Yet he couldn't help the way he felt. There was no time for remorse right now. The fate of the world hung in the balance.

Chapter Twelve

Anuren was not handling the alarming reports well that had begun to trickle in. Pockets of resistance were beginning to rise up and several of the Blessed's processing stations had been destroyed. They thought the beings that may sit on the seat of power for this backwards world were trapped, but there was word of a strange vessel rescuing them. The Jackral had made great strides towards replenishing their food and fuel supply but that was now dwindling. Precious fuel and energy were being used to fight a space battle that there were few signs of being a possibility when the advance team and drones scouted this galaxy. These beings were supposed to be in their relative infancy when speaking of the space worthiness of their vessels.

Now it seems as if they may have been underestimated. Worse one of his most skilled and trusted warriors was on the brink of death. His pack mates were rushing him back to the Blessed's flagship as Anuren thought about all this. The Jackral leader went to his private quarters to watch what he could of Kresh's helmet feed before he went down to determine what was happening. The strange energy signature around the planet was also a source for concern one of which was where Kresh fell. There were Jackral bodies littered around and leading into what looked like an ancient structure. There should be absolutely no technology to speak of there yet there was plainly an energy barrier that repelled their firepower yet they were able to enter on foot and by personal skiff. If he had to make a personal appearance on the surface of this wretched planet, these vermin would not forget it, but then again it would likely be the last thing they saw.

First, he would ensure that they knew he was not to be trifled with. In their guttural language Anruen ordered the Jackral at the communications console "Open a channel to all bandwidths!" Nervously they replied "My lord they won't understand you."

Growling Anuren ran up and lunged at the scared underling grasping his throat in his jaws. The Jackral whimpers as Anuren releases him screaming "Fool! We have their language in our database now and can translate my decree! They will understand and if they do not, we will strike from above."

Ships all around Earth were still battling it out when the transmission went live. Some of the action slowed but most kept going as Anuren's voice came over all channels simultaneously "I speak now to the waste of life force that calls this pathetic place home. I am Anuren, supreme leader of the Jackral race who have come to claim this world and its inhabitants as our rightful bounty. We are the Blessed of the galaxies. Our conquest has never been turned back. Your efforts to stop the inevitable have been surprising and valorous, but in the end will be for naught. As much as I'd like to reward you for your foolish bravery…I cannot. I also cannot allow you to further damage our orbital siege engines and processing vats which no doubt you have noticed on the surface of your soon to be obliterated planet. If you do not cease your efforts, I will be forced to terminate this planet before we can fully gather our provisions and fuel. The choice is yours. Choose your next steps carefully. You can become a part of the Blessed and in some manner live on as a part of our glory, or you can join the oblivion."

After a moment the transmission ended. There was a delay before video was also broadcasts high jacking remaining satellite signals to those who weren't listening via audio devices. Turning to the Jackral on the bridge of their flagship vessel Anuren ordered "Give them a moment to come to their senses. They have to see they cannot possibly defeat us entirely. A few minor victories will matter very little if total destruction will come anyway." Turning to a smaller Jackral sitting at the console which managed the weapons batteries Anuren nods. The young albino female begins to power the main turrets up.

ANCIENT ILLUMINATION III - GODHOOD

From the surface of Earth and all ships nearby the inhabitants of the Milky Way can see various weapons that were previously hidden began to protrude from the hull and bottom of the huge pyramidal ship looming over the home planet. The huge barrels begin to gather energy causing a series of flares also visible by all in the vicinity as well as onlookers on the surface who have come out to look to the stars which had become an amazing light show. As beautiful as it may have been many were filled with dread as the activity was a result of death in the skies above. The onlookers also knew if that held potential energy were to be released, they would be joining them.

* * *

Darius now fully understood the song and language of these amazing creatures. He had spent what seemed like an eternity flying amongst the stars with them and despite all that time out in vacuum he had not tired or even felt hunger. They somehow passed energy to him as they played, nourished him, taught him. This was how he came to fully understand them. The boy was even able to communicate what he wanted. Something in him was manifesting and he couldn't quite understand what it was. His eyes and body now constantly glowed while in space and he was now able to siphon energy from dead or dying stars. He was unsure if that was something his body was learning to do or if this was a residual effect of being in such close proximity to these space creatures the Atlaneans have been using as their ships. Babylon said his people weren't the only ones to do this but they are the last beings given the honor of having these noble celestial beasts at their sides.

If he could pull this off Darius would now carry legacies of two peoples. Babylon was the last to ride in them and have a companion ship. Others were allowed to ride with him of course but no other could fly it as he did and when others from his ancient tribe had come to get a companion ship of their own, the creatures refused. Darius discovered that this was because Babylon was supposed to find them a home long ago but did not return in time because he was off averting a disaster elsewhere. Their home was lost and although they had bonded with the tribe of Atlantis after what they felt was an abandonment had not let another of his people or any other beings' bond with them in that way again.

Darius thought inquisitively as to why they would be so interested in him. Telepathically they told him that he was very different from anyone they had ever met. He was one, yet more than one. They felt he could be the one to finally save them. They needed to find a world of their own. Being out amongst the stars was a joy but very dangerous for their species. Although they could survive out here it was not how they were meant to be. Eventually they will die if another home was not found relatively soon. There was part of Darius that felt very familiar to them. This was also the part that occasionally confused the boy himself. He still did not know where his wealth of knowledge came from or how he could do what others of his kind could not.

Things that lie dormant in him were beginning to wake up. The celestials as he had come to call them promised to teach him to control what was within and he would be able to ingest some of their essence when one of them passed. They also promised to help him save his world and in return Darius was to take them to search for their new home. All of this thinking and telepathic communicating had distracted Darius from what he felt on their way here. His people were in grave danger and he needed to get back immediately. He expressed his understanding and floated back to the companion ship that he and Babylon had come in.

The old man from Atlantis was fast asleep, curled around his trident. When he awoke, he asked "So any luck? Which one will be the vessel to choose you?" Outside of what served as the main viewport was a large gathering of the celestials all a glow like birds showing off bright plumage. Babylon had to shade his eyes, and he turned to Darius for an answer who simply said "All of them."

* * *

The Ryoko-Gekijo had a hard time leaving the Earth's atmosphere. In addition to the usual hardship of making escape velocity under normal conditions there was a war going on all around the planet. Escaping gravity was only one part of it. They now had to contend with falling debris from ships large and small shot out of the sky. Once these damaged vehicles became derelict, they drifted and eventually once close enough the planets gravity well would pull them in sending them hurtling to the surface. They had shields and now weapons but needed to lower the shields in order to fire. Toshi was working furiously to navigate gauntlet of ships and debris as they tried to climb to the void of space.

General Krulak, Ensign Parsons and the rest of their Marines had to nervously standby as there was nothing they could do presently but sit and watch. The situation was made even more incongruous by the fact that they were all in luxurious leather seats. It was after all a large flying theater. The commandant did his best not to follow his internal instincts and begin barking orders. This theater that doubled as a ship was not made for war or some of the evasive maneuvers Toshi was pulling off. The little green guy was making miracles happen on the spot. Takimura was handling the shield systems, while a lithe green skinned woman named Megumi that Parsons was sure he recognized from a performance he and his family had seen years ago operated the weapons system.

Hironike, their leader oversaw it all, and for the first time the Commandant was really starting to respect these beings. This was definitely not a military vessel but from the speed and efficiency they worked together, he could tell they would be deadly adversaries. They conserved energy by powering down the shields so they could make use of the plasma canons to shoot smaller ships and debris from their path. Later they would bring them back up to navigate around larger ships slow enough to outdistance without risk of impact. Throughout the entire ordeal they constantly saw bodies from both the Jackral and united GMC/Kison Askari forces.

They first saw them raining down from vessels that had broken through the atmosphere, then again some were burning up as they hit Earth's atmosphere without the protection of s ship around them, and again once they escaped the planets gravity well bodies were floating in space among the broken space detritus. Ensign Parsons thought the frozen screams on the silent lips he saw would haunt him forever in his sleep knowing the vacuum of space had robbed them of the breath necessary to complete their final moments. His macabre thoughts were interrupted by the announcement made by Anuren. The frenzy in the space battle had slowed a bit and they were able to watch the broadcast on many screens throughout the theater including the main viewport.

Takimura reactivated the shields as they gathered to hear what the leader of the invasion force had to say. After the feed cut out there was a moment of silence until they noticed the largest of the pyramid shaped ships powering an assortment of weapons all aimed directly at the Earth. The Commandant stood and walked over to Hironike who was kind of stunned and angered. "We've got to shut that thing down. Can you get an open line to our forces up here that's encrypted?" the general asked. Hironike looked to Toshi for an answer who nodded affirmatively. Walking back to his men the Commandant quickly thought about something that didn't sit right about the answer he just got.

"Ah Toshi is it? How can you get into our encrypted message stream if its secure from everyone but GMC comm center personnel? I have a feeling I'm not going to like the answer but I have to ask." He added. If Toshi could blush he would have and Hironike answered for him "He's a bit if a tech whiz and just because your people think it's secure does not mean it's secure from him. At this point there's no reason to be dishonest General. He can get the message through. Who would you like to reach?" Krulak thought on it a brief moment before rattling off names "General Jones, Vice Admiral Featherson, and Rear Admiral Halsey for starters. They should be able to remobilize our units and disseminate orders down the chain of command quickly. I appreciate the ride up but I don't think this glorified luxury cruiser will last long in a real scrap up here. If you can, notify the *Ex Wife* so I can coordinate from there."

Confused Toshi blurts "Excuse me sir, you want me to get a message to your ex-wife?" Chuckling a bit Ensign Parsons says "No, that's the GMC flagship. The first of its class to be built. The General wants to coordinate the plan of attack from there." Patting Parsons on the back as he went by the Commandant said "Parsons, you're a Lieutenant JG now. Grimm says you handled yourself well out there, and I know you weren't keen to go. Gentlemen get the word out and please…get me back to the Ex Wife. We need to find a way to blow that thing out of our space and not have it crash to the surface."

* * *

By some strange miracle Sparks was not in vacuum floating among the bodies. As a precaution they had fully donned their armor complete with sealed helmets just in case as the ride had indeed become very rough. Max seemed to be meditating, Bofus was sitting nearly in what could only be described as an upright fetal position with his arms around his legs with eyes shut tight, and the accompanying Kison Askari along with Argos sat as if on a normal Sunday drive. It all amused and annoyed her. She could see ripples of energy mixed with strings of debris narrowly missing their hull. Some of it actually singeing or ricocheting off the hull to minimum effect.

Although not damaging or flight path altering it was still frightening and elicited moments of panic from Bofus and Sparks. The traffic around them began to ease up but the temperature rose in the rear cabin as they began to break through the atmosphere. Even with their helmets on there was a rush of noise as the friction built up in addition to the rise in heat. A wash of relief came over Sparks as she realized they made it through the gauntlet. Now they had to make it to the surface safely, but at least they got this far. Bofus noticed the change and immediately began to perk up. "Hey we made it!" he exclaimed.

The noise from the friction came to a crescendo then relative silence. Peering at an angle through the side portholes Ogun could see the surface. Details of the continents were starting to become clearer. There were some things that they did not have to get close to in order to see they were not out of danger just yet. In fact, they may be flying into more chaos than they left. Pointing Ogun says "We are not out of the woods yet." Those who could not easily see stood up in an attempt to get a peak. Bofus immediately regretted it.

There were what must have been a myriad of ground battles happening all over the globe and there were large swaths of land that looked to be scorched Earth. If the flames could be seen from this high up the fires had to be huge and raging. Bofus wanted to cry but his sadness was quickly replaced by anger. Ogun noticed the change as the usually talkative and boisterous little human started checking his shoulder mounted plasma canon, and then his gravity staff. Ogun nodded to the other Kison Askari who all began performing their own weapons checks. Sparks nerves were beginning to build up again and she was feeling claustrophobic in her armor and helmet.

She retracted her helm and went into Argos's satchel to retrieve the strange flask. The enormous humanoid cocked his head but did not object as he did when Max went for it. Max and Argos took their cue from the other warriors and began checking their gear but everyone also watched Sparks closely to see if she would actually take a drink. She thought of all the craziness happening and said "What the hell." Before taking a swig. She closed her eyes tight as the liquid burned furiously down her throat and then heating up her stomach. Sparks thought she would die.

She saw stars and the heat spread throughout her entire body before settling down. Soon there was a tingle as her ears and head felt lighter than the rest of her if that made sense. She couldn't quite put a finger on exactly what she was feeling. Then suddenly she was just there. Her entire being just relaxed. Staring blankly, she held out the flask, Argos took it and stowed it once again. Max waived a hand in front of her face and asked "Are you alright?" Shaking her head to clear it she responds "I think so. That first part is pure hell, but after that...almost worth it, I think. I'll have to try it again to be sure, and since we're all likely about to die anyway..."

Max slapped away her reaching hand remarking "Argos, I think we may have created a monster. No addicts on my watch." The potential argument was interrupted by an announcement from the pilot "Boots on the ground in ten! When that rear hatch opens be ready double time it out of here. Pretty much everywhere is hot, but I'll try to find us some cover!" Alarms blared and everyone gripped their weapons tight as moments later they were indeed on the ground. The landing was not careful and smooth as they had experienced before in the hangar bays. It was rushed and under heavy fire. Ogun was leading the Kison Askari in a war chant and let out a blood curdling war cry as the hatch slammed down and they all charged out.

Chapter Thirteen

Kresh lay in the infirmary still alive but barely. Anuren stood there watching his brother breathing raggedly with the help of medical equipment. He knows that his brother would rather the pack let him die than to live like this. The others in his group knew there would be fatal ramifications had they given in to those wishes. There was a chance he could live through this and Anuren would risk Kresh's anger if it meant not losing one of the few still alive that knew him as a young pup. One of the Bastet nurses enter the wardroom where Kresh was admitted and checks his machinery. Anuren growls low and rasps threateningly "If he dies…you shall soon follow.

The Bastet are another anthropomorphic humanoid species from the Jackrals' lost home world with one anatomical difference. Their faces have feline features. They're mainly a peaceful race but can fight if necessary. A large portion of their population died when their planet was destroyed. Those that escaped with the Jackral took the role of healers in order to prove their worth so they could survive. There was a growing faction that disavowed the crazy zealots of the Jackral and rejected this way of life that perpetuated conquering. She simply nodded and bowed her head acknowledging the threat but Anuren could tell there was no fear in her big emerald eyes.

As a result of her medical garb that was all he could see of her appearance. Both male and female Bastet were perpetually wrapped from head to toe for religious reasons. At least that was the reason given some time ago. Anuren was too young to know of them when they ran free in their natural states. Things had evolved to the extreme. Kresh's eyes began to flutter open and Anuren went to his side. Anuren sat next to Kresh's bed seeing his extremely dilated pupils. "I know you're in a lot of pain brother, but you don't have permission to die just yet." He said.

The injured Jackral attempted to sit up but Anuren placed a hand on his chest to gently push him back down. The Bastet nurse came by to give him a stern look before leaving them so they could talk. Coughing Kresh remarked "I heard you threaten her, and with that look she just threatened me. Oh, sure they act the pacifists but I've heard the stories passed down for generations about their dealings in bloodshed." It was an old wife's tale about the Bastet race being so guilt ridden that they took an oath to be healers as a way to atone for the lives they took. Changing the subject Kresh asked "How are things on the battlefront? Last I knew before you sent me in to check on that anomaly, we were winning for the most part."

Waiving dismissively Anuren answers "It will be over soon. I announced what these pitiful beings are to do to make their deaths less arduous. They will obey or we will send a salvo down to begin the destruction of their dust rock. It won't last but the sustenance we have gathered will have to do until we get to the next target. The processing vats, at least the undamaged ones are on standby to launch. We can collect them up here once we have cleared the space." Kresh struggles as he is caught between breathing with his injuries and laughing.

Surprised by the reaction Anuren says "I don't see the humor in this." Looking up incredulously Kresh explains "This is why you will eventually lose." The Jackral overlord stands up and was about to protest but Kresh cuts him off "Don't preach to me about a lack of faith! I did not hear what you told these beings but I can guess from previous experience that you did not give them any hope, and that works when you vastly outweigh your opponents. That glimmer of hope is what can keep them in line long enough to deliver the killing blow that they did not see coming. This is what you failed to learn from our forebears. The analytics do not always tell the whole story. You scouted the tech and thought this would be easy. Tell that to whatever it was that we fought in that ancient temple and pray there are no more of their kind. Heed my words brother. Even if you manage to win this conflict eventually your Blessed will become the damned and then you will lose the pack."

Anuren was livid but knew Kresh on some level was speaking the truth. He refused to placate or reason with these beings even if that meant simply misleading them. There was no need. They would either capitulate and die nobly for the cause of the Blessed or they could do so ignobly in a rain of fire. There was no alternative and the Jackral would not even pretend otherwise even if that pretense was for strategic reasons. Stomping out of the infirmary Anuren headed straight to the bridge and the crew there could tell he was in a foul mood. No one said a word or moved a whisker. Turning to his weapons officer Anuren ordered "Find the most populated area on this dust rock and fire one salvo there to be sure that they understood my conditions."

Nervously the weapons officer replied "but sir that area will likely contain some Blessed as well. They are still in an all-out assault on the surface." A crazed look came into Anuren's eyes as he stepped uncomfortably close to the officer and replied "I know. Had they done their jobs this wouldn't be necessary…fire when you have the target solution." There would be no argument that would not end in a death on the bridge of the mothership unless this order was executed. The officer entered the commands into his console and moments later plates shifted on the Jackral ship to allow the barrels of various turrets all be aimed at a single location on the globe. This time when the energy was collected instead of powering down there was a large discharge that went screaming through the atmosphere.

* * *

There was a lull in the action in space while bitter fighting continued on the surface as communication may have been spotty from all the interference. The Ryoko-Gekijo was able to rendezvous with the Ex Wife, and spoke to General Jones via burst messages to Saturn. Hironike could not believe the size of the Centurion class space cruiser. His flying theater fit easily in one of the auxiliary hangar bays. Bodies were being retrieved by both the Jackral and GMC/Kison Askari united forces. The Jackral had puffed out their metaphorical chest before by powering up their largest weapons systems on the capital ship here so everyone kind of ignored it when it began to do so again.

A blinding discharge goes off shocking everyone including General Krulak and all the crew members on the bridge. "What the hell was that?" Krulak asks knowing the answer but hoping he was wrong. They all watched in horror as the blast tears though space, layers of atmosphere to crash into East Asia. The destruction could be seen from space as millions of lives were instantly flashed away. The reaction was immediate as all ships in the area began to swarm the Jackral ships small and large like an angry hornets' nest recently disturbed. The speed and ferocity of the attacks took the Jackral by surprise.

General Krulak snapped out of it long enough to head to the captain's chair so he could try and coordinate and control the unbridled anger coursing through their forces. Too much emotion could lead to mistakes and he needed a way to destroy or disable the Jackral's largest ship before another shot could be fired. General Simeon of the Kison Askari stormed onto the bridge demanding they he should lead a boarding party. Vice Admiral Featherson argued that the GMC special forces should be the ones to handle it, and that dark matter was to be considered a last resort as using it would in fact disable the ship but rendering it listless so close to Earth's gravity well would bring about more destruction than that blast.

Hironike sat and listened to the arguing until he could not stand it any longer "Enough! Our people and our planet are dying while you bicker. I will lead the boarding party, but I need two of your top operators to go with us. General Simeon you are needed to lead your Askari I will ask for two of your young ones, they will need to be fast to keep up. General Krulak I will need to of your mechanicals?" General Krulak is confused as to how the rogue theater troop leader knows about an enhanced black ops unit until he sees Toshi sheepishly trying to hide at a console he definitely did not have clearance for.

Begrudgingly the Commandant says "I shouldn't even be considering this but how do you plan to get through those ships and once near it how can you breach the hull and gain access? You have no idea what the layout is once aboard. Chances of success with a team of operators that have been together for years are minimal, and you want to take a mixed crew. It sounds like a shot in the dark to me." Looking on Simeon interjects "As strange as it may seem I have to agree with the GMC Commandant. I know you can handle yourselves but this is a greater task that will need those of us who are experienced in war. With the added obstacles just mentioned we would almost be better served hitting them with dark matter ordinance."

Sheepishly Toshi straightened up and raised his hand asking permission to speak. Frowning General Krulak shrugged his shoulders exasperated with the whole situation saying "Why not? What do you have to say on it?" When Hironike nodded his approval after Toshi looked to him the Ongakujin tech wiz went on "We need to get in and quickly hack their systems and although I am adept at doing this, we do have a far more viable solution...the automatons. They are after all AI advanced technology that should be able to figure out the language of this alien tech much faster than I could giving us access to schematics in order to find the command deck. I think multiple teams should go. A few to fight and to serve as distractions while a couple groups of automatons go to hack their systems while Hironike and his crew goes in to take out their leader and help take over the ship after the helmsmen or whoever is driving is taken out or coerced into flying away from our gravity well."

They all thought about and continued to discuss this plan while General Krulak asked Lt. Commander Jameson to get a hold of his Mechanics group. The automaton units were mobilized to select a number of groups to coordinate the hacking efforts. Simeon went to confer with Queen Tunisia to select which warriors to send on this mission. They were still having a hard time getting the already deployed units to break off their attacks in order to regroup. They still weren't sure they were going to be able to get any ships especially a group of small ones close enough to pull this off. Any enemy ships they could get their hands on would be damaged and they would not be able to communicate with them in order to gain entry that way.

Athena who was nearby listening but not joining in the discussion, walked up to Hironike who was trying to follow all of the discussion waiting to give input where he thought it was needed. Seeing her approach, he held up a hand and said "Before you ask the answer is no." Smiling Athena adjusts her armor and tightens the wrap on her amethyst locks replying "First I didn't ask anything yet, and second I don't do well with orders or demands." Shaking his head Hironike responds "I know you didn't ask but I already knew you were going to ask to come with me and I feel it's too dangerous. For the same reasons I don't think Simeon should go, your people need you."

As if to emphasize her point, Athena takes out her weapons to check them before adding "Oh I wasn't asking, and I know I haven't been to war exactly but I have likely had more fighting experience than you. I know you are more than assassins. The GMC may suspect but clearly have no idea about your...hidden talents. I know and have witnessed what you have at times displayed though your music and theatrics mask the horror you visit upon those that perpetuate oppressive policy or heinous practices. I am more than a beauty, more than a procurer of sensitive information, or a trophy for wealthy households to flaunt. I am a fighter, and my people are still on the surface of that planet. Angelo and I will either be with your party or one of the others going, and if not, we will form one of our own."

Seeing there would be no winning this argument, Hironike simply nodded as she walked to where Angelo seemed to appear on the bridge out of nowhere. Toshi walked up followed Hironike's gaze and remarked "I guess everyone has clearance now huh?" One of the nearby officers stared at him in disbelief until he raised his hands and walked away. In walked about eight automaton units. They were all marching in lockstep completely in unison. Lt. Commander Jameson commented "Looks like they're taking their attachment to the military seriously. I wonder how effective they will actually be at hacking alien technology to get the information we will need in the time we need it?"

The lead automaton turned to fix its golden eyes on Lt. Commander Jameson before spitting out random facts robotically "Lieutenant Commander Edward Jameson, born in Des Moines Iowa. An accomplished geneticist, bioengineer and recently dabbled in previously unsanctioned technology and biological integrations..." Jameson quickly cuts him off "That's cute and all but quickly pulling up my personal history readily available to anyone with access to a search engine is nothing compared to hacking into an alien computer system in a language that may or may not be translatable to our systems and algorithms." It was obvious from the more natural response from the automaton that it was trolling.

When it next spoke it sounded like a human being as it pointed out "Some of the information I have access to about you was not readily available through general search engines but are in fact kept on an encrypted server where the GMC and other government entities have been keeping tabs on your exploits sir. As far as the language barrier all technology uses mathematics to speak which can be quickly deciphered by us rather quickly. In addition, we have been able to find information recently turned in to a security force group on Earth on a confiscated translation device which was acquired by Kison Tontu warriors during a rescue at one of the invaders processing plants. We were able to get access through this device to their language so that will not be an issue."

Lt. Commander Jameson was obviously uncomfortable about them having access to his information that should have been safe on encrypted servers and he slowly backs out of the conversation. Simeon overheard the last part and corrects the automaton "Don't you mean Kison Askari? We no longer refer to ourselves as just people." Following the retreat of Jameson and then turning his attention to Simeon the automaton replies "Obviously sir not all of your kind feel this way. The information we were able to grift said the device was turned in by a Ragnar who go it from the Kison Tontu that goes by the name of Shajara. Ironically they are known to be a part of extremist groups that would ordinarily be at odds philosophically according to their growing files."

Moments later there was an annoying scraping sound as Sgt. Garrison came in dragging his alloy feet and legs as he walked announcing his presence. General Krulak would have none of it. "Sgt. I would advise you not to scrape up the deck on my ship!" he bellowed. The noise immediately halted as Sgt. Garrison replied "My bad sir! Lt. Commander Jameson said there was a dark assignment for us but would be an extremely joint effort?" Garrison looked around to see who all was there that wouldn't normally be there in a GMC formation or muster.

Lt. Commander Jameson was at the thresh hold to the bridge
entrance but oddly enough would not come in. When he caught
Garrison's eye he nodded as if to confirm that he was in fact in the
right place and then the officer abruptly left. Seeing a rather diverse
group of beings all huddled over a table with a holoprojection
displaying the disposition and deployment of enemy and ally assets in
the galaxy, Garrison walks over to introduce himself. "I'm Sergeant
Garrison, head of the Mechanics unit. Who's in charge of this
cluster…" Hironike quickly interrupts before he can finish "Hironike,
head of the Ongakujin, there is Toshi one of my best tech advisors,
General Simeon of the Kison Askari, and these automaton units will be
split amongst our various strike teams."

Seeming to mull that over Garrison responds "Yeah I was given
the gist of the plan. If you can call it that, but how do we get to their
ship amidst the other ships and firepower in our way? My ship the
Adder has some stealth capabilities but can only take one team, maybe
two. We need to simultaneously get multiple teams to breach their
hull, get in, some will fight to distract so that one or more of the other
teams can get in to take out this Anuren, and possibly the bridge crew.
Then they will have to disable the weapons system or simply fly that
thing away so it's not a danger to Earth and the remaining population
there." Looking to the Commandant he adds "That's a tall order Sir."
The general nods in agreement.

"Yes, son that is a tall order, but the alternative is to let them have
what they want with no resistance. There is no scenario where we do
that, and we survive. I for one will go out fighting. I don't like the plan
but unless you have a better one, we go with this. Mr. Toshi please
elaborate to the Sergeant here on how you plan to get these teams in a
position to breach the hull of that pyramidal beast out there." General
Krulak stated. Toshi took the cue to step up and explain how they
could do it. First, he asked "General Krulak the stealth filaments or

plating in the Adder do you have more we could use?" Krulak shook his head negatively "Not enough to equip similarly sized ships for each team."

One of the automatons perked up and suggested "What about the pods used to deploy our units at Ganymede?" The reminder resulted in visible reactions from the Kison Askari present. Toshi interjected before another argument would ensue "That could work! Of course, we would need to be ejected via torpedo chute from varying angles so that we land at different locations on the hull." Shaking his head and laughing Sgt. Garrison says "Oh, is that all? My boys won't be happy about that." Another automaton responds "Happiness is not a factor or requirement. Following the directives is."

Chapter Fourteen

Max, Sparks, Argos, and Bofus found themselves participating in a mad dash to follow the Kison Askari who preceded them exiting the hauler. Ballistic and energy projectiles were flying everywhere and the air was thick with smoke. Sparks had to immediately activate her helmet to use the breathing filters on it. With that done she should see Max and Bofus had their helms raised as well. For all she knew Argos had a helmet on already under his head wrappings but either way he didn't seem bothered by the conditions. They got some distance from the ore hauler and Sparks could see that it had taken some significant damage on the trip down. It was a miracle they made it. As if on cue a barrage of energy blasts hit it with enough force to knock it on its side.

The pilot and crew barely had enough time to climb out of a side hatch that was now facing upwards before another round of ordinance hit it. This time it was turned into a huge blob of melted slag. One crew member was not quick enough and was fused to the smoking remnants. There was another explosion bright enough to make their helmets blast shield briefly dim. The various units that made it to the surface were beginning to form lines. Orders were being passed on as they were all trying to get their bearings during the chaos they were suddenly thrust into. The area they landed in looked to be fairly urban. The Kison Askari began taking doors off of abandoned vehicles, using them as impromptu riot shields.

The GMC units began giving them cover fire trying to pin down Jackral soldiers and force the chariot Jackral into cover taking away their maneuverability. GMC snipers found their way onto nearby roof tops or any high ground available seeking out sources of counter fire their allies received. What started off slow quickly became fast responses as the battle changed. While still ducked behind their makeshift shields the Kison Askari personal shoulder canons began to auto-fire at the Jackral when they got close. Max, Sparks and Argos settled into a newly formed crater using it as a foxhole of sorts and helped out where they could.

A few of the snipers were taken out as somehow Jackral chariots found their way through dropping off other alien warriors to try and disrupt the new found coordination and it seemed as if they might flank the GMC/Kison Askari forces. Max was using a railgun to take potshots at Jackral that were not completely armored. He was surprised to find some who refused to wear helmets. Three such were dropped nearly on top of them. Max was not going to have time to bring his weapon to bear on the lead invader. As the Jackral warrior went to aim his energy baton something flashed into his chest. There was a resounding clang and he went flying. The second Max was able to shoot in the mouth at close range making his head explode. As the third crested into the foxhole, his head also became a mist of brain particles as hot plasma rushed through it. About a hundred yards away Sparks thought she could see Bofus give a thumbs up as if it was his shot.

With his helmet on and at the distance should not tell if it was in fact him or a short Kison Askari. She had learned that some of the stone people born on heavier gravity planets often had their growth stunted as the skin matured as they got older. The first Jackral was still alive but in incredible pain as whatever Argos hit him with had not killed him but crushed him inside of his armor. Max tried to stand to finish the job when he fell noticing his cybernetic leg had been damaged. Argos finished the job with the largest yet most ornate sword Sparks had ever seen decapitating the wounded Jackral who had retracted his helmet in an attempt to help his breathing. It wouldn't have helped. His ribs were broken, puncturing his lungs. Had Argos not finished him, he would have effectively drowned on his own blood.

Max wasn't sure of what to do or how he could proceed when one of the automaton units showed up with more GMC that had just landed. Seeing the busted leg, the automaton examined it before noting "This is a very old model, but I can fix it. GMC cybernetics leave much to be desired. You would think the government could afford more recent tech." Exasperated Max replied "For chrissake just fix it! I'm not GMC. I'm a citizen fighting like everyone here should!" Noticing the emotional stress in the response the automaton simply says "My apologies." That was when something far off in the distance struck. Everything went white. After a bright flash there was a hint of heat that washed over them. Sparks was sure the blast or whatever happened was on another continent altogether so the aftershock they felt meant anything at ground zero was utterly destroyed.

* * *

Luckily Ragnar found a security forces outpost that was still relatively intact, gave them a copy of the recording for them to disseminate to the GMC and any other authority. Getting into the facility would have normally been dicey given Ragnar and his guilds reputation with local authorities. Finding a group of his brothers had been relatively easy in comparison. There were safe houses that looked abandoned where they were to go to when the big war was to kick off. Well it had not happened between the Guild of the Pristine and all resident mutants as they expected but did with this alien invasion and with much worse results. Some of the guild were caught off guard hearing about their leader fighting alongside mutants but relented after thinking about their current circumstances.

After the information was passed on Ragnar felt it was best to find as many of his soldiers as he could, and look to regroup either with Shajara or any GMC forces nearby. Either would likely be better equipped than his renegade groups which traditionally stole or found black market weapons when they could. He had a strange feeling about trying to hook up with GMC units or even security forces regulars but strange times made for strange bedfellows. Unity was the last thing he thought to strive for but it was likely the only thing that would save them all. The group of fighters he was able to gather made their way to another seemingly abandoned mine.

Shajara and his people were not there but an old Kison Tontu there pointed them in the right direction after some questioning from him. It was obvious some were still suspicious of a known anti-mutant group looking for the Children of the Sun. It took some convincing that there were no ill intentions if Shajara were found, as if on cue there was a loud explosion to emphasize, they were in fact all in danger now. Ragnar thanked the old man without getting his name and they were on their way to another location. Travelling above ground was even more dangerous than before with Jackral chariots flying around looking for more prisoners to round up. The more obvious established areas were all hot with either Jackral patrols or heavy fighting.

Ragnar and his men did their best to avoid the hotspots until they could get with either a GMC unit or Shajara and whatever forces he was able to amass since they last parted. At the fifth mining location they were able to find him. The entrance was heavily guarded although it did not look that way at first. Ragnar thought perhaps the old man had given them erroneous directions on purpose as this latest mine was not active by the look of things. Most of the underground network had been abandoned. At least that's what the stone people had led most to believe as it became very useful when trouble broke out in the past.

There was a heavily forested area leading to the entrance to this last location. There looked to be an abandoned camp fire off to the left. Ragnar sent a few of his men to check it out as the rest of them watched from a distance. The forest itself came alive while the men were checking the doused fire. Camouflaged stone people seemingly appeared out of thin air to surround them all. Ragnar raised his hands and nodded to his people to drop their weapons. They weren't here to fight. Stepping out from the shadows was Shajara's hulking figure covered in moss and other natural elements that helped him blend into the foliage. "Here to kill me yourself?" he chuckled and everyone relaxed. Ragnar's men slowly picked up their weapons but stowed them. Many on both sides felt very uneasy and it showed.

Shajara patted Ragnar on the shoulder roughly, and that's when Ragnar saw the eye patch. "Going for the pirate look?" There was an awkward silence as Shajara didn't immediately answer. Instead he ignored the question quickly walking away. One of his men who overheard stepped in to fill Ragnar in "He dueled the prisoner you questioned. No weapons or armor. Shajara defeated him pretty easily but lost an eye in the process. He has another now but is ashamed of the augment as it is unnatural. For that reason, he is wearing an eye patch to hide it." Hearing that explanation Ragnar chased Shajara down to see it for himself.

"Is it true?" Ragnar asked out of breath as he caught up to Shajara who responded "Is what true? What nonsense have you been thinking on now?" Pointing to the eye patch Ragnar says "The eye. Is it an augment now? You should have let me finish the interrogation." Shaking his head Shajara replies "I tried to stop you from doing something wrong not knowing it was actually me who needed to be stopped. Losing my eye is what I deserved but will need this fake one to be the warrior my people need. When this is over, I will divest myself of it."

Ragnar understood it from his perspective that all beings who purposely augmented themselves were basically cheaters but this was a mutant who already had an unfair advantage so this was no reason for

Shajara to feel conflicted. He was going to explain this but saw from the look on Shajara's face that he would not be swayed by his opinion. He tried to concentrate on the problems at hand. "Are you and your folks ready to get back in the game?" he asked gauging Shajara's reaction. "We are ready to beat these invaders back. There's been reports of GMC units landing in addition to some mixed units a few clicks from here. Something huge hit Asia though, we felt the aftershocks." He offered.

They walked back into the previous chamber that must've been a prep area before going into the mine proper. It was dead silent and the tension was thick as cold peanut butter. Ragnar's men had followed him but he guessed they hadn't really believed the tale of him fighting alongside their traditional enemies. They were lined up against the wall opposite a similar formation of Kison Tontu and other mutants who had come together to fight the invasion. Fearing things might get worse Ragnar addresses his men. "Now look. I don't like having to join forces with the rock heads any more than you do…no offense. The reality is, these dog faced aliens come here, and they don't care about any of us. Mutant or non-mutant makes no difference to em! We are all a food source! We can hash out our differences later, but first we have to survive this invasion. In order to do that we are going to have to stand with those we disagree with first."

Turning to his people Shajara says "I agree. Will you be fodder for these dog-beings or would you rather take up arms with those at least born under the same sun as yourselves?" A loud ragged cheer to fight goes up by both sides in near unison. They gather their weapons and start working on a game plan. As the others are talking Ragnar goes over to Shajara adding "Great talk, though you did sound a bit xenophobic at the end, but don't worry…it's warranted this time."

* * *

Anuren watched the ordinance strike Earth and the chaos it created both on the surface and in space around the planet "See them spread like the vermin they are when you turn the lights on in a dark chamber!" he bellows as the bridge crew looks on. They also noticed the ferocity of the GMC and Kison Askari fighter pilots once they noticed as well. The fighting which paused briefly resumed in space at a fever pitch. Hovering onto the bridge on a gurney came Kresh who noted "It would seem these…vermin have teeth now. With your overbearing manner and the fatal mistake of showing your hand before it's won, you've sharpened them."

Anuren went into a rage and flew across the deck knocking the gurney over sending Kresh flying along with the machinery connected to it. Bastet nurses came running in as alarms began to beep. They quickly righted the gurney, placing Kresh back on it while hooking him back up to the medical equipment. They rushed him out before Anuren could lash out again. Looking around Anuren said "Anyone else want to provide some words of wisdom? Want to gloat over things not going as you think they should? I have a bed next to Kresh's if you do or better yet a one-way trip into the cold vacuum." There was predictably no one who had anything to add.

Looking over at the nervous Jackral manning the weapons station on the bridge Anuren shouted "Fire another volley!" There's a brief silence but Anuren notices the Jackral not moving immediately to execute his command. "Have you all gone mad?" Their leader asks. Finally, one of the more senior crew members stand to try and smooth things over adding "No my lord, it's just that the remaining processing spikes are still gathering fuel from the planets core. Another blast could possibly destabilize them all before we have a chance to gather them along with the food we have processed. Premature destruction would make this trip a fruitless one."

There was a collective mental sigh on the bridge as Anuren nodded acknowledging the truth of why his orders were not directly carried out. "Very well. Prepare my ship and let us remember who we are and why we are here! We are the Blessed whom no one can deny what will be ours. Do not flinch in the face of adversity! These beings seem to think they are the predators here! Show them they are but the last in a long line of prey. It looks as though some of us have forgotten this." Staring out of the front viewport they could see many of the Jackral fighters and even some of the larger troop carriers, interceptors and frigates were being destroyed or pummeled hard.

Not many had the audacity to outright challenge the Flagship of the Jackral or the other smaller but still large capital ships. The Kison Askari Dreadnaught and the GMC Centurion space cruisers were content to sit back watching everything play out. Eventually all of these larger ships would have to come into play. Anuren had prematurely fired his space to surface ordinance but really had no idea what their counterparts were capable of. There was evidence suggesting dark matter capability yet none had been shown thus far.

Perhaps the readings were wrong or there was another explanation for the residue being detected on two of the planets in this galaxy. Either way this gave Anuren more confidence. He agreed not to fire upon Earth again as he came to know the name of this soon to be gone planet, before they had what they came for. None of these beings would be left to tell the tale. That was a strategy the Blessed had come to use long ago. Vengeance was often a great motivator for survivors after all this was how the Jackral became the Blessed in the first place. First surviving what many considered unsurmountable odds after the destruction of their home world. Then upon escaping finding those responsible to pay them back in full. They took their ships and adopted the roles of travelling nomads.

Anuren was the latest in a long line of leaders who had come up with a religion to add confidence in their wild crusade. They found that zealots often did almost anything in the name of a higher power. Especially one that these beings came to believe in after getting through tragedy. Anuren knew this was just one more stop in a long line of others. They had experienced setbacks before to races and beings much more evolved than this ragtag group who had been at each other's throats just before the Blessed came here. Death would be a blessing for these wretches. They would be free of the conflict they themselves create more often than not.

The inhabitants of Earth may not see it that way now but perhaps they will in the afterlife, if it exists for them. Anuren did not claim to know the faiths of all beings in the galaxies. His only concern was with his and the Blessed. He could not fail them. Settling was for the weak and he just didn't see anywhere they could peaceably settle. No race of beings would willingly share their world as they had once long ago suggested to their usurpers. To the Jackral it was meant that they would forever live among the stars plundering what they could from those less favored than themselves. Up to this point that had been everyone they encountered.

Chapter Fifteen

Gathered in one of the larger auxiliary hangars in the *Ex Wife* Sgt. Garrison was trying to finalize their attack plan for boarding the largest of the pyramidal Jackral ship in their space. He still couldn't quite wrap his head around what was supposed to happen. He knew theoretically how things were supposed to go but his gut told him somebody was going to end up a cold smear on the hull. His group was campaigning hard not to draw that detail. They were now going to use modified drop pods shot out of torpedo chutes. That meant those that took that method would be a mix of Sgt. Garrison's group codenamed the Mechanics and automatons.

PFC Long was not happy as he was one of the Marines going with the automatons in a modified drop pod. Another would have Kison Askari with more automatons in case the other group was destroyed in the process. One of them had to be able to access the ships systems. The rest of the motley crew was trickling in for the briefing. Major Vashti entered after leaving his own ship. Sgt. Garrison saluted the Hindi officer greeting him as they stopped by a mobile holostation that would soon show the team a 3D illustration of how things were to happen. "Good evening Major! What brings you to this crazy party sir?" Garrison said.

Returning the salute Major Vashti replies "Good evening Sergeant. Apparently, I am to shoot some personnel out of my torpedo chutes at the enemy flagship." The Major nods towards the rear of the hangar where a group of engineers were adhering plates with the stealth filaments onto the modified drop pods. They also had to be elongated and slimmed down somewhat to fit in the chutes. Nobody wanted a misfire or for them to get stuck. Corporals Aragon and Sims were watching all of this unfold and began to discuss it. "You still want to join this unit?" Sims asks. Watching PFC Long argue with the engineers over whether or not he would actually fit into the drop pod as General Simeon and Muturi of the Kison Askari observed smiling, and the leader of the Ongakuijin suited up in prep for the mission, Corporal Aragon was well aware of how nonsensical this all seemed.

Responding Aragon says "Yeah, I know how all this looks but I am ready to go on this run. Not sure about a permanent attachment though. If this fails or they win it's over for us all anyway. At least we will be aboard the Adder with a bird's eye view of the action. I think you and I along with House will remain there until it's over. I'm augmented but not to the degree Sgt. Garrison, Private Cooper and PFC Long are. That's why they get to ride the torps. Lance Corporals McNamara and Jennings will fly while we provide any support they need from a relatively safe distance remaining in stealth mode. I never thought I would see the day when we would be on an op with stone people and a frickin playwright." Shaking his head Sims asks "Who's the shiny couple?" nodding towards Athena and Angelo tightening down their armor and weapons with Hironike.

Petty Officer House walks over and having heard the last part of their conversation supplies an answer "Those walking fashion statements are Hironike of the Ongankujin, and some esteemed guests from his theater that apparently have some skill I assume. I know she was a labor broker for the rich and privileged not too long ago but her name escapes me. She's a mutant and all but I can't lie...kind of curious." The discussion is cut short as the holostation comes to life. Sgt. Garrison shouts "Gather around for the brief folks!" Suddenly a large 3D map of the Earth and the space around it complete with ally and enemy ship deployments above the table like device.

The still images become animated as the plan plays out in the simulation narrated by Nelson the automaton. Multiple GMC and Kison Askari fighter squadrons are sent in to swarm the flagship to force the enemy forces to react. "We want the majority of their forces worried about attacks from our fighters and ordinance coming from the capital ships which should be firing from a distance. We are not trying to disable the ship outright just want their attention away from the many task forces trying to make their way aboard." In the midst of the simulated battle a line of Praetorian cruisers executes a swift fly by launching torpedoes just below what they think is the bridge area. Nelson continues "One of those cruisers under Major Vashti's command will launch one of the modified drop pods carrying PFC Long, two of our automaton units, Amuzati, and Bulu. The second drop pod should be shot from a different vantage point."

Listening to all this Aragon was trying to put names to faces and guessed that the two extremely short but heavily muscled Kison Askari standing a few feet from Long were the aforementioned Amuzati, and Bulu. He didn't want to offend but could not help but stare. Most of the Kison Askari or stone warriors he had seen were larger than the average non-mutated human but these two were quite the opposite. Aragon had also heard rumors about some of them who grew up or were born on heavy gravity planets had their growth severely stunted since their skin had yet to mature and develop. This had to be the case with them. House noticed Aragon's focus and nudged him to stop the staring.

Nelson's voice continues the narration through the speakers in the holostation "The Adder will look for another breach point to insert Hironike and his team. Sgt. Garrison, Private Cooper, and Muturi will be taking the other drop pod. After all teams are in, The Kison Askari pilot Zurina will be running interference in her stealth ship in addition to the remaining Mechanics unit in the Adder. Try to remain hidden but occasionally fire upon the flagship and nearby Jackral ship in the fight or patrolling nearby. Once inside the task force members will find their way to a terminal where the automaton units can quickly learn the intricacies of the ship's schematics so you can get to the bridge. If any of you are lucky or unlucky enough to find Anuren, he is to be eliminated on sight. Perhaps there are more level headed beings among them that would be willing to negotiate with him out of the way. Get to the bridge and wrest control of this vessel. The Earth cannot withstand too many more salvos from it."

The running images shut down as General Krulak came in asking "Any questions?" There were none. "Let's get to it then…Godspeed!" he added. Everyone went to finish their last-minute preparations.

* * *

The aftershock of the distant explosion had everyone groundside stop what they were doing. There was a stunned silence as it was obvious both sides were frantically trying to find out what just happened. In pockets fighting resumed or had barely stopped. Luckily the automaton fixed Max's cybernetic leg in time for him to be mobile once the firefights broke out again. The fighting was still intense but it was also pretty clear that the Jackral had lost some of their enthusiasm. The GMC and Kison Askari forces pressed the issue to take advantage in the sudden morale change. Finally, able to stand again Max along with Argos and Sparks ran from cover to cover to keep up with Bofus and his stone warrior unit.

Brazenly Bofus had gone ahead of his unit to engage the Jackral who were reasonably more worried about the Kison Askari who were blocking their fire with makeshift shields before doing major damage once in close range both with their shoulder mounted canon and whatever they got their hands on. Sparks's impression of Bofus was changing rather quickly. Sparks had not noticed the baton he was carrying as he jumped from enemy to enemy, but it was literally crushing them when Bofus struck. Nudging Max she said "There's no way he is that strong. Must be the suit."

In between shots Max looked over his shoulder to see what she was talking about. He laughed a little commenting "It's not his suit but a special gravity bow the Kison Askari came up with. Pretty wicked and I bet when this mess is over with, it would fetch a pretty penny in the right market." Sparks just shook her head then began to pepper a Jackral chariot with railgun fire. The action only served to notify its riders to their location as it changed course to come at them. Argos hunched down waiting to spring the moment it got close. There was no need as a group of more heavily armored Marines came through ripping both the chariot and its riders to shreds with plasma fire.

At that the firing stopped for the most part as the Jackral were retreating despite not losing at every flashpoint. Even where they were winning convincingly the Jackral units suddenly broke off their attacks confusing the joint forces all over the globe. "What the hell was that about?" Max asked. Sparks wasn't sure but she was glad for the respite from fighting. They were able to catch up with Bofus and his Kison Askari unit who were grouping up with the GMC units some of which had been fighting for days before the reinforcements came down in the ore haulers. They were taking inventory of wounded and KIA. It was sounding like they lost a lot just getting to the surface. Traffic, weapons fire from the ships and miscellaneous debris was worse than Sparks originally thought. They were lucky to have made it.

There were bodies strewn everywhere and it was obvious from the ongoing light show in the night sky that not everyone had stopped fighting. Looking up Max remarked "Things are still hot and heavy up there. I can't tell who is winning though." There was still an occasional chunk of large debris that would crash to the Earth. Sometimes they could tell whose it was and at other times they could not. Bofus came over, took off his helmet and said "Hey, I think we won!" Pointing Sparks asks "Then what's going on up there?"

ANCIENT ILLUMINATION III - GODHOOD

* * *

The area around the Pyramid at Giza had dwindled down to silence but there were smaller skirmishes here and close to many of the processing spikes as mutant and non-mutant alike begun to chase the Jackral back to them. It looked as if they were going to try and pull up stakes literally and leave with whatever supplies were now gathered. Pharaoh observed this from his vantage point in the uppermost chamber of the pyramid. This gave him an overview of the whole planet as well as the space around it which was ablaze with battle taking place there as things cooled down momentarily on the surface.

This was a surprising turn of events. He had not expected human kind to mount any sort of comeback after the initial attacks had seemed to knock all hope from them. Their cities were ablaze and large numbers had been captured for processing or killed yet they still fought back. Someone surely had noticed. Pharaoh watched a gigantic ball of energy come from what had to be one of the Jackral ships go straight towards the Asian continent pretty much decimating it. Suddenly he was disconnected briefly from the nexus point in the pyramid in the Qin Ling mountains. Pharaoh shook his head to shake the haziness being linked to the global system while the massive doppler like effects of the impact reverberated outwards for miles and miles.

It was almost like feeling attached to the land. Through their connection Malice and Typhoon must have felt it at least partially as they came running into the chamber to see what happened. "Master! What is it?" They blurted in unison. Finally regaining his composure Pharaoh says "Obviously these invaders are sore losers. They've retaliated not knowing that type of force on this planet may destroy it. They're like spoiled children throwing a disastrous tantrum when they don't get what they want. Come to think of it they fit in perfectly here."

Typhoon and Malice were visibly still shaken by whatever Pharaoh had went through. That was a curious thing as he felt as close to normal now as he ever had. Perhaps this made it possible to siphon some of his essence back. There was no way for him to make a full recovery to his original form. In hopes that maybe whatever the elders had done to him possibly wore off by now, Pharaoh was willing to try something. Without telling them his true intentions he said "Come, there is something I must teach you. Never thought there would be a need but these are desperate times. Meditate with me here."

Confused but having no choice but to comply, the two minions stepped forward. The chamber began to light up and three golden throne-like chairs came up from the floors. All three took seats. Typhoon and Malice closed their eyes as they could feel power ebbing and flowing through them. The chamber began to shimmer until it became a translucent tip of the pyramid. Most were too concerned with recovering from the disarray around them to notice. Pharaoh could feel himself getting more powerful as the energy circulated between them, but he could not hold on to it. Cycling the energies through them, he could feel that it was possible to bolster had he wanted to but for all his effort he could not retake what was once given.

Frustration builds up until the connection is broken as Pharaoh erupts "Impossible! I will find a way! Leave me! Useless fools!" Typhoon and Malice were disorientated at the sudden breaking of their link. Groggy they leave the chamber and their master who continues to sulk. Once the chamber closes behind them Typhoon expresses his confusion "What was it we were supposed to learn?" Chuckling in his raspy voice Malice answers "You truly are a fool. No more than an ape even with your newfound evolution. He was using us again in an attempt to gain his freedom from this place he sees as a prison despite having dominion over most of it. He thought he could pull out what he inserted in us in an attempt to restore himself to his former glory. I think our master thought the cataclysmic event could have shifted whatever shackles his elders put on him...alas it did not. Be ready. I can feel things stirring once again."

Angrily Malice stormed off to his private chamber deep in bowels of the ancient place that made their home. Once there he began to coat and sharpen his blades. The blades are the only things that give him anything close to joy, and he was relishing using them again. Typhoon still bewildered at it all went to his chamber continuing to nurse his wounds that were nearly healed with his master's assistance following their latest battle with the invaders that had the nerve to enter the pyramid. There he gathered his weapons of choice but now had some strange new additions.

The ape was particularly interested in the baton like weapons the invaders were wielding. He was normally more attracted to the traditional ballistic and long-range energy projectile firing weapons. This was a mixture of it all. The bulky handle with an elongated nodule felt right in his rough hands. Lightly pressing the nodule produced a blast of energy that emitted from the end of the shaft. It was not that long. The entire device was slightly under three feet in length. Checking to see if anyone heard as the baton bolt hit the wall, Typhoon began to make amused noises as quietly as he could when no one approached to see what was happening.

* * *

The flight back to the Milky Way was going to take longer than the trip out. Darius and Babylon were in the Atlantean's living companion ship, but they had a large gathering of the celestial beings with them. Unlike GMC or Kison Askari ship there was no central system they all linked into to sync their navigation patterns. These beings for a time could travel much faster than most space craft but it could not be sustained as they were organic beings and not simple machines. Darius wondered if they could travel through the ether. When the question was posed to Babylon he said "Never tried wit dis many beings at once! Not sure if they would go for it even if I was willin t try."

Disappointed at the answer Darius understood that it could be a risk. He himself had only walked the void a few times. There was no telling what would happen if some of his celestials got lost in that dimension. After a brief rest they were able to jump to hyperspace again making Darius wonder just how far out they had flown to get them. He and Babylon were able to take turns sleeping on the way out. They were able to do that again on the return trip. The young prince tried to convey a sense of urgency to the celestials as he felt a terrible echo across the vast reaches of space as millions of lives were snuffed out almost instantly.

Being asleep in what served as a rear cabin Babylon watched the boys glow intensified as he began to float. Gently he placed a hand on the boy's chest pushing him back down. It was obvious he was having a nightmare of some kind. Suddenly the boy's eyes opened glowing brightly and Babylon asks "What did you see or hear?" The glow fades as tears well up in Darius's eyes. He looks to Babylon before saying "Death, lots of it. We need to hurry before it's all gone."

Chapter Sixteen

PFC Long was going to look like his code name soon. He was frustrated. Two of the automatons assigned to his drop pod along with the two compact Kison Askari Amuzati and Bulu were already huddled into it. It was horizontally situated in the torpedo chute. All that was needed was for Long to get in the rear of the compartment and await the chance to be ejected at high velocity into a huge enemy ship. The two stone warriors were laughing uproariously at the Marine encased in alloy trying to figure out how he was to fit himself in. Even the two automatons assigned to his drop pod were small in stature. From a distance Corporals Aragon and Sims were watching trying not to laugh. The intercom in their armor blasts Sgt. Garrison's voice "Get your asses to the Adder! We need you to be wheels up as soon as Long gets his can in that other can so Major Vashti can launch him!"

PFC Long turns just in time to see them scurry off. They stomped their way to the hangar bay for immediate transfer from the Praetorian the Major was commanding back to the *Ex Wife* where the Adder was docked. Lance Corporals McNamara and Jennings were there finalizing the preflight checklist. Once back to the Adder Aragon saw Hironike, Athena, and Angelo prepping to do their part. Both Aragon and Sims were still befuddled as to how these three got to go on a military style strike mission with absolutely no experience. There had to be more than meets the eye with them. Either that or they had something on the Commandant which was a possibility. The automatons assigned to them were idly sitting there.

Lance Corporal Jennings walks up to them and asks "You both had flash training for piloting correct?" Both Corporals Aragon and Sims reply "Yes." Lance Corporal McNamara says "Great since you're technically senior one of you can fly this bucket of bolts while we man our newly installed turrets. Plus, our sight augments make us better marksmen than either of you. I know you're not technically attached to us Corporal Aragon, but you're augmented while Sims is not so until Sgt. Garrison returns, you're acting squad leader. He seems to have respect for you so don't mess it up." Aragon and Sims head to the cockpit as Aragon yells over his shoulder "Roger that!"

Aragon settles into the cockpit while Sims sits at the console to his right and slightly behind with the comms equipment. There's a third seat behind that one that's centered between them where Sgt. Garrison usually sits during missions. Somehow Aragon felt that absence despite them not being in the same unit for a while after the initial revolt. Aragon was the one responsible for getting Sgt Garrison back to safety after getting wounded answering a distress call at African mines where the overseer and all the non-mutant workers were found killed. They walked into a meat grinder that day. Now it looked as if they were going to another of a different making.

With the flight check complete Corporal Aragon conveys that to flight control and nods to Corporal Sims who opens a channel to Sgt. Garrison letting him know they are good to go. Sgt. Garrison is also aboard Major Vashti's Cruiser in a different torpedo bay stuffed into a drop pod along with Private Cooper, two automatons and a Kison Askari named Muturi. Muturi is not as jovial as the pygmy twins as Long had begun calling them, but he was also sized similarly. By some miracle PFC Long had managed to manipulate his mech suit to fit at the end of the drop pod, but it wasn't pretty. Amuzati and Bulu let him know about it every chance they got.

Sergeant Garrison wanted to tell them to shut it but also knew levity was often needed during times like this to break the tension. Lives were at risk and not just their own. Billions could die in addition to the millions already lost through this whole invasion. Garrison knocked on the hull of the drop pod to let the artillerymen know they were good to go. They can feel as the drop pod is placed in the chute for launch. The same is happening on the other side of the ship where PFC Long's chute is also at the ready. Now they have to wait for the right timing which in reality may never come. There's never a perfect moment, and the best war plans will go to crap every time once rounds start coming down range.

Back on the *Ex Wife* Aragon eases the Adder out of the auxiliary landing bay and immediately activates the stealth filaments once clear of the massive space carrier. Out in the distance they can see the Jackral ships now being swarmed by both GMC and Kison Askari ships. The fighting is once again hot and heavy. Space is thick with activity. Corporal Sims asks "How and the hell are we supposed to get through all that without getting knocked out? Never mind remaining undetected." Shaking his head Aragon replies "I'm not sure but they said the Kison Askari were going to get us an opening so for now we have to sit tight and wait for our window."

In the rear cabin Hironike, Athena, and Angelo were strapped in and meditating. The two automatons assigned to their team were just sitting there presumably running diagnostics and awaiting the order to go in so they could find an alien terminal to hack. This seemed like a shaky choice to all the automatons but an all-out straight forward attack would be lost in the long run despite several individual victories already logged all over the globe and in the space around it. Due to size and the attrition rate it would only be a matter of time before the Jackral forces were able to overwhelm Earth and its inhabitants.

Hironike and Athena were doing their best not to think about these odds.. Hironike was of one mind and the only thing that concerned him was getting to this Anuren and eliminating him so that hopefully another with more common sense could take his place. If that didn't work, they had to find a way to get the largest ship away. There were more ships that were massive but small in size compared to the obvious mother ship. With that out of the way the Dreadnaughts and Centurion space carriers in the area could take care of the lesser ships. It would also eliminate the Jackrals ability to nearly level a continent as it had already done.

There could be similar weaponry on the other space craft but if so, they had chosen not to use it. General Krulak surmised that if they also had that capability, they would have used it. These being did not seem like the type to miss out on an opportunity to show their strength.

* * *

Simeon rode in Muturi's customary seat in the rear turret of the War Dragon piloted by Nefer with Kamal manning the nav and weapons station slightly ahead of her in the cockpit. Simeon was a bit miffed that he wasn't with one of the strike teams heading to infiltrate the Jackral home ship but had to be satisfied with fighting his way back to Queen Tunisia's flagship. He didn't miss the envious stares of the GMC officers and enlisted as they boarded the Kison Askari interceptor that was docked with the Adder in the auxiliary bay on the *Ex Wife*. No doubt some were going to try and emulate their efforts. Try was the operative word and Simeon was sure Tunisia was not going to share the knowledge gained from the Atlantean shipwrights or Toshi of the Ongakujin. If they were truly allying did that matter anymore?

His thoughts were interrupted by ship particles and plasma fire barely missing them. Nefer's voice blares from the intercom "Look alive General! We are not in a dogfight per se but there is a lot of debris that needs to be cleared as I weave through this mess and dodge enemy fire. I think they know we are coming for them and are trying to eliminate any distractions or threats in the area." The rear turret in the War Dragon gave the gunner control of a laser canon and an astral depth charger with varying ordinances. As Simeon's two hands reached up to grasp the dual trigger mounts a large fuselage of some kind was coming straight for them. Instinctively he pulled back on the triggers and was greeted with a satisfying kick felt in the entire rear structure of the ship as the energy was gathered and instantly discharged blowing the fuselage into heated dust particles.

The ball shaped duraglass canopy could spin and rotate vertically and horizontally one hundred- and eighty-degrees giving Simeon the ability to shoot in many directions to clear debris and even fend off rocket or missile type weapons. The EMP depth chargers were sometimes best for the latter as it could in theory turn off the guidance systems in those at a safer distance. Blasting an incoming warhead could still potentially damage the War Dragon if it was too close when it detonated. He was thinking how lucky he was not dealing with that scenario just yet. Up front Nefer and Kamal were hard at work clearing obstacles. The cockpit had similar swiveling capabilities but was a bit larger and had two laser turrets on the sides of the head of the "dragon".

Nefer quickly called out targets as Kamal would fire on them so she could concentrate on navigating this wild special mine field of sorts. Some of the smaller Jackral fighter ships had taken notice of them and begun to give chase. "We've got company!" Simeon shouted and immediately regretted it but he didn't know what else to say. Nefer must have heard the nervousness in his voice. "Calm down General. I know you haven't had much time in the simulators as you are more of a command infantryman now. Just prioritize the higher threats and work your way to the least. We are almost there. They'll likely breakoff once we get close enough for the throne ships artillery batteries to give us some cover fire." She offered.

Simeon took a moment to relax and realized there was also another button a little aft of the trigger mounts with a head icon glowing next to it. Out of curiosity he pushed it and was surprised as a headset came from behind him going over his eyes and top of his head. Moments later a HUD was overlaid with his view outside of the rear canopy. Immediately data started appearing to him as targets were labelled and prioritized. Finally, Simeon just relaxed and begun firing at the targets suggested by the HUD. Each target was color coded; red were the biggest threats, yellow the next, and blue as the least. Friendly blips signaled allies. Two smaller arrowhead-shaped Jackral fighters came screaming at them from behind. They were firing at the War Dragon trying to gauge the evasive skills of Nefer. Simultaneously two more showed up in front of them in an attempt to pinch down on their perceived prey.

Kamal quickly dispatched one of the forward attackers by destroying it with concentrated laser fire. The ensuing explosion was brief as the vacuum snuffed the flames nearly instantly sending another small smoldering space craft listing slowly towards the Earth's gravity well. The pilot struggled to hit the eject mechanism before entering atmosphere. They didn't make it and likely burned up upon entry. Their wing mate broke off the attack seeing what just happened but Kamal swiveled keeping them in his sights. Nefer flew aggressively to help keep Kamal on target. Meanwhile Simeon fired on one of the two ships behind them before swiveling to the opposite direction keeping the second ship in his sights but since it was some distance further after swinging wide in an attempt to flank them, he opted to drop an EMP depth charger in its path.

The Jackral pilot snarled as if the charge was a dud and simply went wide. The depth charge was programmed to delay detonation until the target got a certain distance past so it would not affect both ships. It would be a bad strategy to disable yourself and your enemy with other enemy ships in the vicinity. A sensor module activated the burst pulse energy once the Jackral ship was the desired distance past it. The tail end of the large electronic pulse catches the rear of the

Jackral ship causing it to shut down. The rear wingman went to see why his partner broke off. It was a fatal mistake. The turn took him back into Simeon's sights who pulled back on the dual triggers obliterating the ship instantly. The final Jackral attacker pulled up on the stick flipping her ship to face the War Dragon on their tail, letting off multiple shots forcing Nefer to swerve as they were grazed with plasma fire.

The lone survivor from the Jackral flight group continued on their way back towards the home ship. Another two Jackral flights soon picked up where the other left off. The new attackers did not last long as Nefer got close enough to Queen Tunisia's throne ship. The Kison Askari artillery units were able to pick them off as they approached. In quick succession eight Jackral fighter ships were sequentially evaporated from the wake of Nefer's ship. Something must have got through because she could see one of her wings were singed and smoking. Luckily, they were now able to get to the dock of their throne ship. Queen Tunisia was waiting for them when they landed in the main landing bay.

Simeon kneeled to her as soon as he stepped off the ramp and saw her. Nefer and Kamal followed suit. "My Queen!" They echoed. Waiving for them to stand Queen Tunisia goes to Simeon placing a hand on his shoulder as he stood. "How did the planning with General Krulak go?" she asked. Nefer took the opportunity to leave the queens presence as fast as she could. It was painfully obvious she felt awkward having told about Tunisia's ill-advised use of dark matter some time back during the tail end of their conflict with the GMC before the accords were signed. Tunisia ignored her and waited for Simeon to respond. He watched as Nefer speed walked out of the landing bay before responding "They are launching a few different stealth attacks with strike teams. It was suggested that I not go so Muturi is on one team and Amuzati and Bulu on another. They are preparing to launch soon from modified drop pods. I suspect it's how they got the automatons on the surface of Ganymede. Let's hope they are successful this time. Hironike is also going to try and take out this Anuren."

Tunisia was obviously surprised at the latest inclusion. "And Athena?" she asks. Simeon nodded "Her as well. She requested not so politely to go along with Angelo well. In other words, it wasn't a request at all." Tunisia knew Athena was stubborn but this was also unexpected. "Out from the shadows and into the light of open war they go." She remarked. Turning she added "Let's go to the bridge and watch from there. Also, we can be ready if our dark matter ordinance is needed after all." Upon hearing that Simeon stopped in his tracks. Noticing his abrupt stop Tunisia says "What? We are at war with another likely more dangerous foe than the GMC. We cannot to afford to fight with our hands tied behind our backs!"

Shaking his head Simeon says "It was discussed and most felt it too dangerous to use so close to our gravity well. That huge ship crashing would cause an extinction level event of the surface, and that's without dark matter being factored in." Rolling her eyes Tunisia responds "Very well." And continues walking. Simeon is now worried that their queen has not learned her lesson. Even worse Darius has empowered her somehow and even if they wanted to stop her, there was a chance they would not be able to. He hoped desperately to be wrong in his thinking.

* * *

Pharaoh could feel something going horribly wrong within the Earth's crust, and only now realized it had to be the giant structures these Jackral as he now knew them had placed around the globe causing it. Reaching out telepathically to his minions he said plainly

"Come we must see to this nonsense." In a few brief moments both Malice and Typhoon were at his chamber doors. It opened to let them in. "What nonsense must we see to Master?" Waiving a hand Pharaoh brings up a world map showing the places the spike structures are placed. "These abominations are doing something to corrupt and siphon matter away from the planets core. We must stop this from happening before this place is destroyed." He says.

Opening up a void portal Pharaoh instructs them "We need to go to each one and at least halt its operation. Expect resistance. I'm not sure if their invasion is failing or some other event has them retreating to these structures which look to be launch capable when the gathering process finishes. If they succeed, they will rip this planet to shreds. I for one do not intend to be here for that. So once again I must delay the destruction of this insufferable place. At least this time it is not at the hands of the very beings spawned here." Typhoon was confused but stepped through nonetheless.

Malice who was more intimately familiar with previous near extinction events where mankind was on the brink of self-inflicted annihilation, knew what their master was referring to. He was not fooled into thinking this exiled ancient being actually cared about the inhabitants of the Earth. The only life that mattered to Pharaoh was his own. Together they exited the portal directly into one of the largest of the spike shaped structures. They quickly made their way to the base of it which was lodged deep into the Earth siphoning portions of the core that was causing the instability Pharaoh felt earlier. It was a slow process which was likely the reason Pharaoh had not detected it faster.

Pharaoh took a moment to study the mechanism before trying to slow the process even further or reversing it. Being on this planet for so long had attuned him to it in ways most supposedly evolved beings could only dream of. He felt that reversing things too quickly could set off a chain reaction that would result in imminent destruction. No doubt there would be someone here that would notice the change in function. He told his minions "Spread out and make sure I am not disturbed while I configure this monstrosity to undo its work without sending us all into oblivion in the process. Eliminate any who approaches. I'll need time."

Happily, Malice unsheathed his black blades and stuck to the shadows. Typhoon did the same thing in the opposite direction wielding his new toys confiscated from the fallen Jackral at Giza. The ape did not relish the idea of combat but was curious to see what these alien weapons would do to their creators.

Chapter Seventeen

There was a burst of forward momentum throwing the drop pod forward that simultaneously forced everyone back once they were launched from the torpedo chute. In the rear of the pod PFC Long was the most stable as his mech suit was tightly squeezed in there. Amuzati and Bulu were having giggling fits while the two automatons were constantly calculating their trajectory. The pod was fitted with external cameras so they could see where they were going. The automatons were linked to the cameras. They were also remotely turning their thrusters off and on in hopes of making them less visible. There was a lot of traffic during what looked like an all-out space battle which in reality was an attempt at a large-scale distraction.

The outer plates with the stealth filaments should not be easily visible, however the afterburn from the rear thrusters when active is a telltale sign of its presence. Something hit them hard forcing the two squat Kison Askari to stop their fit of laughter. The automatons cut the thrusters and things went deathly quiet. They were spinning. PFC long could feel it and obviously so could Amuzati and Bulu who were now trying as best they could to brace themselves. "Temporarily transfer visual to my helm." Long ordered and the automatons complied. At first glance seeing what was happening through the external cameras gave Long a moment of vertigo. He centered his breathing and briefly closed his eyes before looking again.

When his stomach felt as settled as it was going to get, he continued "Slow burn to counteract the spinning so we can stop and get our bearings. I know we are off course. It just means Sergeant Garrison will get there first despite being launched second. That is if Major Vashti was able to maneuver to the other side without being blasted out of space." Once again, the automatons did as he asked, and he was correct they were off course, dramatically so. Long transferred visual back to the automatons since they were likely better at calculating distances on the fly.

They would have to make their way back without detection which in all likelihood result in their immediate destruction. One of the automatons figured they may have found a way to do it without getting obliterated in the process. There was a husk of a disabled Jackral interceptor sized ship floating listlessly nearby. There was a hole in it possibly large enough for the drop pod to slide into. The problem was it was also slightly moving making threading the needle aspect of placing the pod in the hole a difficult thing. Waiting for the drop pods orientation to line up when the hole would rotate so they could enter, the automatons goosed the ignition on the rear burner moving the pod forward but had to stop as it was obvious, they would miss.

PFC Long also cautioned against rushing into mangled chassis because it might look to out of place when it started to move again. Amuzati complained "This is gonna take too long! We need to get there now." One of the automatons looked up golden eyes glowing through the faceplate "I suspect you would like to get there whole and fully functional." Looking on Bulu adds "Good point."

* * *

On the other side of the colossal Jackral home ship Sgt. Garrison and his group were launched out of another torpedo chute from Major Vashti's Praetorian class GMC cruiser. The ship was under heavy fire from smaller ships but the huge plasma canons from the home ship were moving into position to fire at the Praetorian. Major Vashti had to order their evasive retreat nearly instantly after the drop pod cleared the front aperture of the torpedo chute. The ride started off very rocky.

Sgt. Garrison and Private Cooper used their cybernetic legs and arms respectively to keep them stabilized.

Muturi sat forward of them but behind the automatons with their group similarly to how the other group was deployed in the drop pod. He still did not like the idea of being too close to the front when that was likely going be impacting a thick hull of a spacecraft made for interstellar travel. The pod waggled a bit but was not hit or thrown drastically off course. They were able to let the momentum of their launch carry them quite close before having to engage the recently added thrusters. Miraculously they made it to the hull. A loud clang announced their unceremonious arrival. The automatons were watching their flight path through the external cameras and were able to activate the large mag-locks just before contact with the Jackral home ship.

After the clang was followed by an almost immediate thud indicating the mag-lock had been properly activated and was able to find purchase. Sgt. Garrison sighed audibly to which Cooper said "Yeah that would have been a bitch if they were using an alloy where magnets didn't have a similar effect to ours." Looking down at his wrists where there used to be gauntlet like shackles Muturi kind of smiled to himself. That was exactly how his people were able to gain their freedom after discovering an alloy just as Cooper described. Private Cooper was confused by the look on Muturi's face missing the irony totally.

The automatons signaled for everyone to helm up before they opened the seal revealing the cold hull surface of the Jackral home ship. They all nodded that they were secured before a plasma cutter was tested on the hull. It would take a bit of time but the cutters were effectively getting through. They all had to hope none of the Jackral fighter pilots noticed them hitchhiking and blow them off. From a distance they should still be nearly invisible and the fact that they were so miniscule compared to the ship they were stuck to should help.

Sooner than expected the hull is breached and they are able to step inside. Luckily, they are in what looks like a large duct. Private Cooper is happy they didn't immediately walk into an engagement but wished he could have brought his big bad wolf, a weapon specially made for him to carry. It wouldn't fit in the drop pod plus they didn't want to be blowing holes in either the pod or this ship with them in it. Muturi and the automatons kept watch while Sgt. Garrison and Private Cooper placed a cover over the hole they just made. The automatons then went in search of a console to hack with the rest of them in tow. Upon exiting the duct into a hallway what they found instead was a bunch of bewildered Jackral eating in what had to be a chow hall.

✳ ✳ ✳

Word got to the GMC units that the continent of Asia had been hit pretty hard by whatever the Jackral had launched from their home ship and there was likely a danger of them doing so again targeting another heavily populated area of the planet. Max hoped that the forces fighting in space could prevent that. Some of the Jackral forces were retreating to the spike structures so the joint forces on the ground planned to stop as many of them as they could. In contrast there were reports of groups of Jackral surrendering after they found that a lot of their own had died in the massive blast as there were a considerable number of Blessed on site gathering food and fuel at the processing vats.

After overhearing a GMC officer and Ogun discuss what their next move would be Max asked "Processing vat? What are they processing there?" Bofus looks at him and says "Us and anything living here apparently. Animals and people is what they eat."

Disgusted Max says "There's no way!" Sparks responds "Yep, they process all their protein and other nutrients into some sort of meal cubes. We have reports coming in from some of the people freed recently which have been now corroborated by Jackral POW's trickling in. That's why they came here to gather food and fuel." Surprised by her nonchalant attitude about it Max says "It's still gross."

Ogun coming over to get Bofus says "I for one do not relish being on their menu. We are splitting up into hunting parties. All ground units around the globe are doing so with the aid of some supposedly repentant Jackral." Everyone was pretty skeptical about that idea. Seeing Max's recently repaired leg Ogun asks "Will you be continuing or are you all joining up with one of your GMC units?" Angrily Max say's I'm not GMC why does everyone assume I'm a gung-ho jarhead?" Conspicuously looking over his shoulder Ogun glances at a group of Marines some of whom have lost and replace limbs with cybernetics. Sparks has to cover her mouth to keep from laughing.

Frustrated Max stands and walks over to where Argos was securing their gear in an oversized pack, he had fashioned for himself. Sparks looks to Ogun and replies "We will go with you. It's been a good run so far. I didn't think we would make planetfall to be honest. Don't mind Max. He is a freelancer and doesn't take kindly to be associated with the government or any form of authority really. It just so happens that their goals and his align at least for now." Ogun nodded his understanding and he and Bofus went back to their group of Kison Askari to make their own preparations before stepping off. Some would go on foot but a large number would be going ahead to scout out the areas around the processing structures in the chariot like land skiffs taken from Jackral.

This would augment their means of transportation in addition to GMC vehicles, modified hoversleds from some of the Limbia Johari who have resurfaced and basically anything they could get their hands on. Soon there were swarms of joint caravans headed towards all of the local processing structures in hopes of catching fleeing Jackral and freeing people and livestock captured there. Bofus and Ogun find one of the repurposed Jackral land skiffs jumping on it. Ogun takes a few moments to get the hang of the controls while Bofus holds on for dear life. Max and Sparks each take anti-grav hoversleds provided by Limbia Johari. Argos looks around and finds another chariot like Jackral land skiff jutting out of a building it had crashed into.

They all watch amazed as he dislodges it and it begins to float. It bobs slightly under his weight once he hops on but stays off the ground. Similarly, to Ogun it takes him a moment to get familiar with the controls. With that done they head out in search of Jackral.

* * *

On the bridge of the Blessed's home ship Anuren stands as alarms begin to blare signaling there's been a minor hull breach near one of the lower decks' galleys. Pointing to the guards at the entrance to the bridge he orders "Go find whatever this is and take care of it!" They salute and head to a lift that would take them to the level where the breach was. Anuren was getting more and more frustrated. It took them a while to get to the corresponding level where the breach was near. As soon as the lift opened, they could hear a commotion coming from the levels dining area. As a precaution they took out their batons and raised the helmets to their armor as they approached.

The hatch was wide open. The Jackral guards could see there was what looked like a leg laying in the entryway keeping the hatch from closing. There were screams and what looked like remnants of food cubes splattered on the bulkheads. Using the sensors in his helm, the lead guard scans the dining chamber before entering. The screams have stopped but there looks to be five beings inside looking for something. What the Jackral guard sees doesn't immediately make sense. In certain spectrums two of the beings seem to be missing limbs while a couple others disappear altogether and don't show up as life forms.

After explaining this to the others his second replies in hushed tones "It doesn't matter what they are! Anuren ordered us to eliminate them." This was true. The leader signaled for them to clear the chamber and eliminate any inside that were not either Blessed or Bastet. Throwing in canisters with a nerve agent the Jackral were immune to but proved to have adverse effects on other species they previously encountered, the guards stormed in. Unfortunately, this boarding party was helmed as well and the canisters announced the new arrivals. Two energy blasts hit one figure sending them flying to the deck. There was a thunderous crack as an alloy foot met Jackral helmet at high speed sending the guard leader down motionless.

Another baton energy blast bounced harmlessly off an alloy arm before the opposite alloy arm came crashing into the chest of the groups second. Before the guard could recover the remaining automaton rushed in to send a few thousand volts of energy into the Jackral's armor effectively frying him where he stood. Muturi came in between the two remaining guards expanding a collapsible version of the Kison Askari gravity staff and started alternately beating them before using the device to land heavier than normal blows to their helmets crushing their heads inside the now mangled armor.

Private Cooper was quite impressed, he whistled and said "Well that looks like a handy piece of kit." Muturi coolly collapses the device back down and winks, but the face shield on his helmet hides most of the gesture. Sgt. Garrison walks over to the fallen automaton to check on its status. The other automaton reassures him "This unit is still functional. The blast only caused superficial damage and a brief short.

Recalibrating him now." Looking around Sgt. Garrison says "Good we need to keep moving and find a console for you to hack quickly. I don't want to be searching in this labyrinth of a ship for too long and you know more will be coming."

They all agreed. Muturi asks "Any word on the other strike teams?" Sgt. Garrison shakes his head negatively and looks to the automaton in case it has a mode of communication specific to the others on the mission, but that idea is squashed when it notices the attention saying "No word yet. Perhaps being in a large construct as big as this ship is blocking all signals currently." That was to be expected but Sgt. Garrison was hoping perhaps he was wrong on that assumption. They had after all gained entry and he was not too sure that was actually going to work out. There didn't seem to be anything particularly useful in this chow hall so they needed to look elsewhere.

The automaton that was hit by the energy blast had rebooted and was now standing once again after a brief moment for self-calibration. Its golden eyes were open once again and it seemed to be operating fine but there was a big scorch mark on its chest. Private Cooper was peering out of the hatch into the hallway warns "I think more are just about here now Sergeant we need to get ghost." Garrison knew Coop was right and going into that hallway would more than likely force them into another firefight before they could find a terminal or console. An idea hit him and he could kick himself for not thinking of it sooner.

"Let's head back to the giant ducts." He ordered. "Really?" Muturi asked. Sgt. Garrison didn't like being questioned but explained on their way "I was thinking the automatons could scan the ducts tracing the circuitry that has to be in the structure somewhere. The size and direction of the circuitry should lead us to other components. That's the closest we will get to a schematic as the bots should be able to figure out where things vital to the ships systems would be by studying the structure." At the word "Bots" the heads of the two automatons snapped to look at Sgt. Garrison abruptly. Muturi, Private Cooper and Sgt. Garrison were taken aback at the reaction. "Makes sense." Muturi says and awkwardly Cooper adds "No offense?"

* * *

Finally, after threading the proverbial needle with their drop pod, PFC Long and his group make it to the hull of the Jackral home ship. Once the mag-locks secured them the automatons began plasma cutting their way in. They did not breach the hull into a ductway however. They stepped through staring at a group of fully armed and armored Jackral warriors in their birthing area. There was a moment of hesitation before plasma fire burst from multiple directions taking out the automaton who peeked first. Amuzati and Bulu slid out shoulder canons blazing while simultaneously hammering at every Jackral in sight with their gravity staves.

The second automaton with Long's group looked up and shook its head negatively signaling that the damage must be irreparable. Chaos was in progress and there would likely be no ideal time to break cover into the mess. Figuring this was either going to work or not Long decided rationality would get him nowhere in this scenario. By flexing a pectoral muscle, he pressed a special button in his armor stopping the release of his pain suppressors. The transparent face plate on his raised helmet went red, and Berserker stepped in to the fray screaming in fury as he brought his deadly weapons to bear.

Chapter Eighteen

Deep below the Earth's surface in one of the processing structures imbedded into the planet by the Jackral invaders Pharaoh studied large pump like mechanisms that were siphoning material from the planets core, and simultaneously adding a substance not known to this galaxy that acted as a catalyst. The catalyst transformed the materials being funneled into the mechanisms into the fuel necessary for their ships and other large devices the Jackral used. He would be impressed with the ingenuity of it if they were not in the middle of a dire crisis because of these machines and this invasion. After looking over what was most likely a control terminal Pharaoh was able to work out how to carefully begin reversing the process. It would not be a one to one process as not one hundred percent of the material transformed would be restored.

Hopefully enough of it could restore balance to the world. As soon as Pharaoh initiated the reversal despite it being cautiously gradual, alarms began to blare. Malice and Typhoon were waiting outside of the chamber but on opposite sides of the corridor. Feeling a multitude of presences coming Pharaoh shouts to them "Get ready to hold them off! I need a bit more time before I can join you." A mixed group of Jackral and Bastet swarm into the corridor and the Jackral immediately open fire with their baton like weapons. Evading some of the energy projectiles while reflecting others with his blades Malice becomes a dark blur of action.

Amid the commotion Pharaoh could hear jovial gorilla barks as Typhoon let loose with his new found toy. He was alternately shooting energy blasts with the Jackral weapon and bludgeoning any who made it within his reach. The Bastet were not fighting but hiding behind their Jackral counterparts and seeking for an opportunity to make their way into the chamber where Pharaoh was working on the control terminal. It made no difference to Malice who was slicing and impaling the invaders with impunity. The bodies were piling up on Malice's side and he was noticing the Bastet Typhoon was not pursuing. "Why do you hesitate beast?" he screamed.

With the one doorway literally blocked by bodies Malice take the opportunity to switch sides. "I attack those who attack me!" Typhoon responds. Laughing maniacally Malice cuts through the remaining Bastet on Typhoon's side before replying "You fool! They are all here to take what they need and destroy this place. All beings with them play a role in that. Their lack of aggression doesn't absolve them of guilt in being a part of this. If I came to your troop and destroyed all the surrounding foliage leading to their deaths, would you allow it because I had not openly attacked them?" Seeing the understanding and burning anger blazing in Typhoons azure glowing eyes Malice nodded and moved on.

Coming out of the chamber, Pharaoh saw the handiwork of his two minions. Looking to see if there were more ways to enter and finding none, Pharaoh opens another dark portal for them to step into. Just before entering himself, he holds up a hand gathering energy to blast the portion of the mantle this part of the spike structure was sticking into to make it difficult to enter. Satisfied that the resulting pressure would eventually crush parts of this structure over time and prevent it from launching later, Pharaoh stepped through the portal joining his minions on their way to the next site. By the time the material was transformed or as much as was possible the device would be useless and permanently embedded hopefully helping the region's stability. In addition to all the other things going on weather, earthquakes and other environmental variables were coming into play all over the globe. They would have to move faster. Pharaoh was beginning to worry that they would not make it and this was just the first facility.

* * *

The Adder was a lot larger than the space Harrier Corporal had flown before but he was getting used to it. Lance Corporals McNamara and Jennings were in the dorsal and belly gunner positions while Corporal Sims manned the comms and navigation seat in the cockpit with Aragon. Hironike, Athena, Angelo, and their two automaton units were near the rear hatch in armored EV suits equipped with small jetpack units. The time necessary to put this plan into action prevented them from modifying a third drop pod plus this strike team to be blunt wasn't as durable as the others who had both Kison Askari and mechanized recon Marines with them.

Taking a wide approach Aragon goosed the throttle to the max before idling down to nothing hoping their inertia would carry them close enough so Hironike and his team would be able to jump out of the rear hatch and jetpack their way to the hull. Stealth mode was activated and the other reason for shutting down the thrusters was to have a smaller heat signature and lessen the probability of detection. It was for the most part a quiet yet nerve racking ride. Smaller bursts from the attitude thrusters were used occasionally to navigate the dogfights and debris still surrounding the Jackral home ship like a disturbed angry beehive. Lance Corporal Jennings was itching to get into the action. Inside the Adder there was an audible tone as he primed the plasma canons in preparation of lacing some targets. Over the comms came Aragon's voice "Stand down Lance Corporal. You tighten anybody up right now and they're all alerted to our presence. The mission is to go in dark. Now once the cargo is safely aboard, we can light some dog faced aliens up as a distraction."

Disappointed Jennings does not pull back on the triggers "Roger that." He responds. With fairly little to no resistance Aragon is able to nearly sidle up to the Jackral home ship. "Popping the rear hatch."

Corporal Sims announces. In preparation Hironike, Athena, and Angelo all check to make sure the seals are good on their EV suits. They give thumbs up to the camera letting Sims know they are good to go. The rear cabin goes dark and the visors on their helmets activate night sight. There is a moment soon after the rear hatch begins to rise where frost develops on their face shields. The sensors on their suits recognize the dramatic change in temperature and compensate for it defogging the face plates so they can see.

Peering out Hironike can see that they are only seven meters or so away from the hull and there looks to be a lip he might be able to find purchase on. Stepping out he activates the jetpack putting his feet forward in hopes of turning on the small mag plates in the soles of his boots. Word had got back that the other two team were able to securely mag-lock the modified drop pods to the hull so it was reasonable to think he could do so. Relief flooded his body as the mag-plates on his boots stuck to the hull as he landed. Looking back, he watched Athena make her leap of faith. She would have floated by had Hironike not grabbed her directing her feet to the ledge he was standing on. It was Angelo's turn which went off without a hitch. Hironike began slicing into the hull with some plasma cutters as the automatons were making their way over to them.

The second automaton was disintegrated by a wave of energy fire. Hironike tried to cut faster as Athena, Angelo pulled the railguns off their backs to look for where the fire came from. The remaining automaton went to help Hironike gain entrance into the ship before they were all blown off the hull like some space barnacles. There was not one but two Jackral fighters bearing down on them. As soon as the rear hatch closed Corporal Aragon fired up the main thrusters pouring on speed to get the attention of the incoming fighters hopefully taking their attention away from Hironike's team. Pulling up on the sticks the

Adder faces upwards as he climbs towards the fighters. "Mac and Jennings, weapons hot! Light em up!" Aragon screams.

Finally! Lance Corporal Jennings thinks as he locks on to the foremost fighter screaming at the strike team. They could tell the fighters must not have seen the Adder until the main thrusters fired up. Jennings saw the wings waggle a bit as another fast-paced variable suddenly appearing out of nowhere must have startled the pilot. They wouldn't be startled for long as Jennings poured fire into the fuselage of the diamond shaped fighter. The high velocity energy bolts tore away at the ship until it was a floating mess of debris bouncing off the hull of the Jackral home ship. The second fighter broke off its pursuit to avoid a similar fate, but Aragon wasn't going to let it go.

Soon after Lance Corporal McNamara blasted the Jackral wingman out of space. "What now?" he asked. Pushing the throttle forward Aragon says "We go make trouble until we can make arrangements to pick the strike teams up or not if they can successfully take control of that ship and lock the rest of the crew out by some miracle." Corporal Sims brought up the quadrant map featuring all ships in the area. It was so thick with traffic it was hard to distinguish who was who, but looking out the front view port it was easier to identify the ships closest to them. Marking the nearest enemy vessels, he says "Very well, let's go hunting while they try to do their jobs."

Dual tones sound as both Lance Corporals Jennings and McNamara prime their weapons as Corporal Aragon slams the throttle forward and activates the stealth filaments as they search for another target to take down. They run into a flight of Jackral using a solar approach to further hide their presence until the last moment when both McNamara and Jennings open fire on the group. Two are taken out quickly but the other pair were not caught unawares. They split up one leading them while the other hopped to the rear with some fancy flying of their own.

A few well-timed shots let's Aragon know of the danger. "Mac swivel to cover our six! I'll try to lose him. Take him out if you can!" he ordered. McNamara tried to lace the Jackral fighter with high velocity energy rounds but the pilot proved to be a hard target. It juked and rolled back and forth avoiding McNamara's attempts all the while sending fire that barely missed the foils and rear main thrusters of the Adder skimming the hull a few times. Worried Aragon thought perhaps this might be more than he could handle, but he refused to give up. Lance Corporal Jennings was finally able to take out the lead fighter who had proven to be an evasive flier in their own right.

Now with only one fighter to contend with the pressure was off of Aragon as both top and bottom turrets on the Adder were able to simultaneously target the remaining Jackral fighter. Without saying anything Jenning placed fire to the left of the ship well off the mark making them dodge in the other direction. Unfortunately for the Jackral pilot the move placed them directly in Lance Corporal McNamara's sights. Pulling back twice on the triggers sent a high velocity energy beam directly into the Jackral cockpit instantly killing the pilot and rendering the ship a useless piece of smoking space junk. It went directly into the path of another Jackral fighter that was fleeing from a GMC space Harrier. They briefly exploded and the beefier cousin to its atmospheric fighter jet flew through the expanding debris cloud.

Seeing the GMC insignia emblazoned on the ship Corporal Aragon waggled the Adders wings at the pilot who returned the gesture before returning to find another target. "I don't know if they're going to make it out of that ship or if we can even win this thing, but Corporal, you line em up and we'll take em out!" Jennings says. After being sure all systems were still good Corporal Aragon pushed the throttle forward to do just that.

* * *

Aboard the *Ex Wife*, General Krulak and some of his advisors were looking at a digital overview of the engagements going on around Earth. Now Lieutenant Junior Grade Parsons was looking at the same display along with a data-pad that was going through the information using analytics to make sense of it all. The GMC and Kison Askari capital ships were still keeping the attention of their Jackral counterparts but staying just out of range of their weapons. Only when the Jackral ships managed to get within firing range did they engage.

The mission of the larger ships was to keep the Jackral capital ships from firing upon the surface of the planet again while lending support to the smaller allied vessels in need of repair or refueling as they went back and forth engaging the smaller Jackral fighters, cruisers and frigate sized ships. "Parsons, what do your numbers say?" the Commandant asks. Nervously Parsons walks to the center of the war room and with his data-pad highlighted the units deployed in the area to explain what they were looking at "Well sir we are pretty much over extended on these fronts. Reports from the surface say there's some kind of retreat from a lot of the Jackral units after their ordinance drop on Asia. We are holding steady there for now with some of the invaders in disarray but that may not matter if we can't lock down this space and nullify their fire power before they use it again." He asserted.

Thinking all of that over General Krulak looked to his upper brass for their opinions. They bickered for a few moments as the odds of them turning the tide over all did not look good. Some were clamoring for the use of dark matter and again it was shut down because of the danger to Earth it would cause if the Jackral home ship were to crash into it. Angrily General Krulak ordered them to pipe down. To Parsons he ordered "Open a secure line in my quarters to Queen

Tunisia and General Jones back at Saturn HQ!" Parsons was quick to do as ordered replying "Aye sir!" on his way to the comm console in the war room. The other officers grumbled under their collective breaths as the commandant stormed out.

When he got to his quarters a screen came up from the deck with split images. One side had General Jones in his quarters at the recon base and the other side showed Queen Tunisia sitting aboard the Kison Askari's largest Dreadnaught dubbed the Akina Mama, their flagship. "Good evening Queen Tunisia, General Jones." He said greeting them both. "General." They echoed. "As you may already know things look good on the ground for now, though we likely lost millions of lives to that strike to the surface. We think their ordinance may have taken out a lot of their own that were present on the ground when the strike hit. This may be what precipitated the retreat for a lot of their forces but as you likely also know…that may not matter if we can't neutralize their ships up here. Any thoughts?"

Queen Tunisia shifts in her throne-like captain's chair saying "Any word on the strike teams? I know you all shun the idea of us using any dark matter weapons but it may be necessary if they fail and we can't stop them from bombarding the planet once they realize we will not let them have it or us. My people are staunchly against using it as well, but there may be no other choice that I can see." General Jones nodded and said "Hard to believe but I actually side with the Queen on this one." It was a tough decision and General Krulak was hesitant to make that choice because it was likely they could lose just as many lives as they save if the Jackral home ship or even some of the smaller capital enemy ships crash into Earth causing a near extinction level event in the process.

"Some of my staff here actually suggested it as well believe it or not. Two of the strike teams have gained entry and the last one just got to their breach point but contact with them has been nil since they went in. I guess we'll know when they have control or when that things starts firing again. We are busy trying to hold a lot of their assets attention by attacking their ships with the bulk of our Space Navy and Marine assets. We are holding our own but if this engagement continues for too long eventually the numbers will dwindle for us. We have some superstars out there who are kicking ass and taking names but as a whole we are new to this and it's obvious they, are not. If you have anything that could possibly drop a smaller payload than what was used either on Saturn or Earth than it could work. It's imperative that it can be used with precision Queen Tunisia. Target weapons placements and possibly the engines after that. If our boys can't cut the head off of the snake in time, I am sure the officers here will be on board. They're close now to be honest." Krulak explains.

Queen Tunisia nods her understanding. General Jones salutes and signs off. General Krulak returns the salute and says to Queen Tunisia "God help us all." Before signing off as well. When the screen goes blank on the Dreadnaught Tunisia turns to Simeon who had been listening saying "What say you now General? Go to the armory and see what we can make that's smaller than what Nefer and I carried with the Nyuesi Sime. Tell Zurina to be prepared to go on mission." Bowing and placing a fist over his heart General Simeon replies "It is sad that it comes to this. Dark matter is highly volatile even in small amounts but we shall see how small we can get it. We should keep this tech as far away from the GMC as we can should we survive this."

Simeon left the bridge to do as his queen ordered. Tunisia looked at the map of the space war watching how things were playing out. The GMC units were struggling in some areas but more than holding their own in others. The Kison Askari units were not running roughshod through the Jackral space forces but they were doing well for the most part. She wondered why that was. They were just as inexperienced for the most part but had less fear when it came to being in space from the mining expeditions that took place out among the stars for so long. At least now those early hardships were turning into an advantage. She just wasn't sure it would be enough.

Chapter Nineteen

Hironike and the automaton successfully cut their way into the Jackral home ship. An alarm went off as atmosphere vented out into the vacuum and was silenced when the place they entered was automatically sealed off since they did not use drop pods like the other teams which at least partially left the pressure somewhat intact after the breaching. Looking around it seemed that they were in some kind of utility access tunnel. "This looks promising." Hironike remarked looking to the automaton for his response. Athena and Angelo all huddled around the automaton who looked like a person in shock. Angelo gently nudges it asking "What's wrong with it?" Studying its expression Hironike surmises "I would guess that it mourns the loss of its companion back there."

Incredulously the two Limbia Johari echo "Mourns?" Hironike raises a hand forestalling any further objections to the idea of a bot mourning the loss of a bot. "These automatons are highly complex. Likely programmed to think and feel to better understand us. You cannot fully serve if you don't understand who you serve." Athena rolled her eyes and went to take a look around in an attempt to get their bearings. Over her shoulder she says "Yeah well right now it needs to find a way to understand the schematics of this huge vessel for us so we can take out the one responsible for its partner being vaporized."

At that the golden eyes of the automaton blinked twice as it says "Vaporized…yes the schematics. Must find a terminal." Patting it on the shoulder Hironike says "That's the spirit. Angelo follow her but don't stray too far. We will go this way. Come back here so we can figure out which is the best path to take. I am sure someone will come to see what tripped the alarm soon. Let's not be here when they do." Angelo nods and they split up.

Once Hironike felt the bot was as back to normal as it was going to get, he signaled for it to follow him and took off at sprint keeping a low profile and sticking to shadows where possible. The automaton figured this mutated humanoid was running with speed and agility that was quite surprising. There was not much information about the Ongakujin and their typical phenotypes but it was assumed to be pretty close to the non-mutated humans. Either Hironike was an outlier or there was more to them than what was previously known. The Jade Assassin leader signaled for them to stop just short of a t-section at the end of the corridor. Heavy armored boot steps could be heard as well as a deep voice speaking in the Jackral guttural language over the speaker system.

From the sound of things, the group changed direction away from Hironike and the automaton. Turning back to the automaton Hironike asked "Did you get that? Hoping you have at least some of their language from the information we got from the surface." The golden eyes once again began to flicker as it replayed the audio to itself before looking back at him responding "Yes, there have been two more disturbances. All available units are ordered to go to the one of the galleys on a higher deck and one of their troop birthing areas on a lower deck. Whatever it is the speaker was quite angry about it. There was a sense of urgency to his speech pattern."

Smiling through his face mask Hironike says "Let's go see what the others have seen." Heading back near the place they initially entered the ship they met with Athena and Angelo. Athena says "We were about to have a run in before that announcement was made but the group turned around before they saw us." Hironike replies "Same here. The other groups are kicking up dust and making noise which should create a distraction we can take advantage of. Don't shoot unless fired upon. Stealth is the smart play here."

Placing a hand on the deck and the bulkhead the automaton was tracing the circuitry and got a general direction for where the nearest terminal would be. With that done it pointed and said "If we follow this corridor and take two left turns, we should find something I can use." Just as they were about to step off Athena touches Hironike's arm saying "Speaking of shooting I noticed you're not carrying a railgun like we are. How do you plan to take out Anuren?" Reaching behind him Hironike unsheathes a long black katana that almost glows. Angelo in disbelief says "You have to be kidding me." Pulling down his mask Hironike boasts "I bet you whatever libation you enjoy that I handle more of these Jackral warriors with my blade than you do with that trusty railgun of yours. This was forged with the blatanium and some of the new alloys the Kison Askari found on Jupiter. Besides I can take one of their weapons. This will be much quieter."

They sneak off in the direction the automaton gave them, and true to its assumption there was a maintenance terminal there in a small cabin. They quickly went in and the automaton went to work first by trying to type in commands. When that didn't work, he placed a small disk like device on the bottom of the interface and waited. Soon it had access saying "I'm in." Angelo let out a small sigh of relief when they heard approaching boot steps once again. They all froze considering what to do. Hironike raised a finger to his lips before slipping out of the hatch. A moment later there was an audible clang and discharge of a Jackral energy blast then two thuds leading to silence.

Athena was starting worry when the hatch opened and Hironike's head popped in saying "A little help?" In Angelo's direction. Angelo steps out into the corridor to find two large Jackral bodies slumped over with perfect blade sized holes in their chests. There was a scorch mark on the bulkhead but not a scratch on Hironike who simply smiled and said "That's two." Angelo waived him off and helped him drag the bodies into what looked like a utility closet next to the cabin Athena and the automaton was in. When they returned the automaton had a hologram of the ship's schematics up. Studying it the automaton pointed and said "The bridge is most likely here, and we are here." Counting Angelo says "That looks to be about eighty decks above us!"

Hironike claps Angelo on the shoulder saying "Then I think we should move quickly." With the automaton in the lead since he downloaded the schematic, they go about making their way up to the proper level. The automaton remarks "You are both correct."

* * *

The newly upgraded energy canons in the Berserkers arms were ripping through Jackral warriors as energy bolts from their weapons zinged off of his mech suit. The pain made him numb to it all as he cut down any who approached or got within his sights. They swarmed in from the adjacent birthing areas pouring energy blasts into the corridor but were unable to stop Long's advance who continued to mercilessly slaughter them where they stood or laid. Amuzati and Bulu joined in to give him cover fire when needed which was not often as some of the Jackral were fleeing at the maniacal look in his eyes as he screamed and shot his way forward. The arm canons barrels were overheated so he retracted them before reaching behind him. His back casing opened up to produce a huge gleaming ax.

Spinning the ax to reflect energy bolts back at the Jackral as Amuzati and Bulu took turns firing plasma rounds through his legs with the weapons mounted on their shoulders, they made quick work of all who dared stay in the birthing area the strike team entered. Soon there was just a heap of bodies in either direction and rising smoke. Long retracted his helmet and internally pressed the button to resume his pain meds. He relaxed and leaned on the ax as tears welled up in his tormented eyes. After regaining his composure PFC Long went back to check on his remaining automaton who was still with the headless body of the other assigned to their team. Looking up the automaton said "If there were more of the head left perhaps some of the matrices could expand to reconnect and he would be functional until we got back, but there's nothing left of it."

Long nodded and replied "Can you find a terminal before reinforcements get here? We should move." The automaton gently lays the headless bot on the deck before using his hand to scan the deck and bulkhead for circuitry and finds a likely nearby terminal. Long brings his helmet back up and checks the internal HUD to see how long he will have to wait until the arm canons will be cool enough to use again. As the automaton leads the way he says to Amuzati and Bulu "You guys will have to cover us for about one hundred and twenty seconds while my canons cool. Helluva job back there by the way."

They made their way to a terminal and the automaton was able to hack in using the disk like device and found out that the other unit was able to do so as well. Through their mutual connection to the ships system they were now able to communicate and let each other know of their movements. This could be useful later. Long thought as they decided to make their way through the higher decks towards the bridge.

....

Multiple alarms had gone off denoting more breaches and with each report Anuren's anger was rising. These vermin not only ignored his warning but were now trying to storm a vessel of the Blessed. From the reports there was a massacre taking place in one of the birthing areas and Jackral were starting rumors of an armored demon aboard the ship. From other reports another firefight had broken out near the vestibule leading to the main galley. "I guess I will have to take care of this nonsense myself. All who fear any of the vermin we have found here should be ashamed. No longer consider yourself Blessed! I will show you!" He ranted.

Turning to one of the remaining guards in golden armor by the entrance to the bridge Anuren ordered "Lower your helm." When the guard did so the Jackral leader asked "Do you fear any of these beasts?" The guard's lips curled back as he snarled "No my lord!" Seeing the disgust in the guard's eyes at the mere thought of him fearing anything pleased Anuren immensely. Smiling wickedly, he said "Good! Take up your arms and come with me. We shall be the example of what true believers look like. I shall rip the flesh from the bones of this supposed demon who has the audacity to come aboard a Blessed ship without permission. We do not allow our territory to be encroached upon. We do the encroaching."

With that Anuren and the guard left to find the boarding party stupid enough to come to their home ship. When they got to the birthing area it looked like a bloodbath had taken place. There were Jackral bodies everywhere. Some were full of holes from energy fire while others were chopped to pieces somehow. There was an unfamiliar body laying headless near the entrance. Striding over to pick it up Anuren saw there was no blood but burn marks on the chest and neck area consistent with results from their own weapons.

Peering down the neck hole only wires and some strange goo was found. This was a synthetic life form of some kind. "You see!" Anuren proclaims holding it up "They send toys in place of warriors! Let's find the rest of their baubles and destroy them. The processing vats should be nearly full by now. Soon we well leave this cursed place." In the comm node in his helmet one of the bridge crew announces "My lord there seems to be some complications with some of the processing vats, and a possible revolt of some kind…the salvo to the surface likely took out some of our own leading some to surrender or attempt to join the beings here."

There was a long moment of silence as the crew member who called waited for Anuren to erupt. Anuren made an effort to keep himself composed. He was angered at the fact that the bridge crew had obviously been listening to him while he investigated the birthing area. He was angered that these plebs dared defy the Blessed and now his own may be attempting to rise against him for some perceived miscalculation when attacking the surface. Anuren did not dignify them with a response. He simply cut the line and through the body of the synth against the bulkhead before signaling to the guard that they must continue their search. They could not hide on this ship. When he found the encroachers, they would pay a painful price, then it would on to anyone traitorous enough to surrender.

***

Back on Earth's surface Shajara, Ragnar and a rag tag group of their organizations mixed with civilians turned freedom fighters were chasing as many Jackral invaders as they could find. After learning about what happened on the Asian continent, they were not looking for prisoners. There would be no interrogations. In their minds there was no need. The news of why these beings had chosen to come to Earth were clear. Shajara still felt his earlier actions were wrong but this felt right for the most part. The Jackral that did not make it back to the processing structures tried to hide.

The problem was that the beings they were trying to hide from were vastly more familiar with the lay of the land here. Some of these beings especially the mutated had intimate knowledge of the best hiding places within the defunct and active mines, heavily forested areas, abandoned industrial complexes, and the deep underground facilities. Angry at what the invaders tried to do this hunting party went about their business with fervor. Ragnar and his Guild of the Pristine seemed to be in their xenophobic element and it was more than a little disturbing to Shajara how similar they all seemed now that they were fighting alongside each other.

They found and cornered a group of fleeing invaders who tried to surrender and ran when it was obvious that wasn't an option. Holed up in an old industrial building the Jackral were mustering up the courage for a last stand. Shajara's people tracked them here. It would have been foolish to rush in not knowing what they may have prepared. These beings were after all a bit more advanced in general. Behind cover Ragnar and Shajara were deciding how to proceed. "Let me see it." Ragnar says. Glancing sidelong at him Shajara replies "See what?" Checking the rounds in his railgun Ragnar says "You know what...the eye! Take that stupid patch off. Aside from the fact that you look ridiculous, we could probably use it to see how they are set up in there."

Shaking his head Shajara turns away from him brandishing two of the baton-like Jackral weapons but it's obvious he was thinking about it. "I don't even know if it does what you say." He offered. Laughing but trying to remain somewhat quiet Ragnar says "Are you kidding me? You haven't tried it out yet to see what it can do? Boy you are a piece of work! Even after literally losing your eye physically you would rather just use one, lose your depth perception than use a better version? Priceless." Begrudgingly Shajara mutters "Fine." Before removing the patch and looking at the building. It takes a moment for the cybernetic eye to adjust to light after remaining under the patch for so long.

Ragnar watches in unbridled delight as the camera shutter like a mechanical pupil dilates and begins to focus making audible clicking sounds. Shajara visibly shutters at this but continues to look describing what he sees. "There are at least forty or so dog men in there. They seem smaller than the others we encountered inside facilities similar to the one I pulled you from. Two thirds of them are armed by the way their arms are dispositioned as if carrying these." He says holding up the Jackral weapons.

Ragnar thought about the size reference and said aloud what he was thinking "Perhaps they have a caste system where the larger Jackral make up the warriors or leaders but there have to be worker bees in every society that just harvest and gather but don't necessarily hunt or fight. Maybe that's them." Thinking it over Shajara asks "Would you show mercy to the worker bees?" Looking over at his men and comparing numbers Ragnar estimates they have an advantage on this group and thinks they should move in soon before the Jackral have time to devise something nasty.

Turning back to Shajara he says "Hell no. They were a party to all of this and brought it on themselves what's about to happen. They were going to mash me and my people up in paste to eat us! I say we eradicate all the mutts here." Nodding Shajara adds "Do you think it will end if we succeed?" Adjusting his weapon in preparation to charge while signaling his men Ragnar says "They didn't exactly give us a choice."

Chapter Twenty

Corporal Aragon was getting used to dropping in and out of engagements giving Lance Corporals Jennings and McNamara a chance to blow some enemies to space dust before activating the stealth filaments, building up enough inertia before shutting the thrusters down so they could coast with less of a heat signature making it hard for enemies to track it. Word throughout the Jackral fighter ranks must have spread because some were getting wise to these tactics. Coming in with the sun at your back was also proving to be a deadly combination with the tricks he was picking up. Now he had to delay the times of engagement after going stealth. Some of the Jackral were beginning to time when the Adder became briefly visible making for more than a few close calls.

The Adder was made for stealth, brief engagements and getting the mechanics into hostile areas without detection so they could either recon the region of space or a planet for units to come deal with later, or to take out specific targets themselves, but a dogfighting space to space vehicle it was not. They were not meant to take sustained damage. That's what the Space Harriers were for. Aragon had to remind himself that he was not in a Space Harrier which is what he first trained in after his flash training on basic piloting. Thinking about that while they waited around for another opportunity to strike an unsuspecting Jackral fighter in the midst of a dogfight reminded him of his first training flight.

He chuckled to himself and Corporal Sims was just about to ask what was so funny when out of nowhere seemingly the culprit guilty for much of their experience asked "What's good?" scaring them all nearly to death. "What the hell House?! Where did you come from?" Laughing Petty Officer House explains "Did you dimwits forget I was here the whole time? They have a flash training console here in the rear cabin. I've been on it learning how to help repair the augmented Marines in this unit! I am after all a corpsman remember? You guys are hilarious. Mac and Jennings are on the gun turrets and I didn't want to sit on my hands. From the looks of things, they may need some patching up when we get them. If they make it that is."

Continuing to laugh after getting over the initial shock of the situation Aragon says "In a way I was just thinking about you, or rather your asinine prank that almost got us killed. We had not real ammo in the ships we were flying and then the 'surprise' nitro you gifted us finally kicked in…we were high for a first space engagement in GMC history." Laughing with them House adds "Good thing I was strapped in! Wish I was high right now. If not, I would have been bouncing around like a pinball machine. What the hell happened after dropping the strike team?" Sims replied "Just as they were beginning their breach two fighters saw them so we broke cover making us visible in order for them not to get blasted. One of the automatons got vaped. I don't suppose you learned to fix them as well?"

Shaking his head negatively House said "No that information wasn't in the GMC training files. They are products of Koops robotics which I believe can repair themselves. From the sound of it there wasn't enough to repair either way." Both Sims and Aragon nod in agreement. Lance Corporal Jennings pops in over the intercom system "Glad you boys had a cute little reunion but it looks like we have a lot of company headed our way. I don't believe they have a visual on us but we need to be careful here. We've taken some decent hits. Corporal Aragon I know you're senior but I vote we head back to the Ex Wife to refuel patch up and see if HQ has any word. We can remain ghost once we come back out so we're ready to pick up when the Sergeant and the rest are ready for evac."

Goosing the throttle forward enough to get some movement going but hopefully not burning enough to get noticed Aragon gets them heading back towards the GMC/Kison Askari capital ships saying "Agreed. Sims monitor all message traffic in case we get word while we are on route. House keep your eyes peeled on the map and let me know if there's something I need to know while navigating this moving minefield of a battle. Gentlemen stand down on the turrets unless absolutely necessary. You're right we have taken a bit of a beating."

* * *

Ogun and Bofus rode the Jackral land skiff taking out the Jackral unlucky enough to be in their path. Both shoulder canons looked to be on auto fire. They were simply taking out targets as soon as they were within range of the weapons. Max and Sparks would follow up and chase down stragglers with the acquired hover-sleds, any who proved dexterous enough to evade the rapid plasma fire mowing a majority of the fleeing Jackral down. What could have gone either way was now looking like a route on the ground. Argos was cleaving Jackral in half as he flew by on the chariot like skiff with his large ornate sword.

All around them GMC and Kison Askari units were in wholesale slaughter mode. Sparks released the throttle on her hover-sled to watch it all. Tapping a node on her helmet she called out to Max "Stop, this isn't right." Coming to a stop he saw what she meant. As if to further illustrate her point Argos skewers two Jackral at once hold them up briefly before stopping abruptly to send them flying off his blade into a bloody heap some distance away. The whole thing came to a halt as the Earth begins to quake. Large fissures open up in the ground and everyone ran for stable ground. After a few moments the ground stopped shifting.

The Jackral took advantage of the chaos and were out of sight by the time the joint forces regrouped. Ogun jumped off the Jackral land skiff and knelt down to marvel at the giant fissure that allowed the regions Jackral remnant to escape. Even more troubling is that it looked like the fissures were coming from the Spike structures. Bofus looked on as the GMC units went to their field radio operators to see if similar fissures were forming near the other installations. Word got back pretty quickly that this was the case. Now they had to decide if they would continue to pursue if that meant the Jackral would threaten to rip the world apart if cornered. In response to this new dangerous aspect Ogun says "We need to get back on their trail as soon as possible. If they entrench themselves in enough of these structures there may not be much we can do."

Time was of the essence to try and track the fleeing Jackral down before they could set up a planetary self-destruct. They all jumped aboard the various means of transportation they had gathered and begun the chase anew. Bofus was hoping they made it in time. Sparks was just as worried and Argos was secretly wondering if he would ever make it back to his home again or if he would die in this foreign dimension lost to his family forever. Time would soon tell.

* * *

A plan of attack to deal with the Jackral home ship itself if the strike teams could not take over was beginning to take form. General Krulak with his staff working with Queen Tunisia and Simeon with the advice of their elders was going smoothly or as smooth as could be under the circumstances. Word had come back from the surface of the growing danger developing there because of how the spike structures had started tearing fissures in the surface. Currently there was no way to know how deep they were but literally any depth was concerning. Something had to be done before there was nothing to save.

Contingency plans were being made in the event the planet itself had to be evacuated.

So far, they had come up with capital ships from both the GMC and Kison Askari armada approaching the Jackral home ship and its contingent of capital ships as if to engage it. While they begin to trade blows Zurina in her stealth fighter would then launch smaller dark matter missiles into the main engines and again at the main weapons placements to disable its capacity to move or fire upon the Earth. It was obviously a huge risk even if successful but at this point their choices were becoming severely slim. Professor Charles Jones-Bey was one of the few non-mutated human scientists who had the privilege to work with the Kison Askari.

Years ago, he had discovered a genetic link between the mutated races and regular people much to the chagrin of the government who preferred to think of them as either an experiment gone awry or another species altogether. Some despite the changing of time sought to dehumanize them in order to justify using them for their durability and other advantages without affording them rights similar to what regular people were given. Now however the professor was working on something that didn't quite sit well with him. The development of a weapon even if its aim is not specifically to take life was not what he imagined he would ever work on.

Beneath his special hazmat suit Professor Jones-Bey sweats as he watches the technicians assembling the warhead that will encase the supremely volatile dark matter. Previously they had the help of the Atlanteans who were well versed and had ways to house the dangerous substance in ordinance containers of their own design which were proven capable to handle it. This was to be the Kison Askari's first attempt at containing the weaponized version of this substance on their own. A mistake here would have catastrophic results before an assault could be attempted. A rather diminutive Kison Askari was also wearing a thick hazmat suit despite the assumed protection of her already hardened skin. She was manipulating mechanical arms as they assembled the casing around the dark matter ordinance in a containment field as Jones-Bey and other technicians observed the process.

He was not familiar with the clear substance the casing was made of. Curious Professor Jones-Bey asks "Why not simply use the ordinance already assembled? Miss…" Taking a brief moment to steady her hands the Kison Askari turns to correct him "Doctor, actually. Doctor Jami, and we needed to produce a smaller warhead than what was used earlier. The Atlanteans provided a portion of our dark matter arsenal as well as substance needed to create the containment capsules but it is a finite amount we have in store. Babylon himself provided them but he and his people have disappeared once again." Charles Jones-Bey was even more intrigued with this Kison Askari now and couldn't help pestering her despite the gravity of the situation.

"That all sounds quite troubling. I was not aware the stone people had their own doctorate programs." He added. Annoyed at his statement and that he was breaking her concentration she spat back "I have a Ph. D. in physics and astrophysics which I studied while on other planets while having access to all the information available on Earth yet some still question us despite us having the ability to have more practical application when it comes to dealing with what goes on among the stars. We are more than hard skinned brutes!" Raising his hands Jones- Bey says "I meant no offense just that I was unaware, and I have spent considerable time with your people."

Chuckling Dr. Jami says "Spoken like a true academic who hasn't had to deal with the real world. Make yourself useful if you're going to stand around and pick up those lenses please?" The professor went to pick up a strange pair of goggles and placed them over his head and when looking at the tools and substances in the containment field it looked as if he were looking at a negative photograph. Seeing that he had the lenses on she further instructed "Now, there's a dial on the right side that should let you switch to different spectrums. Change it until the clear elements of the material of the containment capsule looks solid and the dark matter should have a glow."

Professor Jones-Bey rotates the dial until it looks as she described and gives a thumbs up. "Good, now I am going to take these three especially shaped pieces to enclose a portion of the dark matter in the capsule. When I seal it there should be no glow coming from the tip of the warhead. When that's done a vacuum will be formed on the other side of that wall taking the remaining and unused dark matter back into the reservoir leaving just the capsule." After the explanation she went to work. Even without the lenses Professor Jones-Bey would have been hard pressed to take his eyes away.

It was obvious that Dr. Jami was working with surgeon like precision as she used the special mechanical arms to first displace some of the dark matter with the encasement pieces before nudging just the right amount of the dangerous substance where she wanted it. Inside the suit sweat beaded down her ebony calcified skin as she placed the third piece to enclosed the warhead before pressing the button that activated the vacuum. Jones-Bey watched the swirl of glowing dark matter leave the chamber all except what was in the spear shaped capsule. With that done she asked "See if you can find any crack or fissure no matter how minute that allows the slight glow of the dark matter to shine through. If you find any, I need to apply more sealant."

Professor Jones-Bey looked for any such tiny fissures and found none. There was another dial on the left of the lenses that allowed him to turn the image of the capsule so he could look at it from varying angles and still no glimpse of escaping light could be found. Satisfied he said "None that I can see Dr. Jami. What is the capsule made of?" Taking off the helmet to her hazmat suit she replies "That is a trade secret and the reason your GMC cannot control dark matter. It is a secret that must not leave this facility which is why I did not name it for you. I know the Queen has allowed you and other exiles to come with us, but that doesn't mean I trust you. That's earned over time. Thank you for your help. Time is short and we have to assemble at least eight more if you have time."

Some of what she said hurt but he understood why she felt as she did. In response he said "Of course I have time. At least tell me what we are calling these warheads?" Before placing her helmet back on she turns to Jones-Bey and says "These are Assegai warheads named after ancient spear heads used by a great leader in history. Unfortunately, he was known for his lust for warfare. Hopefully these can lead to the end of war." At that they went about assembling the rest needed for the mission.

Zurina and Nefer were being briefed on their mission as Simeon explained the best way to approach the Jackral home ship. Ordinarily you could approach warships either head on or by flanking them to get the best target acquisition of their weapons placements but this ship had shown the ability to move various artillery barrels and turrets. The salvo shot at the Earth's surface had come after a majority of the ship's armaments had moved to the underbelly of the ship before discharging a huge energy blast of some kind. Despite knowing she would be the least visible space craft out there Zurina was getting plenty nervous.

The added danger of carrying more than the small single pilot fighter ships usual inventory of munitions all of which are to be dark matter ordinance made the task even more worrisome. Watching a digital rendering of how things were supposed to go did nothing to alleviate that worry. Plus, there was obvious tension between the two pilots. Zurina had remained loyal to the Queen the entire time and

Nefer who had expressed her concerned at Queen Tunisia's perceived wanton use of dark matter ordinance during the last conflict with GMC forces.

General Simeon saw the attitudes and didn't care either way. The current situation is what mattered most to him. The past was just that the past, and if all three strike teams and these pilots failed then none of it would matter any way. He said as much to them "I don't care about what happened before or what misgivings you may have about each other and your relationships with the Queen. It is beyond imperative that you succeed if the others we have sent on mission fails to secure the controls to that Jackral home ship. Are we clear?"

While still giving each other side eye, Zurina and Nefer echo "Crystal General." Starting up the rendering Simeon points out the maneuverability of the large ship's weapons. "This is footage of when the ship fired on the Earth following Anurens proclamation. Watch as the weapons move in unison to relocate before firing. You will need to keep watch on where the weapons move. We want those largest barrels rendered useless before heading to the rear of the ship to disable the engines if we are not able to gain control of the ship. We are waiting to hear back from them or get some sort of signal when they succeed or fail."

They all watched in relived horror as the energy charged up before it was discharged to the Asian continent ending at least millions of lives in one shot. There was an opportunity perhaps once the barrels prepared to fire for Zurina to hit them at the last minute but that might be another huge risk if the dark matter in any way increases the lethality or blast area of the energy discharge. While discussing this its' decided it would be better to disable the weapons prior to them firing. If it's done while the weapons are discharging it may indeed disable the weapons but may also destroy all the ships both enemy and allies in the process.

They left the briefing to go down to the hangar where Zurina's Nyuesi Sime was being fitted with the Assegai warheads. Begrudgingly Nefer nodded to Zurina before going to her War Dragon as she prepared to fly with her running interference and just to be a good wing woman in general despite not agreeing with all of this. It wouldn't matter much if they failed. All would be getting a one-way ticket to oblivion if that dark matter were mis measured and there was an amplified interaction with the Jackral weaponry. Kamal was waiting at their War Dragon when Nefer got to the hangar bay. General Simeon met with her as she was in her pre-flight checklist. Seeing him she called down "You have some last orders, General?"

Shaking his head, he replies "No, I was wondering if I could ride in the rear turret again. I rather enjoyed it the last time and Muturi is already on the Jackral home ship. I know I am a General now but if this may be the last fight, I would rather have an active part in it." The ramp lowered and he came aboard.

Chapter Twenty-One

Sergeant Garrison, Private Cooper, Muturi and the two automatons made their way back towards the duct system where they entered the ship just outside one of the galleys. The automatons scanned the circuitry in the bulkheads and had easily traced heavily cabling most likely to carry both power and data to a nearby service terminal. More alarms went off as occasional fire was being thrown their way from other ships now. Sergeant Garrison was glad for the misdirection but also hoped they didn't do their jobs too well and seriously damage the ship with them aboard it. When he expressed that particular worry one of the automatons was quick to remind him "That's not likely to happen as we have nothing powerful enough to outright destroy a ship of this size. At least not in one or two salvos."

Garrison mumbled back "Thanks for the tip. Now do we have the schematics yet?" After a few moments the other automaton pulled up a digital display for them to look at which conveniently had their current location labelled on it as well. Private Cooper stood watch while Muturi, Sgt. Garrison and the automatons studied the schematic deciding which direction to go next. "Looks like the bridge or at least part of the weapons station should be here a good distance below us. I don't think getting to the lift is the right play however since it's likely heavily guarded now that they know they have company. Can you tell what the maximum capacity is for largest of the ducts on this space tub?" Garrison asks.

The automatons go through and analyzes the schematic as thoroughly as possible labelling the one with the largest capacity for them to squeeze through. Seeing what's highlighted Muturi says "That one looks promising and we have a few stops pretty much at most ten levels below us what is it?" Looking at each other before looking back at Garrison and Muturi the automatons chorus "Waste management chute." Studying the schematics further they could tell where the other breaches occurred and one went over to activate the small hack disk realizing this had already been done twice which is why they were able to easily read the system.

They were also able to now link up with the other automatons who had got in but was as yet unable to manipulate any of the ship's operating systems. The automatons' eyes flickered repeatedly in response to the loss of two of their units. When the expressions on their normally blank brown faces went suddenly sad Muturi asks "What's wrong?" Looking at him they respond "Two automaton units were damaged beyond repair in the other breach attempts." Private Cooper looks back responding "Oh crap." At that Sergeant Garrison looks up as they hear armored footsteps nearby 'Couldn't have said it better myself. Let's move. Lead the way my robotic friends to the crap indeed." After ducking into a corridor before they are discovered they step off lead by the automatons. Confused Cooper asks "You couldn't have said oh crap better? What's that mean Sergeant?"

Smiling cruelly Garrison says "You'll see." Looking to Muturi for answers but the Kison Askari shrugs muttering "Waste management." Cooper was still confused but didn't like the Sergeants smile…not one bit.

* * *

Corporal Aragon had managed to make it back to the *ExWife* and dock in one if the landing bays with the GMC Capital ship flying as if it were in a game of chicken with the Jackral home ship. It would approach until within weapons range and then back off but stay close enough to keep the ship from firing on the planet again. It was an absolutely crazy game. One they would ultimately lose if the Jackral decided to fire with its largest weapons batteries. For some reason they were not electing to do that. Part of that reason was the multiple ships small and large all around it flying, fighting, shooting and just being a nuisance for the Jackral fighters and warriors manning the artillery units and plasma canons.

Their lack of focus was a testament to the efficacy of the strike teams now aboard the Jackral home ship. Aragon hoped Sergeant Garrison and his crew were doing well in there. Meanwhile he Corporal Sims, Petty Officer House, Lance Corporals Jennings and McNamara had to see to the Adders maintenance to be sure they were ready to head back out for the strike teams evac. They were sure the modified drop pods would not be reliable modes of transportation off the ship. In the hangar bay it was a swarm of activity with Marines and other personnel running to get tools to fix ships or dragging hover-sleds with fuel to ships. As they thought the Adder had taken a beating, but should be ready to go soon. At least that was the word they got from Sgt. Roscoe Brown the local grease monkey on this particular hangar deck.

Corporal Aragon was going through all the diagnostic checks while Sgt. Brown was shoring up the plating on the hull making sure to replace patches where the stealth filaments had been melted off. After finishing he yelled "It's not perfect but it should keep you hidden when you need to be! All I have left to do is hammer the mounts on your rear main thrusters back in place. Looks like you were zigging when you should have zagged a bit." Laughing despite it not being particularly funny considering the circumstances under which the mounts became bent They all went about resupplying the ship.

Lance Corporals Jennings and McNamara had to go stand in line to get more ammo and power supplies for the turrets. Jennings remarked "I remember my great great great grand pops talking about the days where the only kind of ammo you needed were ballistic rounds. This is ridiculous." Confused McNamara looks at him and says "Yeah but your great great great grandpa likely wasn't fighting in zero G's with plasma and laser fire coming at him. How is it you spoke to him? How is he?" Chuckling Jennings replies while pushing a full hover-sled back towards the Adder "Oh he's long dead but we have one of those virtual memorials with some of his memories and it's got an interactive AI so it feels like he's there with you. Kind of creepy if you ask me."

When they got back to the Adder, Aragon informed them that new orders had come in. They were to form a joint flight with one of their Space Harriers and two Kison Askari vessels. One was a War Dragon and the other was a small fighter with stealth capabilities similar to the Adders but with an extremely deadly payload. If the strike teams were unsuccessful the Adder, Space Harrier, and War Dragon had escort duty. Other flights could be called in to pave the way giving the Kison Askari fighter a shot at disabling weapons and then main engines. "Lovely." Lance Corporal McNamara says. Jennings asks "Anyone know who the jarhead pilot going with us is?"

Walking up in a smart looking GMC flight suit with helmet in hand was a redheaded Marine with two silver bars on his armored shoulder paldrons. He says "That would be me. Captain Maplethorpe." Sticking his head out of the rear hatch to make sure he heard correctly was Corporal Aragon who looked none too pleased with that choice. Coming out to briefly salute and greet the Captain, Corporal Aragon says "Good to see you again sir! At least we have real rounds now." After looking at him strangely Captain Maplethorpe says "Straighten up and fly right Marine. We have a job to do." The officer shakes all of their hands and heads back to his ship in prep for the mission. Lance Corporals Jennings and McNamara notice the awkwardness of the exchange.

Petty Officer House and Corporal Sims are obviously trying not to laugh as they all get back aboard the Adder. Sergeant Brown slaps the fuselage and goes to the front of the Adder signaling a thumbs up to Aragon as he straps in to once again do a pre-flight check. Over the intercom in the Adder McNamara asks "So we just gonna ignore all that or is someone going to fill us in on what's up with you and the captain back there?" Everything checked out and it was obvious Corporal Aragon was stalling, so Corporal Sims chimed in "Have you boys had the pleasure of trying Nitro or gone to a Nitro club?" At the silence he assumed they had not and continued.

"If you haven't and we all survive this I implore you to try it. We found out about using nitrous oxide in varying mixes as an alternative to spirits and other libations since getting the supplement treatment from the GMC. Now these clubs have mixes like ambrosia, old school joviality, and the like to make you go through different emotional stages similar to being high or drunk without some of the usual side effects if it's prepared in the correct lab but I digress. The good doctor here scored a batch of canisters labeled "Surprise" which he bestowed on us during some off time and we took it while in our barracks on Saturn. We thought it was a dud. Turns out the reaction is time delayed and it doesn't tell you when the effect will release."

Finally, as they are taxiing to leave the hangar Corporal Aragon finishes the tale "What he's not telling you is that we were in our first real flight time training session when the stuff kicked in since our flash training. Captain Maplethorpe who was then First Lieutenant Maplethorpe was my flight master sitting in the second seat while I was on the sticks…high as a kite!" They all kind of laugh as they are given permission to leave the hangar. Thinking it over Lance Corporal Jennings puts two and two together "Wait a minute. Didn't we get ambushed after the big flash training push by the rock-heads?"

House jumps in "Whoa, whoa whoa! Stow the negative euphemisms Marine. You are astute in your estimation on the timing of this event which is what made it all the more hilarious since my dear

Corporal Aragon survived the unexpected experience of being high with very real, live rounds being fired at him while only having tracer rounds to fire back with. The aforementioned Captain Maplethorpe has been none too pleased ever since witnessing Aragon laugh, cry and go through nearly every emotional spectrum while avoiding fire from hostiles in space craft." They laughed a little more until the gravity of the situation hit them. Both Aragon's training mishap and their current situation.

They pulled away from the *Ex Wife* and waited for the rest of the flight to join them. Control acknowledged their positioning and ordered them to cloak and back away as far as possible from them as the other assets would be joining them soon. Seeing as things had gotten dicey with the capital ships all baiting the Jackral home ship as well as trying to distract it Aragon didn't mind putting some distance between them. They would be getting up close and personal with them soon enough. Soon he saw a smaller but bulky space Harrier come out and vector near their location. Assuming it's Captain Maplethorpe, Corporal Aragon double clicks his mic on the tactical frequency and there's a double click in return.

Corporal Aragon reveals the Adder briefly so the Captain knows where he is before they get moving. They hold their positions awaiting their Kison Askari counterparts. They would not have to wait long. All Lance Corporal Jennings could manage was "What the..." as the Kison Askari War Dragon approached. The long sweeping wings combined with the length of the fuselage and swiveling cockpit made it look very much like its namesake from a distance. "Never saw one of these in action Jennings?" Corporal Sims asks.

Chuckling Jennings replies "Nope and I am sure if I did, I would think I was high. Must admit I'm kind of jealous." They all kind of ogled the ship until Captain Maplethorpe broke the silence by opening up a channel saying "This is Oscar three Mike, who is the Kilo Alpha in the War Dragon?" Making sure his mic was muted McNamara says to the Adder crew "Boy listen to Cap Maplethorpe being all official!" Simeon in the War Dragon responded to the Captain "This is Oscar...the hell with all that! This is General Simeon but Simeon is fine for now. We can worry about military bearing and platitudes if we survive without becoming space dust."

Captain Maplethorpe was about to respond when Corporal Aragon jumped in "This is Echo four Alpha in the Adder. Glad to have you with us General. Aren't you a bit high up in rank to be going on a fly by the seat of your pants kind of mission Sir?" Everyone got a slight laugh out of that but Simeon was cool about it saying "I wasn't supposed to be on this mission but there are privileges to being high ranking. I can do what I want pretty much. The only one who could deny me is the Queen and she doesn't know I'm here. I figured if this is our last rodeo so to speak then I wanted the best seat in the house. Nefer is a great pilot and Kamal has shown an aptitude at gunner. I will do my best at rear gunner on this strange boat. Zurina should be here soon in her Nyuesi Sime. It has similar stealth capabilities to your Adder which I assume is near since I can only see your Space Harrier."

After a moment there was another voice on the frequency "Sorry I'm late! The packages I carry can be a bit touchy. Don't want one of these babies detonating before we want them too." Captain Maplethorpe agreed with that sentiment wholeheartedly "Roger that. When do we go in? It's your payload that will have to be delivered." Zurina chimed back in "For now we wait. Comms should go between the War Dragon and the Space Harrier from now on. There are reports that some of the Jackral ships can triangulate and find some of our stealth ships when transmitting but not receiving. We have lost a few already. The Adder and I should double click to acknowledge and triple click to deny or ask for a repeat. Captain Maplethorpe I was briefed that you would be with us. When you get the call from the *Ex Wife*, we go in. Here's to hoping we never get it."

Disappointed but understanding the gamesmanship of it all they did just that, wait. Mock sleeping Lance Corporal Jennings muttered under his breath "Hurry up and wait."

...***

The remaining automaton with PFC Long's group stated "We should be a few decks below the bridge now." They were pinned down and Long once again had to wait for the canon barrels in his arms to cool and recharge. Amuzati and Bulu looked beat down and tired. The automaton had various scorch and burn marks all over its head and body but was still functional. Looking down at his chest plate and the rest of the mech suit his torso was housed in, Long could see scorch marks and pitting as if acid had started corroding it.

They were all ducked down behind large containers in what looked like some kind of cargo hold. Just when it seemed the Jackral were about to close in and end them there was a large explosion on another deck which shook the bulkheads. Most of the Jackral search party ran off in the direction of the disturbance. Some stayed to move in on their prey there. Amuzati tightened his grip on the gravity staff he was holding. Raising it up he saluted Bulu who returned the gesture. Turning to Long they both whispered "Amandla."

In a low hushed tone, the automaton said "There are approximately eight or nine combatants headed this way from varying directions. This cover won't last if we stay here." Long nodded as an indicator light came on letting him know his arm canons were ready for use once more. He looked towards Amuzati and Bulu giving them a quick salute saying "You two are weird as hell, but if I don't get a chance to tell you later. It's been a pleasure doing business with you.

Semper Fi." With that Long kicked one of the large containers they were hiding behind which slid into two Jackral warriors pinning them against the bulkhead.

Taking up a discarded Jackral baton Bulu came out slinging energy projectiles everywhere while his shoulder mounted canon on auto target took out enemies on either side of the strike team. More Jackral swarmed into the cargo hold. Amuzati activated his canon to compensate for the extra targets. PFC Long simply shot, pummeled or cleaved his way through the Jackral until a small dark object came in affixing itself to his chest plate. There was a burst of energy and his systems went dark. Unable to stop himself Long crashed to the deck like a metal fallen oak tree.

The automaton picked up two of the Jackral weapons and began pour fire into the incoming swarm taking many out, and then bludgeoning some as they got closer. Inside Long's helm he could see the system had rebooted but he could also see that they were about to be over run. Amuzati and Bulu were acquitting themselves well as was the bot, but it might not be enough. Bulu was hit in the midsection and went flying just as the tone along with the message "system online" flashed across Long's eyes.

The internal AI spoke "Your pain meds are about to run out. Would you like to resume pain reduction or enter Berserker mode? Blink once to accept meds, blink twice to skip this dose." Long blinked twice and the face shield went red once again as the mech suit came online. By this time there were Jackral atop of the suit beating him with their weapons. There was a hydraulic hiss as the arms of the suit pushed up with enough force to throw them off some hitting the overhead hard enough to break necks. Bulu shook his head and got back to his feet. Pointing in the direction they should run Amuzati began firing again as he picked up the automaton which was struck down just before Long was EMP'd.

They found a lift and despite the risk they entered it. PFC long retracted his helm and told Bulu "Just hit buttons until this thing stops." The squat Kison Askari went about doing just that until the automaton pressed the button on the bottom row furthest to the right. The lift came to a full stop as they stared at the console with nearly one hundred buttons lit up. They looked on as the automaton began to self-repair as it muttered "That should have been your first choice."

Chapter Twenty-Two

Sitting on the Kison Askari throne ship *Akina Mama* Queen Tunisia waits watching how this will all unfold. There was a nervousness about the air. They knew Zurina, and Nefer should have met up with the joint flight as a contingency if the strike teams failed. The queen was confused as to why she had not seen her top general Simeon in a while. Njemba was standing near the royal guards looking especially guilty. Finally, unable to ignore the obvious she asks "Njemba, where is Simeon?" If the large Kison Askari could blush, he would have.

Njemba begins to stammer and Queen Tunisia interrupts him "Let me stop you there. I know you're his understudy, aide or whatever your role is for the general, but if you lie to me you will be relegated back to mining duties should we survive this ordeal. Dishonesty will not be tolerated." To emphasize her point her eyes began to shimmer and glow. The royal guard took a few steps away from Njemba. Taking a deep breath before replying Njemba mumbles "General Simeon is on board the War Dragon piloted by Nefer." The Queen stands "I'm sorry did you say on a War Dragon?" "Yes, my Queen." Njemba confirms.

Thinking it over she decides to move on "Very well. It was foolish of him but I understand. Make sure the order goes out to all War Dragons, Kitanas, and Shibokaze class ships to head out in support of this mission. Hold the Azriel class and Morning Stars in reserve. We might need them for cleanup when this is finished." The bridge crew set about executing her orders and Njemba is happy not to be under such heavy scrutiny now that the queen knows the truth of Simeon's whereabouts. He hoped the old man knew what he was doing. Time would tell.

The ships Queen Tunisia ordered out to the special battlefield came flying out of the gaping launch bays of their throne ship and it caught the attention of the Jackral fleet who answered in kind sending forces of their own in the direction of the Kison Askari ships. Tunisia was feeling good about all of this until she looked down at her most recent reports showing their forces were down about fifteen percent since beginning this large-scale engagement. The Jackral of course were also taking losses but it was impossible to know how many since they had no way of gauging how many ships they began with. The GMC forces were reporting being down twenty five percent which did not bode well. They would not be able to keep this up indefinitely. Those strike teams had to get control of the Jackral home ship soon or they would be forced to try and disable it.

She toyed with the idea of going to her own Nyuesi Sime. They likely could not stop her now but she was sure Darius didn't imbue her with some of his power for her to abuse it. Tunisia was determined to be a great example of how to lead her people from now on, and not give in to impulses no matter how satisfying they might feel to live out. She just hoped there would be a people to lead once this ship were taken over or disabled, if either could be achieved.

* * *

Athena and Angelo were following Hironike's lead as he skulked from shadow to shadow taking Jackral warriors out with quick efficient but most importantly nearly silent attacks. They were just about to the bridge and they guessed the other strike teams were near as well for there were often multiple disturbances and alarms going off at once where groups of the Jackral were forced to go see what the problem was. Many times, Hironike would just wait to nab an unsuspecting Jackral at the rear of the formation. His blade was swift, often slipping silently through armor and organs depriving the victim of the air necessary to cry out. By the time the group noticed their numbers had dwindled it was too late.

They would either finish the group off before they travelled too far or a depleted group of Jackral ran into the buzz saw that was one of the other strike teams. Hironike seemed to know when it was best to cut off their pursuit letting them go to the new disturbance and never over extending their strike team. Angelo appreciated this most because he was not a fan of Athena coming along on this mission in the first place. To take stock of the options they had left, Hironike decided to head to another maintenance closet with the help of their remaining automaton who quickly found one nearby. From there they should be able to figure out where the other strike teams were and how many guards were on the bridge. The crew seemed to be worked up in a frenzy which helped them feel out the coming and going of the Jackral.

From what the automaton could gather there was something happening in one of the main lifts and oddly enough a trash chute. Waiting for another group to pass so they could continue unnoticed Athena asked "Why a trash chute?" Looking back at her Hironike smiled saying "Pretty smart actually. Nearly every deck on this ship will have some sort of refuse or waste to get rid of. The trash or waste ducts would give them access to most of them. Now they might be crazy to navigate depending on how the flow of their trash travels but it could cut a lot of guess work out of maneuvering through such a large vessel."

Seeing as they were already in EV suits, Athena considered the possibility of that strategy, but the thought of what they would likely find in those chutes made her glad her team had found another way to the bridge. Once they made their way to the maintenance closet, the automaton began searching the system for any information it could find on the whereabouts of the other teams in relation to the most recent disturbances. For all they knew there could be other strike teams aboard. Desperate times call for desperate measures and all that.

* * *

Although they wanted to sit out the battle until they were called upon, the two flights of Jackral fighters heading their way had other ideas. Corporal Aragon was the first to notice but forgot he was supposed to remain radio silent. "Um…we have some hostiles coming our way. They don't look like they want to talk." Captain Maplethorpe was quick to remind him "Secure that noise Adder! All comms goes thru me or the Dragon, stick to our six but don't decloak." Maplethropes Space Harrier shot forward towards the Jackral fighters and veered right.

Nefer did the same but chose to go left to split the two flights of Jackral fighters. Zurina easily stuck to Nefer's tail and Simeon could kind of tell where she was as the hull of the Jackral fighters were blurred where her Nyuesi Sime blocked them. She was surprised when the Kison Askari General began to fire around her ship at the enemy. Two of them were destroyed quickly forcing the other two to back off. Captain Maplethorpe took out one of the fighters from the other flight and was still in pursuit of the second with the remaining two on his tail. Unfortunately, he did not have a rear turret like the War Dragon did.

The two Jackral fighters giving chase were taking pot shots at him every chance they got. Corporal Aragon in the Adder decided to remain on Captain Maplethorpe's six but from either above or below so that the Space Harrier was never in his line of sight. Making sure that only his internal channel was open for communication he says "Mac and Jennings when you have a clean shot take the two out on the Captains six, then maybe we can swing back for the two on the War

Dragon that seem to be hanging back." There were dual tones as both dorsal and belly turrets signaled, they were primed and a chorus of "Rodger that."

There was staggered fire as the Marines each waited for clear shots to pull back on the double triggers sending hot plasma rounds into the cockpits of the two Jackral fighters turning them both into space junk. The brief explosion of its wing mates made the lead Jackral fighter hesitate. The slight slowing was enough for Captain Maplethorpe to get a missile lock. With tone confirmed he pulled the trigger. Just to make sure Maplethorpe broke off in the opposite direction and came around pouring laser fire into the nose of the Jackral fighter slowing it again as the missile caught up to it ripping the ship apart. Flying through the smoke and debris Captain Maplethorpe opened up a channel to the War Dragon "General Simeon I don't know about you but I would rather do this than wait until we are called upon. We will eventually be targeted anyway sitting in a holding pattern around the battle."

General Simeon replies "I agree, but what's your plan of attack? We are not supposed to just jump into the fray." Maplethorpe continues "You are correct sir, but we can stay on the fringes of all the major engagements and push forward as if about to join. When some of the Jackral fighters see us, they will break off to pursue as we pull away. If we can lure small groups like those two flights with no more than eight in a group, they will have a numbers advantage but not know about the two stealth craft with us. Zurina, double click to confirm that you have more onboard weapons in addition to the ugly stuff."

Zurina assumed he was talking about the dark matter ordinance. She did in fact have laser canons she could use as well. She quickly double clicked her mic to give them a non-verbal response. With that confirmed Captain Maplethorpe said "Good, let's see who we can lure to their doom, shall we? Aragon, good shooting back there. Glad to see you have your head on straight this time." Corporal Aragon double clicked his mic acknowledging the compliment and they all pushed forward to seek out more targets until they were called.

* * *

Laying down Sgt. Garrison was staring over the precipice at the drop into the waste management duct that went quite a ways. The rest of the strike team low crawled beside him to take a look for themselves. They could see there were hatches on each deck below where waste and other biproducts entered the conduit that would flow down to where ever the end of the line was for the ships waste. Seeing the automatons crawling up to the edge Sgt. Garrison says "Take a look and see how far down you think the hatch is where we can enter the bridge level is."

There were no signs of the Jackral thus far but Muturi and Private Cooper were keeping watch just in case on both the levels above and below them. The automatons looked back at Garrison and chorused "The bridge level should have an access point eight decks down at the hatch to your far right with the hexagonal symbol above it." Following where they were pointing Sgt. Garrison nodded and asked "Is it possible to mag-lock on the alloy surfaces here?" The golden eyes of the automatons began to flicker as they communicated with the bots with the other teams.

After a few moments their eyes stopped flickering and they both echoed "Yes, the team with the Ongakujin head was able to do so on the outer hull in their breach attempt, so it stands to reason we should be able to do so here." Thinking that over Garrison remarks "The band leader...right. I find it curious how a musician rates going on an op like this but I guess that's above my paygrade. Alright everyone, prepare to scale the bulkheads of this duct until we reach that hatch with the hexagon above it there."

Suddenly large cylindrical canisters came rushing down the duct. There was a pause then another rush of the objects came at high speed. Following the trajectory of the objects in their downward flight Private Cooper asks "What was that?" Muturi shrugs but answers "Most likely...crap." Sgt Garrison looks to Muturi to ask "Your boots do have a mag-lock function to them yes?" Shaking his head affirmatively Muturi says "Of course, some of the mines I've worked have zero G environments. Wouldn't want to fly away while collecting ore stuck in large asteroids." As if to prove his point Muturi activated the function on his boots and began to make his way down.

Another wave of trash came hurtling down the chute and Muturi ducked down to make himself as small as possible hugging his knees. Shaking his head Private Cooper went next mumbling "We should have taken another rout and used wraith suits." Chuckling Sgt. Garrison says "Quit griping and get down to that hatch! Just make sure to avoid the flying crap. From what I heard the latest wraith suit didn't work out for the poor sucker wearing it." At last they were all making their descent when alarms began blaring.

A deep sonorous gruff voice began spewing warnings in the Jackral language. Not understanding they yelled up to the automatons for a translation while ducking and dodging waste canisters. The automatons which were the last to begin the climb were able to alternately switch the magnetic function off and on at a high rate enabling them to basically slide and stop at the target hatch before the rest of the team. Once at the hatch they began trying to open it while explaining "Apparently us being in the waste management duct is a violation. Dumping waste not in the regulation containers is prohibited."

After seeing what the automatons were able to do Sgt. Garrison was able to do a similar act seeing as he had cybernetic legs and the controls were integrated with his neural network. There was not much room on the ledge where the automatons stood. The alarms kept blaring. Soon hatches above and below them opened up. First there were Jackral helms staring at them from all angles. Next came energy fire. Predicting what was about to happen next Private Cooper disengaged the mag-lock on his boots so he could free fall the rest of the way barely catching on to the ledge. Sgt. Garrison and one automaton helped him up while the other was still working on the hatch.

Inevitably with the Jackral firing down the chute some of the canisters were hit sending waste flying everywhere below. Looking up Private Cooper yelled "Jump! I'll catch you." Muturi looked up in time to see a large canister heading his way explode into a spray of muck. Just as he was about to get slopped, he disengaged the mag-locks on his boots going into a free fall while shooting upwards with his shoulder canon hoping to stave off any nasty debris following him. Leaning out Cooper was able to grasp the falling Kison Askari by the harness which luckily didn't snap. Private Cooper then set him on the already crowded ledge and saw that the automaton was still having issues with opening the hatch.

Frustrated Cooper used his cybernetic arms to pry the hatch open. Muturi stepped through firing at a group of Jackral that were waiting on the other side. One of the automatons were immediately blasted and went flying down the chute along with canisters and free-falling waste. Sgt. Garrison snatched back the remaining automaton from a similar fate as it was watching its companion fall not paying attention to the hail of fire now coming their way from inside as well as from the decks above and below. They scrambled into the corridor returning fire as they went searching for some cover.

There was none to be found unfortunately. They would just have to fight their way through. Energy blasts filled the corridor and many of the bolts were being blocked by Private Coopers arms. The armor casing of the rest of his suit however was not as strong as the alloy his arms were made of. He stumbled after a myriad of successive hits. Sgt. Garrison dragged him down another corridor when they got to it hoping for a spot they could regroup. Seeing Cooper down enraged Muturi. The small warrior roared as he extended his gravity staff while simultaneously firing his shoulder canon and waded into the Jackral.

Ducking down the corridor pulling the automaton and dragging Private Cooper, Sgt. Garrison could not see what was going on but could hear screams, weapons fire hitting the bulkheads and bouncing off armor. Since it continued, he assumed Muturi was somehow holding his own despite being vastly outnumbered. He was grateful for the cover. At the end of the corridor he had chosen was the entrance to a lift. They were currently on the desired deck but needed time to regroup and with no other choices getting in was really their only option so he could check on Cooper's wounds. The bot looked to be in shock and he wanted to wait but wasn't sure if Muturi would make it to them in time.

He pressed what looked like the call button and went back to the end of the corridor to check on Muturi. Things hadn't gone silent so he was obviously still putting up a fight somehow. Calling over his shoulder to the bot Garrison said "When the lift gets here put Coop on it and see if we can patch him up. I'll be right back. Need to make sure this crazy little bastard doesn't get himself killed!" The lift opened and the automaton was thankful when PFC Long's faceplate went from red to clear as he saw Cooper was down. "You may want to help the others." The automaton stated as it dragged Cooper into the lift.

Chapter Twenty-Three

Anuren and a few of his elite guards were rushing through their home ship, and at each turn seemed to be too late in finding what or whoever was causing the disturbances. Frustrated they go from piles of Jackral bodies to more piles. Running back towards the bridge so they could simply watch footage of the incidents and gauge where the intruders are going the Jackral leader is nearly taken out by railgun fire. A plethora of high-density high velocity rounds hit Anuren's armor with such force that he is forced into the bulkhead before going to the deck.

One of his guards returns fire but is quickly taken out as his helm was retracted when the firefight began. When Anuren looks back to check on the downed guard he realizes his head is missing, the blood pooling on the deck causes another Jackral guard to slip. The Jackral leader ignores the pain in his chest that has to be deeply bruised beneath his armor and gets a glimpse of some of the culprits. His attention goes to where the initial fire was coming from and sees two humanoids in armored EV suits but there must be something strange with the faceplates. Picking up a discarded Jackral weapon Anuren fires upon them forcing them to take cover having come out of a utility room nearby.

A few rounds come back his way forcing him to get low as well. Railgun rounds tear into the bulkheads, and into other Jackral who ran to join their leader. From a low vantage point he watches the infiltrators run down the corridor. Coming out of the utility room is what looks like another synth being like the one Anuren discovered earlier and an armored green blur. In the wake of the latest phenomenon a slew of Jackral bodies drop, necks sliced through armor plating that should have protected them. That was concerning but they could not let them roam free now that they had finally pinpointed the troublemakers.

Slowly composing himself Anuren yells "Catch them!" They gathered up all who could give chase and ran after them. Athena and Angelo were at the end of a t-section near the main lift with their weapons trained on the opposite end of the corridor. When the running Jackral became visible they opened fire once again. They dove to the ground to avoid being riddled with holes. Hironike hides among the shadows waiting for his opportunity but Anuren is slow catching up with the other Jackral as if he wants to see how they will be attacked before coming forward himself.

Angelo and Athena are doing a good job laying into them taking most of the combatants' attention. The automaton is trying to remotely get into the ships systems being so close to the bridge as well as having a few of the mini units already attached to several consoles, the bot thinks it should be able to brute force their way in. Hironike hopes the other automatons are somewhere joining the efforts. In this moment he had to concentrate, slow his breathing to become ultra-aware of his surroundings. There was a lot going on and he could now see Anurens aura even through the bulkheads. This opponent was not to be underestimated. The Jackral leader was patient and so Hironike had to be as well. He sheathed his special blade and waited.

* * *

Down several corridors from where Anuren was giving chase to Hironike and his group the lift hatch opens up. PFC Long steps over Cooper looking back as he did so in hope that the Marine would make it. Amuzati and Bulu followed after him as the Automaton inside the lift got up to help the other drag Cooper who was still conscious into the lift. Cooper was in immense pain and it felt as if some of his armor and prosthesis had been fused to him in ways they weren't meant to be as a result of all the energy fire he had taken. As the hatch to the lift slid closed, he passes out from shock. The two automatons look oddly comforted by being reunited with another of their kind. They set about hacking into the ships systems and try to keep the hatch closed while the fighting continues outside. Their golden eyes began to flash again simultaneously as they echo "At least we are all on the same deck now."

PFC Long can hear the weapons fire and some maniacal screaming from another Kison Askari warrior. He doesn't understand the language but recognizes it as something similar he had heard Amuzati and Bulu yelling during earlier fire fights. He rounds the corner and sees Sgt. Garrison imploring Muturi to come back "We can recover in the lift. Make a plan!" Muturi is hearing none of it and is firing away with both his shoulder canon and a Jackral weapon while also beating down any who comes within reach of his gravity staff. More and more Jackral are swarming in. Long knows this looks as bad as there's no way for them to win a close quarters battle in such small confines. There's no cover to speak of and the numbers will overwhelm them soon.

Anuren and his guard change direction after hearing the ruckus Muturi was raising. Athena was glad for their sudden change in plans as it looked like Angelo had been hit in all of the commotion but she was just now noticing and felt bad. "Are you ok?" she asked. Stubbornly Angelo nodded pointing back to Hironike who stepped out of the shadows and seemed to re-enter them again. They decided to follow from a distance with their remaining automaton bringing up the rear. "Neat trick. You should ask him to teach us sometime." He added. Gripping her railgun Athena replies "It's likely not a trick but tech of some kind. One of Toshi's toys no doubt."

They hear more energy fire and screams mixed with battle cries from both groups. The corridors are filled with smoke occasionally lit with energy or plasma fire. Athena and Angelo have resorted to low crawling and have lost sight of where Hironike went. She is sure he went into the chaos and worries for him. When she attempts to move forward, she feels Angelo firmly grasp her arm cautioning her to wait. Angrily she does so having found a recess in the bulkhead that would give them some cover. After a moment the automaton catches up to them and huddles with them while alternately peaking down the hall. They were situated just before the opening of a t-section. Since they weren't moving or firing a group of Jackral came barreling by missing them completely headed towards the fighting.

Out of the smoke behind them PFC Long seemed to just materialize as his faceplate went from clear to red. Athena and Angelo sat mouths agape as they saw Long enter Berserker mode, the canons came out of his arms and shoulder plates lighting the corridor up ripping through the Jackral that just ran past them. Some of the super-heated energy and high velocity ballistic rounds wound around Sgt. Garrison who was further down the hallway striking more Jackral who just got within reach of Muturi fighting to his last breath. Sgt. Garrison instinctively hit the deck turning to see not only Long but a new arrival of Anuren and his guard behind him.

Amuzati and Bulu tore through the remaining Jackral still standing around Muturi as Sgt. Garrison tried to warn Long "Look out!" he screamed as energy rounds rained in from behind pushing Long forward who turned with the barrage and unsheathed his ax from a compartment that opened in his leg spinning it. The motion began reflecting the energy projectiles being fired his way taking out many of the attacking Jackral. Pointing Anuren orders "Shut down these toys and trinkets!"

As Long charged forward there were a plethora of small disks that came flying adhering to the overhead, bulkhead and decks. There was a simultaneous flash as all of the disks lit up with electrical discharges. Once again Long's mech suit went limp and crashed to the deck. Sgt. Garrison jumped up and ran forward without thinking. As he crossed the thresh hold where the disks had landed his legs went limp causing him to fall was well. The lights and systems for the corridor went out leaving only auxiliary emergency lights on. Still smoky and mostly dark all noise had died except for coughing from Jackral recovering from their injuries. Amuzati and Bulu were trying to remain quiet but still check on Muturi. Both were glad not be cybernetically enhanced they slowly inched their way towards where they thought a corner was to find cover before the lights came back on. Everyone seemed to be listening.

The silence was broken by deep laughter. "You see what happens when you take their toys!" Anuren proclaims. Some of the Jackral still unsure join him in laughing. As the lights begin flickering there are multiple loud thuds as armored bodies begin to fall. Angrily Anuren growls and begins firing down the corridor towards where he last saw Amuzati and Bulu not knowing they had moved. The lights are not completely back up so the darkness is pierced intermittently by energy fire briefly giving them a glimpse of a small silhouette which induces more fire as more bodies fall. Hironike uses the dark and the panic to his advantage slicing through the Jackral elites surrounding Anuren. He saves the leader for last.

The hydraulics in both Sgt. Garrison's legs and PFC Long's mech suit hiss as they are both close to coming back on line as the lights flicker more as stability is coming back to the power grid in the corridor. The lights come back up fully and Anuren sees the two mechanics about to rise. Retracting his helm, the Jackral leader screams "I don't need toys or tech to kill these vermin! I am Blessed!"

rushing to take them out he doesn't see Hironike until the last second while stepping over Jackral bodies.

Had Anuren followed through with his baton swing he would have likely taken Sgt. Garrison's head and helmet clean off but had to change directions to swing at Hironike catching him awkwardly in the midsection. The blow messed with Hironike's sword aim taking off Anuren's ear instead of beheading him. There's an awkward moment as Sgt. Garrison and Long are finding their feet as Hironike hits the deck. Anuren squeals in a strangely familiar way blood spraying from his head. The Jackral leader recovers and goes in to finish Hironike off when his head explodes and as a railgun round flies through the back of his unarmored head spraying the overhead and bulkhead with Jackral brain matter.

Wiping off skull fragments and burned fur, Sgt. Garrison follows where the round came from to see Athena far down the corridor peeking out of a recess in the prone firing position barrel still smoking. She gives a thumbs up as Angelo pulls her back. A few moments later they come out asking "Is it safe?" Dusting himself off further Sgt. Garrison says "I think so." PFC Long was moving to ensure all of his suits systems had recalibrated and were fully functioning after the unplanned shutdown. Hatches at all the entrances to the corridor opened and more Jackral came piling in. They all stopped at the sight of the body of their headless leader.

Sgt. Garrison and PFC Long were about to light them up when Hironike slowly grasped their weapons and lowered them saying "Look at them. They are defeated seeing the fall of their leader. No need to fight anymore." Many of them fell to their knees and began keening. Bastet began to enter as well which none of the strike teams had seen before now. Watching it all Long comes up to Sgt. Garrison and whispers "When he got cut, I swear he yelped like my dog back home after someone stepped on his paw or something...weird."

Hironike, Athena, Angelo, Sgt. Garrison, and PFC Long escorted the remaining automatons to the main console on the bridge to see if they could gain control of the Jackral home ship. The crew there having received the news of Anuren's fall did not give any resistance but did not offer any help either. They just watched crestfallen. Kresh at the back of the gathering crowd around Anuren's body silently made his way to the main lift where an automaton was dragging Private Cooper and Muturi with the help of Amuzati and Bulu. The fighting looked to be done and Kresh had not agreed with all of Anuren's tactics but he refused to simply lie down for these beings.

Once he got to the fighter hangar bay, he could tell the news had spread quickly as pilots, mechanics and crew in general were standing or sitting staring off aimlessly contemplating the futility of it all. One pilot didn't bat an eye as Kresh put on a flight suit and jumped into the stretched disk-shaped fighter that was ready to head to combat. Only after the ship powered up and left the hangar bay did anyone glance in his direction but no one sounded the alarm or mentioned an unsanctioned launch. Back on the bridge the automatons were trying their hardest to brute force control of the ship after the more sophisticated strategies had been tried and failed.

They were able to stop a signal that was jamming external communications so Sgt. Garrison could get through to the *Ex Wife* and tell them the status of their mission. When speaking to General Krulak, Garrison stated "Target is down, and the rest of the combatants at least for now are standing down." The Commandant liked the sound of that as did the bridge crew and others within earshot. General Krulak then ordered "We will have our birds on standby to disable the weapons in case someone there is still feeling the need to exact revenge. You keep working on flight systems and report back when you have control. We need that ship away from Earth as soon as possible."

"Roger that." Garrison responded and relayed the directives to his people who were keeping watch over the Jackral seemingly still stuck in shock. The automatons who were now fluent in the Jackral language were asking for help but got no response to their inquiries. One of the Bastet who had come on to the bridge told the automatons "They are still trying to get over their failure. It goes against their entire existence up until now. They truly believed victory was their destiny in all their intergalactic endeavors. With each victory it confirmed their self-proclaimed status as Blessed. This day proved that to be a false claim. Beware, some will lash out when that reality hits them."

The automatons acknowledged the input, translated it to the strike teams and went back to work on the ships systems. Thinking all that over Sgt. Garrison commented to Long "Some of these aliens might be feeling froggy again when that epiphany hits. We need to call some back up to come in, in case that happens. If they all rise, obviously we won't be enough." Overhearing Athena and Hironike agreed so the calls were made for reinforcements from the Ex Wife and other capital ships to come handle potential backlash for Jackral who didn't think this battle was over. A slew of modified Night Eagle troop transports and Ore haulers from the GMC and Kison Askari forces were on their way to the Jackral home ship.

Meanwhile the fighter, interceptor and frigate class GMC ships were having an easier time in mop up duty after news of Anuren's death must have spread through the ranks of the ship captains and fighter pilots still out fighting or patrolling.

* * *

Just outside of the bulk of engagements Captain Maplethorpe, and Nefer were still baiting Jackral ships into engaging them thinking they would have a larger numerical advantage than they actually did as the Adder flown by Corporal Aragon, and a Nyuesi Sime flown by Zurina accompanied them both in hiding using similar yet different stealth tech. They had all fallen into a rhythm with The War Dragon and Space Harrier mainly becoming bait for the Jackral fighters to chase only to find themselves sandwiched between two sets of enemy ships, one of which could fire both fore and aft.

The action was dying down as the Jackral ships broke off their pursuit early when Captain Maplethorpe got the call from the Ex Wife to begin their run on the Jackral home ship. The GMC officer then relayed the message to Nefer and the other ships in the group "HQ says their leader has been taken out which may be why some of their fly boys have less enthusiasm now. We still have assets aboard their ship with more on the way but we are cleared to disable weapons placements while they work on the flight controls. Zurina take out the biggest turrets first and save the remaining dark matter ordinance in case we have to take out the main engines if they fail to gain control. Do you copy?"

After a moment Zurina double clicked her mic to confirm that she understood the orders and they changed direction headed for the massive Jackral ship in the middle of a still raging but dying down battle. Some ships continued to fight while others just floated. Some of the Kison Askari and GMC craft were still targeting them either way as no official surrender message had gone out. The main turrets which had been fired previously were still aimed at Earth's surface and luckily still grouped into position on the belly of the Jackral home ship.

Opening fire Captain Maplethorpe and Nefer in her War Dragon with Kamal on front laser turrets and General Simeon in the rear gunner's spot teamed up to try and clear a path to give Zurina a good shot. With that done she fired four of the Assegai warheads straight into the cluster of turrets gathered on the belly of the Jackral home ship. There was a brilliant flash then a blossom of purple that spread over the turrets and some of the ship's hull along the bottom began to disappear as well. Just as everyone watching began to worry that the ordinance had done its job too well, it oddly started to dissipate some. Readings suggested it was not safe to be in the affected portions of the ship, but it was unlikely the dark matter would destroy the huge vessel and send it crashing into the Earth.

Chapter Twenty-Four

Everyone's attention was taken from the controlled explosions happening on the belly of the Jackral home ship when a myriad of large things came out of hyperspace. They were being thought of as things since some looked like ships while others similarly shaped looked more like glowing sea creatures flying through space. Corporal Aragon was afraid at first that perhaps some residual effects of prior nitro use had taken hold of his brain giving him strange visions. He was relieved when others in the Adder began commenting on the phenomena, and there was a buzz going through all the various communications frequencies.

The GMC, Kison Askari and Jackral alike were all trying to figure out what these new arrivals meant. One of the Manta shaped ships looked familiar to General Simeon and he called in to the *Akina Mama* to see if his hunch was true. "Akina, this is General Simeon. Can you patch me through to Queen Tunisia?" he stated nervously. There was a brief pause before Tunisia's voice came on the line sounding obviously annoyed "Simeon, glad to hear from you. Your aide Njemba has been sweating profusely while trying to cover for your absence. Are you out flying in the battle when you should be here coordinating our forces with me?"

Hesitantly Simeon apologized so he could get to his reason for calling her "My apologies my Queen. I felt I would be better out in the field, and I am not piloting. I left that for Nefer who is more experienced. The reason I called was to ask if any of the new ships looked familiar to you? Not the large glowing organic looking things but there's smaller one with a bluish hull like what I saw Babylon in before. Any word from him or his people?" Taking a moment to look at the group of new vessels which were simply flying through almost playfully as the battle came to a halt as all ships were observing them.

There was one smaller vessel that did look familiar to Tunisia but there was a strong pull to another and when she realized why she felt it her heart rose. There was a larger more organic looking ship that glowed more than the rest of them. Soon Queen Tunisia knew what she felt was her connection to Darius. The prince was somehow aboard that vessel. "I do believe that is Babylon's ship and somehow the brightest one is being flown by my Darius!" she exclaimed. Immediately she ordered for the *Akina Mama* to hail Babylon in hopes he could confirm or even speak with Darius. One of the Jackral ships did not seem to be as enamored with the new arrivals as everyone else seemed to be. It began approaching while picking up speed. "What is that fighter doing?" Queen Tunisia asked to no one in particular.

***

Kresh was in fact not mesmerized by this new group of ships and in fact wanted to go out in style. The old warrior had no intention of surrendering as many were thinking of doing now that Anuren was gone. Nobody had the stones to rise up and lead them after all they had been through? That was pathetic and Kresh would not live in a world where they were defeated or the Blessed became the Cursed. The Earthling imbeciles would never gain control of their Jackral home ship, and the processing spikes would continue to harvest until this planet was an ashen husk. Kresh would leave them to it, but before he did, he would take some of these magnificent glowing things out with him.

Some looked like they could be beasts and he thought of them as such. The brightest one seemed like a good enough target for Kresh to take his frustrations out on. One of the oldest warriors in the Jackral legion wished he could see the dumb look on the faces of the Earthlings when they figured out the controls were DNA locked to

Anuren, some of his crew and in his armor which was likely inoperable once he was killed. The controls were normally handed down to the next in line for leadership. In his greed and ambition Anuren had never named a successor or had any pups that Kresh knew of. This planets destruction would be glorious. Kresh throttled forward with all of his weapons armed poised to open fire as soon as he got close enough.

With a war cry Kresh opened fire causing the ship/creatures to scatter. The thrill of feeling super-heated energy rounds pumping out of the Jackral fighter was exhilarating. Many of the vessels were quick enough to spin away from the incoming fire but for some reason the ship Kresh wanted to destroy simply stayed in place as if nothing in the world could go wrong. That angered Kresh even more. Despite it having no real effect the old Jackral warrior clenched harder on the triggers as he pushed the throttle all the way forward. Finally, the vessel in question turned as if to flee only to turn completely around to come at the Jackral fighter head on.

Kresh welcomed the challenge. He would not turn away and was ready to accept this worthy death taking another brave being or beings with him. The energy blasts holes in what was the closest approximation to a cockpit, then a strange aura formed. Kresh's ship was floating through what looked like debris of the destroyed ship when suddenly he was face to face with a young Kison Askari free of any mechanized armor or even an EV suit with bright glowing eyes full of a fury he had never seen before. There was a bright flash as something flew from the boy's hands directly into Kresh obliterating him and his ship leaving only Darius floating there sadly looking in the direction of his lost celestial.

* * *

Queen Tunisia was watching all this transpire along with everyone else who witnessed the arrival of the celestials. Her heart swelled with joy when she felt the connection with her son and just as quickly dropped when that connection was suddenly gone. Then inexplicably after the vessel Darius was aboard was destroyed and he seemingly disappeared the connection was there again and he appeared to fly into the Jackral fighter blowing it to pieces with something that shot out of his hands. Everyone was seeing this and were just as confused as she was. Njemba walked up to her and asked "My Queen is that…Prince Darius?" Coming out of the perplexed trance she was in Tunisia replies "I think so, but he has no EV suit. In vacuum. Flying no less. How is that possible?"

Nobody had an answer and speculation about the boy's true origins would once again run rampant amongst their people. Interrupting their thoughts was Babylon's voice and visage becoming the overlay on the *Akina Mamas* front viewport. "Not sure if we are just in time or too late Queen Tunisia. You look well all things considered. The boy felt something was wrong here and I knew you wanted him away, but this is a lot more than I had anticipated." He remarked looking at the many ships surrounding the Earth as well as the trauma the planet was going through even now that could be seen from space. That meant things had to be extreme at surface level.

Looking up Tunisia spits angrily "Never mind that! What have you done to my boy Babylon?" Standing to come closer to the viewport as if it made a difference Babylon says "Come now. You always knew the boy was special…different. We just didn't know how or why and we still don't. B'sides you don want to ave this conversation wit everbody listnen." That much she knew was true. In response Queen Tunisia said "Just bring me my son and get him out of there!" Babylon nodded his understanding and signed off.

Darius must've sensed his mother's worry because he was already on his way to Babylon's ship and once he came aboard, they headed straight for the *Akina Mama*. Just as one call ended another one came in. The Ex Wife was calling in to update them on the status of the strike teams and odds they would be able to take over the Jackral home ship. Queen Tunisia took General Krulak's call but was short as she couldn't wait to get to the main hangar bay where Babylon and Darius had just landed. General Krulak was a bit perturbed but understood. The strike teams had yet to crack the nut of hacking into the ship's systems but at least there was more back up aboard the Jackral home ship and the other ships were simply standing by.

The automatons meanwhile were trying repeatedly and failing to get into the ship's systems and one of the Jackral finally told them about the master switch that was in Anuren's armor. Apparently, there was some AI within the armor that knew when he gave orders to the bridge crew. With that artificial cognizance now disabled and control had not been assigned to an heir or next in command prior to Anuren's death it could not be passed after the fact. Not to mention the mechanism within the armor itself may have been destroyed during all the fighting or when he was finally killed. They had gone out in the corridor leading to the bridge to retrieved the armor to see if they could perhaps reactivate or maybe reverse engineer something that would work. Nothing thus far was successful.

The gathering of enemy forces aboard the Jackral ship was beginning to make the Jackral nervous and resentful. They were lost now and bereft of leadership. Some were thinking they could still fight despite not having control the home ship which was now in a perpetual holding pattern around Earth wastefully burning fuel and this close would eventually drift into the gravity well. The last possibility for some of the remaining Jackral warriors seemed a fitting end to the one planet that had finally thwarted their conquest.

ANCIENT ILLUMINATION III - GODHOOD

* * *

Back on the surface weather conditions began to add fuel to the fire as the instability within the Earth's crust started to worsen. Earth quakes, series of severe storms and hurricanes ravaged the planet as everyone scrambled to stoutly built shelters. They were unsure if they would survive at all if these conditions continued. The hunting parties had evolved into rescue parties which took in all beings, but once within the confines of the shelters throughout the world tension built up once the beings from Earth learned that Jackral and Bastet from the invasion forces as well as those that were trying to retreat to the processing vats were now seeking sanctuary from conditions that likely would not exist had they not come to Earth in the first place.

Oddly enough at Ogun's command Bofus found himself watching over a group of Jackral prisoners. The GMC and Kison Askari forces had taken to separating the alien beings from understandably angry inhabitants of Earth. People were enraged and some were of a mind to exact some revenge on the aliens responsible before they all likely came to their untimely demise. Ragnar agreed with this sentiment but would lose in any attempt to win out even with all of his forces reunited against the Kison Askari and GMC which were now loosely acting as if they were on the same accord. The irony of that was not lost on him as he watched the joint forces patrol one of the largest reinforced shelters with enough room to house the Jackral invaders separately.

"House" was putting thing rather kindly. They were prisoners and knew it. Sensors showed that some of the spike structures were strangely more stable than the others and they had no record of GMC or Kison Askari scientific groups doing anything at those sites. Whatever had been done there needed to be duplicated soon. All the gathered science groups had the opinion that even if that were done there was no guarantee the stability would hold or for how long. The world was in a panic and for the first time they had to contemplate leaving their home planet.

Unbeknownst to them the newfound stability that was spreading to some of the Jackral dig and processing sites was due to Pharaoh and his minions void walking to each of them repeatedly slowing the work of each Jackral construct, but it was not halting it altogether and there was a possibility the damage was too far gone. The whole ordeal was beginning to tax all three of them. Sparks sitting outside the facility Bofus was tasked with patrolling was beginning to wonder if any of this mattered or made any sense. Multiple times now it seemed that her life and universe was being torn asunder and there was very little she could do about it. Max felt her frustration and came to sit with her but stayed silent knowing nothing he could say would fix things.

Argos did the same plopping his huge bulky body down on the other side of her. Sparks took off her helm and gauntlets watching the crazy light show that was going on in the sky. She leaned on Argos and he seemed not to mind. Max took his cue from her and began taking his armor off and just took in the sight of the night sky as time went by. Argos sat up slightly tilting his head to the side looking at them both. The movement forced Sparks to sit up. She was about to ask what was wrong when he began to take off all his layers of clothing. Not sure of what to say Sparks simply sat there open mouthed.

Slowly and methodically Argos unraveled heaps of wrappings beneath a large leather like tunic. Turns out he was not armored after all but clothed in a copious number of layers. There was at least a helmet especially made for his large head and the goggles were incorporated into that. The helm hid his eye color which was an angry red like his skin tone. He stood up looking every bit the mythical creature of some kind. He was heavily muscled with a map of scars all over his body. Sparks was sure he couldn't be from this planet but if that were the case why weren't more of his kind discovered?

His oversized pants and boots now that she could see them more clearly had armored plating stitched into them which offered some protection. Mouth still agape she turned to Max and said "There has to be a story behind how you two came to be partnered up. Is he an alien of some kind?" Looking over at Argos and the at Sparks Max replies "He wanted to show you his true self before we all died. That definitely means he likes you. Yes, there's a story to how we met but I doubt we will live long enough to give you the whole tale. That huge ship there looks to be getting closer to us and the planet sounds and feels like it's given up on us. No, I don't think he's an alien despite the size, skin color and what look to be tusks. I think he's from another dimension that kind of exists here as well."

Max's observation looked to be coming true the Jackral home ship did seems to be looming larger by the minute. At least they had front row seats to the end of the world she thought. The other nonsense Max was talking seemed too crazy to be believed but then again everything was nowadays.

* * *

In the main hangar bay aboard the Akina Mama Babylon was making his way down his ships ramp as Darius came running down to greet his mother. Queen Tunisia also ran to meet her son at the bottom hugging him fiercely. "What were you thinking? I saw you out there with no EV suit! Saw the ship you were in destroyed. I thought I had lost you my son. Don't do that ever again. Promise me! I didn't even know such a thing were possible." She was in tears but joyful at being reunited with Darius who accepted the loving. Looking into his eyes she could tell he felt guilty for making her worry.

Babylon stood back giving them their space to enjoy the moment only speaking when Queen Tunisia finally looked up at him to ask "What happened?" Turning from her to look directly at Darius the Atlantean responded "I'm not too sure. We were in separate ships, and young Darius has yet to explain to me exactly what happened." They both look at the boy expectantly. Tears welled up in his eyes which began to glow as he gathered his thoughts to explain.

"Everything happened so fast. We came out of hyperspace and the celestials were happy at first then they saw all the fighting and destruction happening both out here and on the planet. They began to kind of dance to comfort themselves and it seemed to stop the fighting momentarily. Then the one ship came at us and started shooting." As Darius was reliving the incident tears flowed more as he continued "He shot and killed one of my celestials and before I knew exactly what I was doing I void walked as Babylon showed me."

At the last comment Queen Tunisia shot a suspicious glance at Babylon who recoiled a bit but asked Darius "Please continue?" to try and take everyone's focus off of him. Catching the silent exchange between Babylon and his mother Darius went on "As the celestial was destroyed, I opened up a portal to leave where I was only to step out in front of the ship attacking me, gathered my anger I guess…and threw it at the ship." Njemba, Queen Tunisia, her royal guard, Babylon and other Kison Askari within earshot of the story tried to digest what it meant. Who was this boy really? Why hadn't any of these abilities manifested in any others of their race? What would the other beings of this galaxy think once the story spread? It was inevitable the news would spread. Nearly everyone no doubt had footage of the attack on the new arrivals and the results.

Queen Tunisia finally composed herself to ask Babylon "Did you know he could do this? Why would you teach him this void walking?" Thinking it over and fully understanding why this would worry a mother, Babylon replies "I had no knowledge of the boy's capabilities and suspect there is a great deal more we will discover about him as time goes on. As for the void walkin, I had a feelin he could andle it as there are not many who can anymore since de ancient one separated himself from our societies in general. It is possible had I not shown Darius, he might not have been able to escape de attack."

The ire in the Queen's eyes died down some but it all still bothered her. She stated flatly "Very well." And they all went back to the bridge to see what the overall status of things were presently.

Chapter Twenty-Five

With the strike teams mission over for their part Hironike, Athena and Angelo caught a shuttle back to the *Ex Wife* to get back aboard the Ryoko-Gekijo as everyone else was trying to sort things out. Earth was not exactly safe, there was still the question of their status after the revolt and their return to Earth which was under investigation prior to the Jackral invasion. Athena, and Angelo were already out of their combat armor/EV suits while Hironike still wore his cyber-ninja like suit of armor which was drawing stares from both the GMC personnel and the Kison Askari they passed on their way to the Night Eagle troop transport they were assigned.

Athena recalled putting her hand on the covered hover-gurneys carrying Private Cooper and Muturi. The two had fought well to all accounts and there was still life left in them but they were in critical condition. She wished them a speedy recovery. It was obviously touch and go as to whether they would pull through. It was still amazing to watch the celestials as they had now come to be known as fly through the bevy of ships now swarming around Earth. As they made their way to the *Ex Wife* an unannounced group of Jackral fighters and larger ships launched from the Jackral home ship. As fast as they streamed out of the huge ship, they all turned about and slammed straight into the left side of the main rear thrusters of the Jackral home ship.

There was an explosion killing them all instantly and disabling the functionality of the ship itself causing it to list closer to the Earth's gravity well. The final act of defiance likely would result in a death knell of not only all those aboard the Jackral home ship still not under control of the automatons desperately trying to hack into its systems to avoid exactly what was happening. Everyone who witnessed this was taken by surprise of the act itself seeing these Jackral commit a mass suicide before correlating the end results.

The Jackral still dazed by the loss of their leader and predicament of now being helplessly stranded simply sat watching while the GMC and Kison Askari forces scrambled to come up with a plan to avert this growing disaster. As soon as the Night Eagle Athena, Hironike, and Angelo were aboard landed in the auxiliary bay large enough to accommodate the Ryoko-Gekijo on the *Ex Wife*, they scrambled to get back to the theater/ship. Waiting for them was the rest of the Ongakujin traveling with them as well as Major Vashti fresh off his mission of getting two strike teams onto the Jackral home ship. "Welcome back! Congrats on a semi successful mission." He said in greeting.

Grateful for the warmer reception than the last time they had spoken Hironike replies "Thank you, but I was wondering if our involvement was enough to wipe away the question of our loyalty and therefor regain our previous status in this crazy society moving forward?" Chuckling Major Vashti says "I am not sure you're aware although you should be, but we have much bigger fish to fry so to speak. If we cannot stop this ship from crashing, or the Earth from breaking apart if we fix that issue, moving forward will have extreme complications. You are fine as far as the GMC and Global security forces are concerned for now. Just know that since you aren't working for us in any official capacity that most won't know of your deeds this day. Nothing personal just protocol, plus being the head of the Ongakujin affords you a sort of celebrity status and we wouldn't want to jeopardize that should we all survive this calamity."

With that Major Vashti and his retinue of Marines stepped off back to wherever their orders carried them as it was obvious despite the relative success that some of the military no longer looked at the Ongakujin the same. For entertainers' black ops missions was a difficult cross over to get most to wrap their heads around. Nodding his understanding Hironike went to board the Ryoko-Gekijo with Athena and Angelo not far behind.

Waiting on the bridge were Toshi, Takimura, and Megumi who all respectfully bowed to Hironike and the others when they entered. "Congratulations on the successful hunt Hiro, but it may not be enough from what we have seen." Toshi says. Nodding towards Athena Hironike responds "Thank you but the kill actually belongs to the lady. Queen of the Limbia Johari is full of surprises." The gathered Ongakujin look at Athena with a newfound respect and some with suspicion. Walking over to a three-dimensional model of Earth and the space around it complete with ship dispositions Hironike asks "I take it you've been monitoring the automatons progress with respect to hacking the invasion ship?"

Coming up beside him Toshi answers "Yes and I have no clue as to get in. Unfortunately, as you may have heard we have some other issues resulting from the mess they made of the Earth. Which is on the verge of being compounded by the uncontrolled ship being partially disabled by the group kamikaze run." Athena and Angelo came to take a look when she noticed him wincing. She placed a hand on his shoulder letting him know she would be fine. Hesitantly he went back to the quarters they were using to address his injuries suffered during their stint with the strike teams. Hironike noticed the silent exchange and remarked "He's a loyal one." Smiling she responded "He is that. He can be a bit jealous as well. Angelo knows I don't always agree with your methods, or how some have used the information we have provided in the past. Now none of that may matter if we can't solve this."

Megumi and Takimura stepped up to the display nodding in agreement. Turning to Athena Hironike says "Let's make a pact then. If we somehow make it out of this without losing the world we have come to know as home, we will try to find a means to get what we need done without assassination. The caveat will be that if no peaceful remedy can be found, you let us do what we must. You know our history, how we came to be as we are and why your peoples are linked to ours." Thinking it over Athena reluctantly agreed. It felt as if she had nothing to gain or lose given their current circumstances. In order for any of it to matter they had to survive.

* * *

Darius waited patiently as the leaders of the GMC, Global Senate, Kison Askari elders and Queen Tunisia bickered via video conference as to how to move forward to solve their current problems. They couldn't seem to agree on what methods to try first or who would be responsible for which steps in each proposed process. Babylon was there basically for moral support and guidance if asked. No one asked. The people of Atlantis were not yet recognized by any other governing body aside from the Kison Askari and they had remained untethered to the often fighting or arguing societies of Earth. Ironically this was a case for them having good reason to remain aloof for all this time.

The young prince was getting more and more angry as these beings were refusing to listen to each other. Time was slipping away. Whatever the solution was, this was not it. Darius politely asked to be excused and Tunisia seeing the frustration on his face nodded thinking he would go play and she was trying to stay abreast of the conversation. Four huge Kison Askari with the gold and silver etched into their skin marking them as royal guard tailed Darius to his quarters. Politely the prince said "A little privacy please? I'm tired." Bowing the largest guard stated "We will be just outside if you need anything." They all left to wait just outside the hatch of the Prince's quarters aboard the *Akina Mama* standing watch.

Once he was sure they weren't going to come in the room, Darius sat down to think of how to handle this. He knew his mother would be angry if he just void walked out of there, but there was likely no other way he could escape without his guards knowing. Sitting with his legs crossed he concentrated for a while. During this meditative state a portal opened up. Before he knew it, he was up and stepping through it. Light flared around him as his eye began to glow as he stepped out of the portal he summoned into the void of space. Off in the distance he saw the Jackral home ship continuing to list as the gravity well of planet Earth was beginning to pull the ship to it.

There was a mass of ships all around it as well as a gathering of capital ships observing. They had tried to use large tethers with some of the larger capital ships in the area but the tethers broke despite being in vacuum which should have nullified a lot of the weight. Another issue was that having part of the main thrusters still active was contributing to the ship leaning towards Earth. Darius also saw the group of celestials that had come here with him. Gathering himself he flew over to them. As soon as they felt he was near the surrounded him and began to glow as well. The large manta shaped space creatures seemed to know what he needed without him having to ask. Darius had become better at understanding their mode of communication which kind of telepathically sent visual messages, but he was unsure he could accurately convey a message to them.

They floated together over to the surrounded Jackral home ship which was now beginning a slow entry into the Earth's atmosphere. Some of the celestials knew they would be lost in the process of what they were about to attempt. When Darius tried to emphasize this, he felt them comforting him, ensuring that they knew sacrifice might be necessary. As long as he promised to uphold his end of the bargain, they would do what had to be done here. En masse the celestials gathered around and began pushing the Jackral home ship away from the Earth. Some of the smaller beast sadly burned up by partially entering the Earth's atmosphere. Others were just badly injured but were large enough to survive. Not all of the celestials had plating to make them look more like inanimate vessels used as means for transportation like Babylon's ship. Eventually they did get the ship far enough away that it was no longer in danger of crashing.

* * *

Morbidly mesmerized by the Jackral home ship coming dangerously close Bofus, Ogun, Sparks, Max, Argos, and literally the entire planet watched as it looked like an eclipse as the ship loomed large casting a deadly shadow over the planet. Oddly the view of their impending doom took a strange turn as what looked like glowing space beasts that would be more fitting for an ocean gathered around to push the huge ship back out of their atmosphere and into the vacuum above them. There was also a bright but very small figure that hovered near them but didn't get involved directly. Everyone looking up at this saw it as a blurry smudge of light unidentifiable to the naked eye.

Those aboard ships in space watching from the opposite perspective could identify the figure quite easily. Most were simply shocked, but there was one aboard the *Akina Mama* who was absolutely horrified. Queen Tunisia was sitting in her captain's chair on the bridge of the Kison Askari flag ship simultaneously terrified for her son and smolderingly angry at the royal guard who would pay dearly for losing track of Darius. All Babylon could do was sit quietly. He desperately wanted to comfort or advise her but knew from the look on her face that this was not the time.

General Krulak's voice was the first to break the awkward silence "Is that Prince Darius with those things?" Begrudgingly she replied

"Yes, General. I believe it is." Also on the bridge of the Ex Wife was Lieutenant Junior Grade Parsons who was there for administrative purposes but couldn't help himself adding "So, I mean yes that's the Kison Askari Prince but are we not going to mention that he's not wearing an EV suit, or armor that I can see, and he's what flying?" The other GMC personnel shot glares at him for speaking out of turn with so much top brass present including the commandant. That didn't deter him at all. He figured this was the end of the world as he knew it. Nothing worse could come of him speaking his bewilderment as most had to be feeling the same.

The young officer continued despite the stares "I mean plus he's glowing like a lot. Nobody finds that weird? I mean is this something they can all do now? Could have been useful." Frustrated General Krulak interrupts him "Parsons! Give it a rest!" Sheepishly Parsons obeys muttering "Aye sir." Before going to sit at a nearby console to make himself look busy while still keeping an eye on the main viewport through which most of the crew were watching the new arrivals push the Jackral home ship away from their planet. The relief they felt was short lived as calls from the surface came in announcing the stability issues the planet itself was still going through. They weren't sure when but it was likely things would go critical soon if they didn't act fast, and the world's top scientists who had gathered when the crisis in the spike structures was discovered to be causing the sudden shifts. They were stumped.

* * *

Corporal Aragon docked the Adder after Sgt. Garrison, PFC Long, Private Cooper, Muturi, Amuzati and Bulu had been shuttled to him from the Jackral home ship. Cooper and Muturi were still on their hovering med-gurneys in critical condition and unconscious. A group of Kison Askari had come to take Muturi to the *Akina Mama* where their own facilities would be better at caring for the warriors' wounds and help him recover if he made it through. Amuzati and Bulu went with him but promised Long they would keep in touch and report on his progress asking that he did the same with Cooper's status. PFC Long promised that he would do so and watched them leave. Sgt. Garrison told Long to head inside the Adder and prep for takeoff back to Saturn so they were ready when the time came adding "Make sure Aragon didn't mess up my ship."

Then he followed the medical gurney to sick bay ensuring he knew where Cooper was going to be kept. There was suddenly a commotion happening but he was too preoccupied with the status of his men to worry about it. The last bit of scuttlebutt he heard between leaving the Jackral home ship, and arriving here was that things weren't looking good on a few fronts so he couldn't worry about it now. Any solutions to the large problems were well above his pay grade. As long as he could get his boys healthy and functional then they could go about tackling problems they were familiar with. Finding enemies to shoot, uprisings to put down, and recon missions were his jam. Catching falling ships, the size of large metropolitan cities, or figuring out how to stop a planet from breaking apart from the inside...not so much.

＊＊＊

Darius figured he might as well face the music now. He promised his group of celestials that he would be back and void walked back into his quarters aboard the Akina Mama. Inside his room Babylon and Queen Tunisia sat waiting. Well Babylon was sitting and Tunisia was standing there looking painfully beautiful in her flight suit inlayed with gold and silver. She decided to change out of her ceremonial dress when contemplating taking out her Nyuesi Sime to make Darius come back. Babylon rose when the portal opened giving the room a soft purple glow and the prince stepped through it.

Tunisia ran to him and hugged him crying. "Why would you do that when you know how scared I am for you? Our people already suspect you are not mine and a demon seed, or whatever such nonsense they spew about when they think I don't hear them." Looking guilty the boy replies "Mom, I had to. You all were arguing and they could help. They said they would help as long as I kept my word to help them. I didn't mean to scare you. You don't have to be scared. You can do it too. You just haven't tried." Confused she takes his face in her hands.

"Who is they dear one? What is it you think I can do?" Bringing up a monitor showing the celestials he explains "Them Mom. They're my friends and they helped me move the ship. I have to help them find a home now, and you can walk the void as I do…it's why I shared. So, you would be protected and they would have to listen to you even if they didn't agree. As long as you don't give in to fear or anger again. They will see what's within you is right."

Now she was even more confused and looked to Babylon for help. He explained the situation with the celestials and their search for a new home world, and convinced her not to be too harsh on the royal guard who were unable to stop the boy from void walking since they didn't know that was an option in the first place. After a while she relented but scolded them nonetheless. The Queen was determined to get the idea of going away again with these space creatures out of his head, but the boy seemed hellbent on it.

Chapter Twenty-Six

In the rear most sick bay on Saturn at the GMC facility there PFC Long waited outside one of the larger operating rooms where Lieutenant Commander Jameson was working on Private Cooper. They were trying to save him from succumbing to injuries sustained while infiltrating the Jackral home ship. The corpsmen and other medical staff were not pleased with Longs' presence but the young Marine was unrelenting. They were even less enthused with his huge hairy beast being there as well, but all were too afraid to tell either they had to leave.

Obediently Teufel sat by his master taking up an uncomfortable amount of space in the hallway. Corporals Aragon and Sims were curious as to Coopers status but were also leery of Longs' ability to control the beast if things went wrong so they waited at a respectful distance, and refused to admit their fear. "You can come down here and pop a squat with us Corporals." Long remarked. Laughing nervously Corporal Sims replies "We are good. I think I might be allergic to be honest." Aragon just shook his head and waived. Lance Corporals Jennings and McNamara were getting supplies for the Adder.

Much of the galaxy was still trying to recover. Sgt. Garrison was now unfortunately up to his elbows in paperwork. The repairs and medical attention he and Long needed was minimal. Koops executives were not happy about the losses of the three units that went with the strike teams. Dr. Mwamikazi wished to be notified next time the GMC risked such an expensive asset the way they did. General Krulak intimated that it was first and foremost a necessity to the survival of all who resided in the galaxy. As far as he was concerned for the amount the GMC was charged for use of the automaton units, they could do what they wished with them.

Lieutenant Commander Jameson came out of the operating room and was surprised to see them waiting there. "So, this is what has all the nurses in an uproar." He commented noticing Teufels bulk sitting down next to PFC Long. The bulkheads seemed to shake as the beast began to growl low. Wary the medical officer looked at Long saying "I suggest you keep that thing under control. I am intrigued by its physiology and would love to study it but it's a risk having it here. We've discussed this before. As for Private Cooper, we've done what we can. It's up to him to fight now." The rest of his staff slowly left the operating room not taking their eyes off the beast until it was well out of sight.

The news seemed grim, and not what they wanted to hear, but Corporals, Aragon and Sims went to relay the news to the others in their small unit. Corporal Sims called over his shoulder "Long, can you even take nitro or does that suit rid your body of certain stimulants other than your pain meds?" Confused PFC Long replies "What's nitro?" Chuckling as they go around the corner Corporal Aragon says "You will learn Marine! I will teach you!"

* * *

Back on Ganymede at the Kison Askari new home facility there a similar vigil was being held by Amuzati and Bulu. They were waiting to see if Muturi would recover from his wounds. Their answer unfortunately was obvious from the doctors coming out of the medical facility where Muturi as well as pilots and other askari involved in fending off the invasion were being treated. The two stood as soon as they saw the medical crew come out. Their faces told the story that needed no telling. Before they could ask there was a loud wailing sound and they turned to see Muturi's wife and children who had witnessed the same doctors exit. Some of the medical staff went over to embrace the mourning family. Amuzati and Bulu had no words of comfort to give them. It was true that Muturi had gone out like a true warrior but they knew well that this was not the time to tell that story. His wife and children least of all would want to hear it with their grief so fresh in their hearts.

It was better to leave them to it. Placing hands on them gently as they left was the only comfort, they could offer at the moment to let them know, they knew Muturi, or at least shed blood with him briefly in their people's time of need. Gatherings like this were happening literally all over the globes on Earth, Saturn, and Ganymede. Many would not live to see the progress that was yet to come. Many that made it would not be so sure it was all for the best.

* * *

It took them a couple years to melt down the Jackral home ship giving them enough material to use the strange new alloys and other materials to patch the Earth together. Simply pulling out the large spike structures would have expedited the planets' demise. Strangely it looked as if the planet was now beginning to mirror their society. The core was still in place but much of the surface was now a Frankenstein like patchwork of both natural areas mixed with new alloys that had machines beneath regulating ever shifting tectonic plates. Earth was never a perfect sphere, but now it was even more warped than before. It was now basically the largest space station known to anyone here.

The few exceptions were Babylon, Pharaoh and the still present celestials. The remaining Jackral had been transported to Saturn. It turned out their musculature was used to a similar gravity of Earth making the conditions there ideal for detaining them. Stripped of their weapons and armor they were forced to help in the rebuilding operation resulting from their actions in the invasion. This was determined after a lengthy trial to decide what to do with them. The proceedings were broadcast and there were plenty of differing opinions as to what should be done with them now that they were basically stranded there. The Bastet were another issue altogether seeing as they might have been unwilling accomplices.

Protests demanding the Bastet be freed and integrated into society was stirring up more controversy while some were very uncomfortable with trying to let strange alien beings live among them when they were having a hard-enough time getting used to the normalization of mutated humans that had been with them for centuries. Unsurprisingly Ragnar and his Guild of the Pristine were staunchly against any integration program. Although the cat-like anthropomorphic alien species were viewed as less threatening there were many who did not trust their side of things told during the trial.

Many felt that not enough was done to stop the Jackral during what must have been decades if not centuries of conquests. The Bastet were being held at new facility at Earths' new lunar station. Millions of lives had been lost in the process and there were those who wished to simply kill them all and not waste resources housing and feeding these invaders. It was an ongoing societal debate that was confusing and complicating an already evolving global and now galactic society. Things would only get more difficult before they could be ironed out. One thing that would not change…greed.

The Kison Askari were allowed to start a rather lucrative business reinvigorating the niche in personal transportation, but there was a mad scramble for alternative resources recently acquired. Namely the tech and material from the confiscated Jackral ships, armor, and weapons. Predictably the GMC and Kison Askari split anything that had military applications. Queen Tunisia conceded that bargaining chip in light of her previous actions and the relative non action against her since she had been reinstated as Regent which was looking more and more like a permanent position. Darius was not only growing in stature but also in ability as he became more comfortable with testing them.

Queen Tunisia often tried to convince him to try new things in secluded areas or at least away from prying eyes that constantly followed his movements. The boy who was growing fast and fast approaching his father's stature seemed unphased by the scrutiny. The problem was that the Kison Askari who were already suspicious of him and his relatively unheralded birth to his rise to the throne ignoring the need for secrecy when traditionally royal families within the stone peoples often found themselves targets of the government bodies headed by non-mutated Earth born humans. The same happened to prominent families of the Limbia Johari, Ongakujin and other lesser known families with extreme mutations in their gene pools.

The economic and societal scales were tipping and it was not going unnoticed. Pharaoh took his minions and did what they could to help avert or slow what would have been a cataclysmic tragedy if the Earth had been allowed to self-destruct. Now the ancient being of light had gone back to ground having his minions once again help observe and manipulate things where they could. They had to be more careful now that some knew of their existence including the Jackral and it bothered him that he was still ignorant as to how exactly he and the prince of the Kison Askari were connected, but there was no doubt they were. The ancient one was still determined to find a way off this desolate rock. The boy may hold the key to his escape. Occasionally he would void walk to speak with him when he felt he was alone. Often making it seem like a dream sequence.

The prince seemed determined to go off on some mission now that things were stabilizing in the Milky Way with his people in a better place in society than they have had in a while. Pharaoh didn't want him to leave before he had a chance to take advantage of his inexperience. It was obvious he had little idea of what he was capable of. That could be useful. With the addition of the Jackral, Bastet and materials new to the Milky Way inhabitants' things were again becoming interesting, but not enough for Pharaoh to be content to remain here. The other beings of his kind must have forgotten him and he resented that fact. This miserable species had to be leaps and bounds beyond their realistic potential they would have reached had the illuminated ones not visited millennia ago. As of this time no one had returned even to observe to see if he had in fact enlightened them. Perhaps something had happened to them that Pharaoh was unaware of.

Could he be the last of their kind? Had intergalactic marauders have come to his home world and wiped them from existence leaving him stranded perpetually with no one able to restore what was initially taken from him so long ago? That was impossible. His kind had evolved to a point where physical means of transportation were virtually unnecessary. That very ability was what they had stripped from him. Although he was forced to use a corporeal construct, he could still walk the void but could only do so on Earth. Try as he might he could not figure out exactly how they had done so.

There was one being here who might be on the verge of discovering or evolving to the point Pharaoh's beings had. When thinking about that it was a sad and pathetic idea. All these years and only one of them was close to ascending as the illuminated ones had? There had to be another explanation. If this Darius ever reached his full potential, he would be considered a god among these others. Perhaps that was the answer. If Pharaoh could convince Darius he was the reason for this miraculous transformation then maybe out of gratitude the boy would help him escape this fate.

That was a far better alternative than letting the boy go off and help some comparatively mindless beasts find a new home world of their own. Malice and Typhoon much more in tuned with their master's vibrations caught most of these thoughts as he meditated. They still despised each other but were also wanting this being out of their proverbial hair and would do whatever was necessary to be rid of him so they could move on with some semblance of a life on their own terms rather than this perpetual servitude.

***

On board the Akina Mama which was now orbiting the Kison Askari home facility at Ganymede Darius sat in his quarters staring at his father's ceremonial cape and shackle set. He and Queen Tunisia had just come in from a flying session. Tunisia did not like to do it often and was in fact unaware that she even could until he told her that was part of what he had gifted her. When she did so it was in her full flight suit including her helmet. Darius would tell her the helmet was not necessary. She knew this but also did not want her identity known as the whispers about him were stronger than ever.

Especially since he was no longer trying to hide his abilities. Darius was filling out and looking more and more like the elder Omega they had lost not long ago now. The light in him that sometimes shined through was the only difference. Sticking her head in his quarters she asks "Will you ever wear it? I know your father would have loved to see you in it." Darius smiled at that. Standing to feel the fabric and the alloy of the large greaves and gauntlets he replied "I don't know. It's like he was not so subtly announcing his status as a royal while simultaneously reminding himself and others of what had become of his people."

Coming to stand in front of him Queen Tunisia holds up the cape portion to his broadening shoulders she states "We should not forget where we have been. Nor should we let those who placed us there forget. Lest we end up back there again." Shaking his head Darius replies "Careful mother that we don't hold ourselves there mentally. We are beyond those times now with assurances that our contributions will be valued as they should be. We have our own table. No need to ask for a seat at anyone else's. When I return, I will decide if I can wear these. Right now, I am beyond them for I have a responsibility to the celestials."

She knew this answer was coming and her own eyes flared briefly with light before gaining control of her emotions. "What about your duty to your people? They will need you, and you are the true heir here." Standing to leave his quarters Darius explains again for likely the thousandth time having similar debates "If not for them, there would be no people here for me. No Earth where our people began at the very least. The Jackral would have eventually turned their world siege machines on our newest colony on Ganymede before leaving, and I am not sure we would have repelled them. Even in defeat they likely would have destroyed everything in final protest. Our people don't seem too accepting of me, and I feel like the non-mutants are just waiting for the upper hand to be back in their possession. It's tiring and honestly you all here are well-equipped moving forward. Once the celestials are placed, I will return."

He was right. They were well positioned now, but that didn't make her feel any better about him going off on his own. She was getting used to her new abilities but she somehow knew he had a much higher potential which he felt a need to explore. The fact that he was still so young made him being right about all of this that much more maddening. Queen Tunisia also knew that him getting a firm control of his abilities would make him a better ruler when he returned. At least that's what she told herself.

The bottom line was that she could not stop him. He wanted to go and was powerful and cunning enough. It was best to let him go in hopes that he would return of his own free will. There was also truly a debt owed to these celestials as he called them. Tunisia had been aboard the celestial ship that Babylon often travelled in as well as another that Darius had now adopted since his original celestial had been destroyed. If she were being truly honest with herself, she wanted to go with him, but duty demanded that someone stay and look after the Kison Askari and with the heir gone she promised to do so while he was away.

It felt good to sit on the throne and to have her concerns actually heard. She was not only the voice of her people but of all the mothers, sisters and wives out there. Queen Tunisia took solace in that as her son took to the stars with his celestials. The Kison Askari waited his return. There was another audience with the GMC scheduled and she sat on the throne in a chamber similar to the one they had constructed on Jupiter where the Jovian accords were signed years ago. Sitting in one of her long black bejeweled gowns as the overhead screens made it look like the night sky were overhead and not miles of rock, mantle and planetary crust she waited for the most recent representatives.

Finally, more masked senatorial proxies showed up complaining about hidden Jackral alloy caches not being shared. Leaning down from the dais Queen Tunisia let her eyes glow ever so slightly as she denied hiding any such materials since the Kison Askari now had full control of the resources they produced through their mining facilities. She was insulted that they had the nerve to ask where her son was. Queen Tunisia answered "That's really none of your business but since you must know. The prince is off studying. We will let you know when he returns. I know you only ask since you don't like the answers, I give you. Perhaps you think it would be easier to manipulate a younger mind?"

Tunisia felt that if she could see their faces beneath the masks they would be blushing with embarrassment. They quickly ended the proceedings and left Ganymede with no more real information but were glad to be away from the queens discerning gaze nonetheless. She and her people did have things well in hand for now. She hoped Darius found whatever it was that he was looking for and returned soon.

Epilogue

Sparks had no idea what they were doing in the middle of nowhere. Things had been getting particularly hot with the addition of new alien species in the mix and Argos finally revealing himself. As expected, suspicions arose. He wasn't technically a mutant, yet he wasn't non-mutated human either. People on all sides began to inquire as to his origins and Max wasn't well equipped to answer them. When they're curiosity couldn't be satisfied people demanded Argos be detained despite the many times, he had in fact fought on their sides, once with the Kison Askari on Ganymede when the GMC assaulted their new facility, and against the Jackral invasion force on Earth.

It didn't matter now. Interest groups who got hold of the information and images of a being with unidentified origins ran wild with the potential for another invasion by the new species. When that story gained traction demands from not just interest groups but government officials came calling. Despite the language barrier Sparks and Max could tell it all saddened Argos. He revealed himself thinking it was basically the end of the world. Max set about making sure his black-market enterprises would thrive in his absence. He was disappointed because things were especially booming in light of all the potential new inventory he could broker. Now he would have to leave all that in the hands of a longtime acquaintance as he made sure his closest friend returned home safe.

They were out in the Mohave desert in what looked like an abandoned warehouse. Sparks was starting to get annoyed with the lack of explanation from Max who was rummaging in the large bag Argos perpetually carried. "What could possibly be the reason we ran from civilization to come here for?' she asked. Looking up as Argos watched almost as confused as Sparks was Max said "He might not

remember but he was sent here a while ago as a baby…with this."
What he pulled out wasn't all that remarkable.

The object looked like a trinket sold at an antique store. Max help
up the round bauble with strange runes etched into it. It had tarnished
over the years obviously and Argos seemed not to recognize it at first
until the object touched his red hands. When it fell delicately into his
hands the object immediately regained its luster and the runes lit up.
The warehouse took on a blue glow as a portal opened up behind
Argos and he turned to look upon a verdant forest that spread far and
wide as they could see. Sparks could not believe her eyes. The portal
opened to a vibrant beautiful place that seemed almost primordial
until she noticed structural buildings near the river bank.

Tears welled up in Argos's large eyes as he recognized the place
from which he came. Max stood to awkwardly hug him. "You need to
go back now. You've saved my hide more times than I can remember
but things are getting too hot here. These people will not simply let
you be. You've weathered the storm for me here so if you need, I will
go with you." Argos looked down at Max's cybernetic leg as if to hint
at something. Laughing Max says "Yeah I guess it's my turn to stick
out like a sore thumb." From the look in Argos's eyes there was more
to it than that but he patted Max on the shoulders and walked through
to the other side.

Taking up some of his weapons and other gear Max turned to
Sparks looking at his stuff adding "Not sure if any of this will work
over there or how I will get more ammo but you can never be too safe.
Take care of yourself Sparky. My boys will take care of you should you
need anything. You can have the ride." Sparks just shook her head
looking at the view. "The world here has been going crazy as it is. You
think I would let you enjoy all this without me? I don't even know if I
fit in here anymore. I'm coming."

Before he could argue Sparks shoved Max through the portal, jumping through after him.

Pharaoh felt the rip open and close in the interdimensional fabric separating realms. Perhaps there was another way to restore him to his former glory.

* * *

For months Darius travelled with his group of wild celestials. He had come to know them as individuals. They had found a plethora of worlds which either didn't suit them or the inhabitants proved to be hostile. He did not want to leave them with beings that would prove to be unwelcoming or combative. Darius had some of them fitted with plating to give the celestials a protective hull like the one that remained with Babylon. Not all of them accepted this treatment but he made it clear that it was necessary for protection. Travelling with or in the celestials was becoming easier and Darius was completely comfortable flying on his own. For the longer distances he did rely heavily on his celestial.

Pharaoh had appeared to him recently and it was obvious the exile was trying to use him for his own gains. What that was exactly had not been made clear. The knowledge of this ancient being existing in Darius's mind was confusing and made no sense. How could he possibly be aware of someone who predated him by not only generations but massive eras. It was also obvious that if he did not return soon the stability Darius left could be shattered at any moment if Pharaoh chose to lash out. Sitting in his celestial thinking this over, he was searching for a place to take them.

Instantly a place came to mind and his instincts told him to void walk there first, but he ignored it. In his mind's eye he could see a city of light having no idea why it was familiar to him. He decided to take them there and see if the inhabitants would accept these wonderful creatures. Telepathically Darius communicates the coordinates to his celestial and the rest of the group. When they ask how he knows of this place there's no answer he can give them. Warily they get together and prepare to enter hyperspace. Looking at his father's gear that he took with him, Darius hoped the celestials' trust in him would not be betrayed when they got to their end destination.

Closing his eyes, he could see where they were headed. He could see a city of light where both the architecture and the beings that lived there shimmered gloriously. All structural buildings were made so you could see clearly into them. Darius realized it wasn't the buildings at all that shined. It was the beings within them. The dwellings simply served to exhibit all of the ancients that lived there. There was no need to hide. They were perpetually on display.

Suddenly a flood of memories that could not be his own came to him instantaneously. It was information overload and he had to snap out of it in order not to go crazy from the number of images, thoughts, and life experiences threatening to overwhelm him. Standing he decided to walk over to the cape and tried it on. It was a bit long. After a moment he could feel his body straighten and grow until the hem of it was now off the deck. Stepping into Jared Omega's boots he could feel there was a lot of room in them. Oddly his feet grew until the alloy tipped boots were filled. His calves swelled slightly to fill the matching greaves.

The wrist gauntlets sans the glove portion seemed a bit much. He knew they were ceremonial but for some reason he could not bring himself to put them on. He could almost feel his mother's disappointment. There was a soft warbling sound as his celestial was warning him that they were close to the targeted destination. Leaving the ceremonial wrist shackles, he went to what acted as the front viewport and was not disappointed at all. The planet looked like a huge living jewel. Light swirled within and around it. There was nothing quite like it. From far off distances beings must see this as a giant star or even a tight knit nebula. So much light shone from this place that it created shadows and silhouettes from other celestial or stellar bodies in the vicinity.

He could sense the joy emanating from the group of celestials with him. They were chattering nonstop telepathically and he had to concentrate to shut them out. One question was being shouted repeatedly which translated to "Where are we?" He asked them to wait near the planets moon so he could go down and get the lay of the land so to speak. Taking only the next celestial that had chosen him, they made planetfall without incident.

Darius could feel the approach of thousands of beings and it took him a moment to realize he could see them. It did not bother him in the least that not one of them were humanoid. Watching in amazement these living breathing balls of light approach as he stepped out onto the surface for the first time, his celestial asked once more "Where are we?" As the question bounced around in his mind, he took a few more steps dropping the helm his mother slipped into his things Darius replied "Home."

ROD VAN BLAKE